THE
LIGHT
OVER
LAKE
COMO

OTHER TITLES BY ROLAND MERULLO

THE
LIGHT
OVER
LAKE
COMO

A NOVEL

ROLAND
MERULLO

LAKE UNION
PUBLISHING

Published by Lake Union Publishing, Seattle

www.apub.com

Amazon, the Amazon logo, and Lake Union Publishing are trademarks of Amazon.com, Inc., or its affiliates.

ISBN-13: 9781662510786 (paperback)
ISBN-13: 9781662510793 (digital)

Cover design by Shasti O'Leary Soudant
Cover images: © Evelina Kremsdorf / ArcAngel; © Geoffrey Kuchera / Shutterstock

Printed in the United States of America

For
Pat and Art Spencer
Vivian Leskes and Frank Ward

One can't govern for so long, and demand such heavy sacrifices from the people without provoking some sort of indignation.

—*Benito Mussolini*

AUTHOR'S NOTE

This story is based closely on the actual events of the last weeks of Benito Mussolini's life. I have imagined some of the other characters, and I have changed some names and slightly altered the actual chronology for narrative convenience.

—Roland Merullo

One

April 1945

"You'll be all right if we leave you for an hour, Mother?" she said. "To get the sewing?"

Her mother leaned back against the sofa cushion and answered in a voice barely above a whisper. "Yes, of course. Yes, go. I'm fine, yes."

"Do you want to lie down or sit up?"

"Fine sitting. Go, Sarah; be careful. Go, Lydia, sweetheart. I'm fine."

Sarah adjusted the blanket around her mother's knees, kissed her gently on both cheeks, lifted Lydia into the stroller, and set off. It was the first week of April, and the Swiss city of Bellinzona, 250 meters above sea level and surrounded by mountains, had so far been only lightly touched by the warm currents of spring. The air was cool and crisp. Lydia, wrapped from toes to chin in the blanket Father Alessandro had given her, blinked up at Sarah from the stroller, eyelids drooping.

"Dormi, tesoro. Fai un sonnellino."

At the word *sonnellino*—nap—a smile touched the corners of the girl's lips. She blinked twice, slowly, mouthed *"Mami,"* and let her eyes close.

As she had since Lydia's birth, eighteen months earlier—a wartime birth, in a foreign land—Sarah felt torn in two, as if great coarse hands had hold of each arm and were tugging her in different directions.

Behind her now in the farmhouse's small stone outbuilding, her mother was probably already asleep, wrapped against the April chill and perched on the old leather sofa like a skeletal bird. Without Sarah to care for her, Rebecca would no doubt have heeded the summons of the grave months ago. An Italian Jewess who'd slipped across the border with her pregnant daughter, Rebecca had no legal status in Switzerland, no friends there, no relatives besides Sarah and Lydia, almost no strength left in her arms and legs. Every Sunday when Sarah made this trip, she hoped, half guiltily, to return and find that her mother had passed peacefully into another world. But Rebecca's withering flesh seemed glued to iron bones. She'd survived eight grueling months hiding in a friend's attic near Lake Como. And then, accompanied by her daughter, she'd somehow managed to climb to the Swiss border and make her way down a mountain path to this cold outpost. Every harsh kilometer of that trip, and every day since they'd arrived in Switzerland, Sarah had carried the weight of her mother's survival on her shoulders.

At a year and a half, Lydia's needs were different from those of her grandmother, but, of course, Sarah was responsible for her survival, too. Lydia had learned to walk only a few months earlier but seemed to be making up for the late start, clomping as fast as she could from room to room of the small house, leaning into a clumsy trot in the yard, falling, crying, standing up, hustling here and there as if searching for the father she'd never met. Most afternoons, as Rebecca napped, Sarah took her daughter for hikes up the stony paths that led into the hills, tiring her out so she'd sleep through the night, and, at the same time, strengthening their legs and lungs for a journey Sarah had been secretly planning for the better part of a year.

Now, pushing the stroller along the path, she tried for the thousandth time to put that journey out of her mind. She willed herself not to think of Luca, Lydia's father, not to imagine walking back over the mountains to Italy, not allowing herself even to hope for the end of the war. *Now,* she said to herself, *now is what matters. Now.* But beneath the duty to her mother and Lydia, she felt something else, more selfish—the pull of her lover, of home, of a life that had nothing to do with Nazis and Fascists and war.

In front of her the path sloped downward. It soon changed from dirt to gravel, then to small, neatly set cobblestones that led all the way to the church square. That uneven pavement caused the stroller to bump and shimmy, but instead of waking Lydia, as Sarah had at first worried it would, the irregular movement always lulled her daughter deeper into sleep. The girl didn't stir or mumble. She lay still, her face framed in black curls and set in a lovely, perfect peace that Sarah could no longer even imagine.

When she reached the church, Sarah could tell from the building's silence—no bells yet, no parishioners near the doors—that the Catholic service wasn't over. It seemed to last a different amount of time every week. She pushed the stroller in slow orbits, around and around the stone patio.

After several circular trips, she became aware of a woman about her own age, watching her from a bench. Sarah tried to ignore the woman at first—was she a spy, a policeman's wife, one of the many Bellinzonans who were less than happy to have Italian refugees in their lovely city?— but the woman stared so persistently that at last Sarah looked up and made eye contact. The woman was waving her over. "Come, sit by me," she called, in accented Italian. *Vieni, siediti vicino a me.*

Sarah pushed the stroller over to the bench and sat at one end. The woman seemed friendly. No German spy or Fascist operative would be so poorly dressed. "I've seen you here before," she said.

Sarah nodded, watching her, trying to parse the accent. Not the Swiss-Italian everyone else in the city spoke—not exactly.

"I see you here every Sunday."

"But I've never seen *you.*"

The woman shrugged. "I mostly try to be invisible, like you. You don't say hello to the people you pass. You keep your eyes down, as if you have to watch your child every second or someone will steal him away."

"*Her*—she's a girl. Lydia."

"You have the war hanging all over your spirit like a ragged gray cape. You're Jewish, aren't you?"

"What makes you say that?"

"I've seen you talking with the priest, but you never go inside the church. Why else would you be here, and with a small child? I'm Jewish, too, don't worry. From Austria."

"Here legally?"

"As legally as you." The woman put a hand on Sarah's arm and smiled her sad smile. "I'm Marlena." She gestured to the stroller. "Such a beautiful child you have. I'm jealous. Is the father here, too?"

Sarah shook her head and felt Marlena squeeze her arm, then let go.

"Alive, at least?"

"I . . . I think so."

"Then I'm jealous again. My husband waited one day too long to leave Austria. One day. He got me out and promised to join me after he'd helped his brother get away. That was four years ago."

"Perhaps he's still alive."

"Four years of silence from a Jew in Austria doesn't translate into 'alive.'"

"I don't know, I'm sorry, I—"

"Where are you from in Italy? I'd like to live there after this is all over. I can't go home."

"Lake Como. Near Menaggio. A village called Mezzegra."

"Lake Como! We stayed there on our honeymoon. So beautiful. You can go back now, you know."

"Not yet."

"The fighting's moved north of there now. The war's nearly over. You should go back and find your man."

"The priest told me there's still trouble around the lake; it would be too dangerous to go back. And my mother is here with us." She gestured up the long hill. "She's very ill. Are you sure? About the war?"

"Mostly sure, yes. Everyone says the Germans are being chased home to die there with their Führer."

At those words, Sarah felt the sudden disintegration of the thick wall she'd built to keep her thoughts from traveling east toward Luca. She turned her eyes to the church. The building's imposing bell tower and gray stone walls seemed cold to her, and the Swiss people seemed cold and alien. The food, the language, the landscape—alien and cold, all of it. She shifted her gaze again, due east, studying the gently rising plain that led to the foothills, and beyond them the mountains that marked the border. She wished more than anything that she and Luca had made some plan to meet after the war, something other than a last kiss and a hasty *ci vediamo*. But they'd all been frantic on that day, listening for German patrols, Luca already a partisan fighter, she herself three and a half months pregnant, her mother so frail she'd barely been able to stoop down and pass through the small square opening Luca had cut in the border fence. No amount of pleading had been enough to convince him to join them. "Go, go, go!" he'd said, his face contorted and his fingers clutching the chain link. There had been no dreams of the end of the war then. No thought of making plans. Nothing but a world filled with terror and blood, and a crazy rush to leave.

"I think every day about walking back and finding him. I walk the hills to be in shape." Sarah gestured to the stroller. "Sometimes Lydia walks with me."

"Then go."

Sarah thought of her mother and shook her head. "I can't," she said. "Not yet."

"Don't wait too long." Marlena got to her feet and glanced down into the stroller. "Don't make the mistake my husband made, that's all. The war's over. Who knows what the Swiss are going to do now with their illegal Jewish visitors? Who can ever say?" She tapped the handle of the stroller with one finger and hurried across the patio without saying goodbye. Just as the first church bell sounded, Sarah watched Marlena disappear into one of the narrow streets in the town's gray center.

5

Two

Luca Benedetto knelt at the side of the spring-fed pool, washed the last of the dried blood from his hands, then took off his clothes and lowered himself into the freezing water, letting out a strange guttural noise as it enveloped him. The noise surprised him—he'd trained himself to move silently through these trees; was he growing careless now, at the very end? But no one would hear him in this place. He was fifty meters uphill from the ruined cabin where he'd hidden Sarah in the early part of the war. Moss in a thick carpet on the roof, front door leaning sideways on its remaining hinge, the interior a gloomy cavern of cobwebs and mildew. One iron bed with a sagging mattress. One unbroken window. A three-walled outhouse.

He returned to the cabin from various engagements, never for more than one night. It was his way, the only way he had, of trying to maintain a connection with Sarah. If all had gone well, she'd have a child by now. *His* child—female or male, he couldn't know. She and her mother would surely take good care of that child. There was food in Switzerland; some danger and difficulty perhaps, but no war. Except in the highest mountains, winter would be over. Soon, May would arrive—Sarah's favorite month—with its longer days and warmer mornings and the promise of life bursting from the gardens and fields, from every branch of every living tree.

He lifted himself out of the pool with his one good arm, dried himself with a scrap of towel, and ran his hands through wet hair. Earlier that day, he and his band of partisans had ambushed three German soldiers who were fleeing a battle, twenty-five kilometers south of where Luca now stood. He'd stationed himself and his men and women on either side of a narrow stretch of road near the city of Como at the lake's southern tip. There was intense fighting farther south—American soldiers with their tanks and artillery, and Italian partisans in the hills with their stolen rifles, pistols, and knives. The Americans killed and were killed in great numbers, the partisans in twos and threes. At this point, Luca found it impossible to understand why the German generals kept fighting. Their evil cause was lost; anyone could see that. Between the invasion of Sicily in July 1943 and now—the fourth week of April 1945—the Allies had fought their way steadily up the peninsula, enduring hellish casualties but pushing the fearsome German Army north and north and north, bombing their supply lines, capturing their officers, weeding them, house by house, from the big cities: Catania, Messina, Naples, Rome, Florence.

Luca knew this because, less than a month earlier, he'd made contact in a safe house in Milan with an American scout, a true warrior. Caplan was the man's name—a Jewish name, he said—and his job was to slip behind the German lines, collect as much information as he could, and carry it back to his superiors. He and Caplan had shared a simple meal and a few stories. Thanks to a Neapolitan mother, the American spoke Italian almost without an accent, a skill that made his scouting work slightly less perilous. Exactly one day older than Luca, Caplan had left a fiancée at home near Boston. He wanted information on German artillery emplacements and troop movements in the territory between Lake Como and Milan, and Luca had been happy to provide it. In return, the American had made him a magnificent gift from the safe house storage: a lightweight, portable automatic rifle and four boxes of ammunition. "It's an MAS-38," Caplan told him. "Use it well."

Luca had not yet grown immune to the act of killing another human being, but he could feel how far he'd moved in that direction, how almost ordinary it had become to rip the life from another body with bullets or a blade, and to spend a few minutes at night cleaning dried blood from beneath his fingernails. He'd become accustomed to waking before dawn, not knowing if he was about to witness his last sunrise. He kept reminding himself that the cause was just, perfectly just, that Mussolini and Hitler were twin demons who had to be stopped, for the sake of Italy and for the sake of the wider world. But what he and his people had done during the day almost always tormented him in the night. He'd awake covered in sweat, in the forest, in a hidden cabin, a secret apartment, and have to steel himself to do what his superiors ordered him to do.

That morning, he and some of his band of nineteen men and women had ambushed a motorcar with three German officers inside. The Nazis had been fleeing the battle, leaving their underlings to fight, saving themselves . . . or so they'd believed. The call had come on Giovanni's radio. Solana and Eleanora had dragged stones and branches into the road to slow the motorcar down—a tactic they'd used more than once—then they'd all worked together to fell a larger sapling to stop the vehicle entirely. Luca had waited behind a stone the size of two kitchen stoves, waited and listened and watched, and when the vehicle came to a stop, he'd stepped out from behind the stone, five meters from the men, and slaughtered them with the magical weapon. He and Giovanni and the women had started to do what they'd so often done: relieve the bodies of their weapons, search the vehicle for food. But a small flame licked up from above the car's left rear tire, and Luca shouted for them to run. Seconds later the motorcar exploded, sending pieces of body and metal flying into the trees and skidding across the road. By the time the smoke turned from black to gray, the partisans were gone, slipping away like forest creatures, Giovanni and Eleanora to a comrade's house in Cadenabbia, Luca and Solana up the steep hillside to this ruined cabin.

Washed and dressed, Luca returned to the cabin and told Solana, who'd been resting, to take her turn. By the time she came back he'd made a small fire in the old woodstove, dumped a can of soup into a rusty pot, and torn the small loaf of bread in half.

There was little need now to worry about being discovered. The Germans—so ubiquitous at one time—had long ago ceased patrolling the higher wooded terrain. They were fighting in the cities, or running for their lives, streaming up the *statale*, the lakeside road, in long, heavily guarded columns. When he and Solana finished eating, they took turns relieving themselves—she in the smelly outhouse, he in the trees—then wrapped themselves in blankets. He lay on the floor, she in the bed. He was close to sleep when he heard her say, "Come and lie here with me, Luca."

"That I cannot do."

"One night, please. I can't forget what I saw today. The pieces of body, the smell of burning flesh."

"After all these months of it?"

"After all these months of it. Today especially, for some reason. Please make love to me."

"You know I cannot."

A long silence. He pressed his eyes tightly closed, tried to imagine Sarah's face, to remember the feel of her body against his, to convince himself she was waiting for him, still.

"Just a little comfort for us after . . . everything."

He squeezed his eyes more tightly, made his good hand into a fist. No.

They were quiet for several minutes, and then she said, "Just hold me. We won't do anything. Just lie here. I'll turn my back. I have all my clothes on. Just please hold me."

He climbed onto the bed, and she turned away from him, keeping the blanket wrapped around her. He covered them both with his blanket and nestled against her, his body insisting, insisting. *No*, he thought. *Not in this bed where Sarah and I made love. Not anywhere. No.* He wrapped his good arm over her, held her against him, and willed himself not to move. He could feel her sobbing. She lifted his fingers to her mouth and kissed them, then set them back again. For a long time they lay like that, and then he could tell from her breathing that she'd fallen asleep, and he turned away from her, moved to the floor again, made himself as comfortable as possible there, and dreamed that he had a son.

Three

Enzo Riccio lay on his back in one of the many luxurious bedrooms of the Villa Feltrinelli, looking up at the ceiling and wrestling with the idea of betrayal. Moonlight leaked into the room through the curtains that covered the three-meter-tall windows, and he could see pieces of light reflecting from the facets of the chandelier. He tried to focus on those small glints, on the incredible idea of a chandelier in a bedroom—anything to keep the other thoughts at bay. He knew that the house—a lavish, castle-like brown stone structure that sat on the shore of Lake Garda—had belonged to a wealthy family before the Germans requisitioned it. Feltrinelli was the family name. Lumber merchants. Where were they now? he wondered. Murdered? On the run? In prison somewhere? At another of their properties, perhaps in neutral Switzerland? Had someone betrayed them when the occupation of Italy began? A jealous neighbor suggesting to the SS officers that there was a glorious mansion they might use to house their special guest?

The chandelier began to tremble, tiny movements caused by the heavy footfalls of a man pacing restlessly in the bedroom above. The man was Benito Mussolini, the Nazis' "special guest" at Lake Garda, Enzo's boss, and a person he'd once idolized. *Il Duce*, everyone called him. *The Leader*. For fourteen years now, in his position as senior aide, Enzo had served his *Duce*, the architect of Italian Fascism. Enzo knew more about Mussolini's romantic escapades, more about his dietary habits and health concerns, more about his volatile moods than anyone on earth with the possible exceptions of his wife, Rachele, and his young mistress, Claretta Petacci. For the first twelve of those years, Enzo had felt himself in the presence of a living god, one of history's great men. And then that idolatry had slowly eroded, evolving from the first doubts to pity, disdain, and finally, disgust. Now there was nothing left of the good feelings for Mussolini, nothing besides an old shell, a kind of armor that stood between Enzo and a fate he did not want to imagine.

Il Duce was pacing his bedroom at this hour—two a.m.—because, from the first day of their arrival at Villa Feltrinelli, nineteen months earlier, the founder of Fascism had felt like a prisoner here. And *prisoner* was very close to the correct term. There were forty SS guards on the grounds. A defensive bunker filled with antiaircraft artillery. One German officer in particular, SS Lieutenant Fritz Birzer, had been ordered never to let Mussolini out of his sight. After Hitler's commandos had rescued the deposed *il Duce* in a daring mountaintop raid, the Führer had flown him to Germany and hosted him for ten days, bringing Enzo and a handful of other German-speaking associates there as well. By then, Mussolini and Hitler had become close as brothers, their fates knotted tightly together, but they were far from equals. It was clear to Enzo that Mussolini felt humiliated by the Führer's hospitality. Torn suddenly from power by his diminutive king, shuttled here and there around Italy for weeks like a guilty captive, rescued at last from a hotel at the top of the Apennines, *il Duce* was putting on a brave face for his German host but seemed to Enzo a broken man. "I've done my work," he said once, when they were alone. "I invented Fascism. I built it from nothing into a movement that changed Italy forever, changed the world. I should be allowed to rest now. I must be allowed to rest."

But Hitler had other ideas. After one in a series of exceedingly awkward dinners—Mussolini eating almost nothing, Hitler the vegetarian slicing up his food and chasing various exotic medications with gulps of mineral water—the Führer had said, "You must now return to Italy, *Duce*."

Mussolini's stony expression split open, for only a second, in what seemed to Enzo pure shock. *Il Duce* recovered quickly, set his lips, glared down the long table. "I believe I can be more effective from abroad," he said.

Hitler was shaking his head. "No, no, *Duce*, listen to me: if you don't go back, your supporters there will refuse to fight. And if they refuse to fight, we'll lose Italy. And if we lose Italy . . ."

Even Enzo, an aide, not a military man, could have finished the sentence. At that point—the end of September 1943—Germany was already being pounded by long-range British and American bombers. If those Avro Lancasters and B-24s could take off from Genoa and Milan instead of London and North Africa, they could carry heavier loads and be more easily accompanied by fighter planes. Hitler's dreams, already tarnished by Churchill's stubborn resistance, by Russian victories in the east and Allied progress in the south, would crumble to dust.

In the end, Mussolini hadn't been offered a choice. Hitler had ordered him back to Italy and, after allowing him brief interludes in Rome and Verona, decided to install him at Lake Garda in the relative safety of the country's northern tier. As if to soften the blow, Hitler had named his tired friend the leader of an artificial duchy called the Republic of Salò. Ministers were appointed, stationery printed; Mussolini even started dating his letters "Year of the Fascist State XXI" instead of 1943, in reference to the time that had passed since 1922, when he'd ascended to power. But it all had the sour taste of pretense. *Il Duce* passed his days reading, playing tennis, organizing his papers, arguing with his wife and then slipping away to spend time with his young Claretta, who'd been conveniently set up in a house not far down the shore.

Italy had fallen anyway, Enzo mused, in spite of *il Duce*'s return. It had taken almost two bloody years for the Allies to battle their way northward from the southern shore of Sicily. But now they were less than two hundred kilometers south of Milan and Lake Garda.

The pacing in the room above continued. A flake of plaster broke loose from the ceiling, glided down in the moonlight, and landed on Enzo's forehead. He took it between thumb and forefinger and crushed it to powder. He turned onto his side, but couldn't make himself fall asleep. A thought had been planted in his mind, a terrible possibility, and it had taken root and sprouted. He was in a position to pass on information about Mussolini's plans for escape, and he was trying to decide whether the idea of doing that, an idea that grew more enticing every day, was being nurtured by an unfamiliar urge toward goodness for its own sake, or by something as tawdry as mere self-protection. The will to remain alive.

It didn't matter, he decided. He should try to sleep, maintain his deferential act in the Villa Feltrinelli, come to a final decision in the morning or later in the week.

A knock on the door—three hard raps—startled him. "*Il Duce* wants to see you," a voice called through the wood. "Immediately. Are you awake?"

"Yes, awake," Enzo called back, wondering if his great leader had suddenly developed the ability to read minds.

———

Enzo washed and dressed and was in the villa's elegant library within ten minutes. He waited there tiredly, held in a harness of worry, running his eyes over the floor-to-ceiling bookshelves. On a cherry side table, someone—Mussolini himself, perhaps—had propped up a framed photo of the uniformed *Duce* speaking to the crowds in Piazza Venezia, years before. Enzo couldn't help but wonder what Mussolini thought when he looked at that photo. The high point of his life, those years of glory must have been. And now . . .

Ten minutes, fifteen minutes. He waited sleepily for half an hour in the silent room with its Persian carpet and book-lined walls, wondering if the important meeting would be something more than another conversation about operational details. Mussolini was mercurial, optimistic as sunrise one day and cloaked in gloom the next. Though *il Duce* seemed to approve of Enzo's work, seemed to find him indispensable, in fact, it was the *seemed* that mattered, and Enzo worried that his imagined disloyalty had begun to show on his face or in his words. Three times people had tried to assassinate Benito Mussolini since he rose to power in 1922. Three times he'd survived the attempts. *Il Duce* had a nose for betrayal, a sixth sense.

At last, the heavy wooden door swung open and Enzo stood.

"Sit, sit," *il Duce* said. Enzo sat. Mussolini started pacing the room, hands clasped behind his back. *"Ascolta,"* he said. *Listen.* "Listen carefully."

"I'm listening, *Duce*," Enzo said, but Mussolini kept pacing, buried in thought, and wouldn't look at him. "I want you to arrange certain matters. Barrazino, our hapless underminister of the Interior, informed me today that the war is lost. There's no hope for victory now, he said. None. Hitler himself must know it."

Il Duce walked over to the windows and stood there, looking out at the moonlit lake, flexing his hands behind him. "What I'm going to do is I'm going to tell Scavolini to summon all the fighters he can, our best men. We'll head north into the Valtellina and make a last stand there, a last stand for Fascism. Will you come with us?"

"Of course, *Duce*. You don't have to ask that. I—"

"I'll speak to Rachele, but I want you to talk to Claretta. Go see her tomorrow. Tell her she has to leave, soon, as soon as possible. I'll make the arrangements. She should go to Switzerland. She'll be safe there."

"She'll want to stay with you, *Duce*."

Enzo saw a violent shudder pass through Mussolini's hands and arms, as if he were holding himself back from another eruption. *"Lo so,"* he said sharply. *I know.* He whirled around and drilled his eyes into Enzo's. "I want you to tell her to go, that's all. In the morning, first thing. Will you do it or not?"

Enzo stood, made a half bow, and said, "Of course, *Duce*."

Mussolini waved an arm—in thanks or dismissal, Enzo couldn't tell. He returned to his bedroom and for another hour stared up at the chandelier, wide awake. Time after time, *il Duce* had promised to return Italy to its Roman greatness, make it a leader of the world again, respected by all.

What was it, Enzo wondered, *that made me so eager to believe him?*

Four

The clanging church bells echoed against the facades of Bellinzona's stone buildings for half a minute, subsiding one by one into a cold Swiss silence. Sarah wheeled the stroller around to the church's rear door and waited there. In her kerchief, long borrowed dress, and the worn work boots she'd found at an outdoor market, she felt like some kind of beggar woman, and hoped none of the parishioners leaving by the front door would see her there. She had never felt welcome in this country.

Lydia stirred, pumped her knees once as if trying to wriggle out from beneath the blanket, then uttered a tiny sigh and went still again. Sarah pushed the stroller forward a meter, then pulled it back. She watched the heavy rear door. Another few minutes and she heard the *clank* of the metal latch and saw one side of the double door swing open, and there was Father Alessandro, jowly, red faced, holding a bulging cloth bag in one hand and smiling at her as if she'd come to prepare his lunch.

"Ah, le mie belle donne," he said, much too loudly. My beautiful women.

Sarah winced.

The priest stepped down onto the cobblestones and came toward her, holding out the bag. "Plenty of work this week," he practically shouted.

Sarah gestured toward the stroller, but it was too late. Lydia cried out and sat up.

From the day they'd arrived at the rear door of his church, having slipped across the border from northern Italy—Sarah more than three months pregnant and her mother as weak and brittle as a stalk of corn in a frozen field—Father Alessandro had been almost preternaturally kind to them. He'd found a nurse for Sarah's ailing mother; found a midwife to deliver Sarah's child; found food and clothing for them; let them live in the rectory, at first, and then, after Lydia was born, arranged for them to move to the stone cottage on a hillside with a sweeping view of the Alpine uplands. He'd even managed to arrange for Sarah and Rebecca to earn a few francs every week—sewing aprons and repairing clothes for the locals—always presenting the work in this same cloth bag.

He'd seemed, at first, to want nothing in return. But over the past few months, Sarah had begun to feel a certain kind of need emanating from him. It wasn't sexual, exactly, but a smoking loneliness she could almost smell and almost taste, and she sensed it again now as he handed her the sack of clothes, reached out and twirled a finger in one of Lydia's dark curls, offered an eager smile to his *beautiful women*.

"One day I want you to come to Mass," the priest said. "You won't understand the Latin, but just sit in the back and listen to the lovely music. Lydia will find it comforting!"

"Thank you, Father, I need—"

"And, who knows? Perhaps some part of our beautiful faith might attract you!"

"Yes, thank you. I need to get back to my mother now. I—"

"Ah, how is she?"

"Not well, Father. I think she's close to the end."

"She's in my prayers every hour. Tomorrow, I'll come and visit." He reached out and put a hand on Sarah's shoulder, brought his face close, smiling, nodding. "Tomorrow in the morning, I'll come."

"Thank you, Father. I have to go back to her now."

"Good, good. Can you carry the bag and push the stroller at the same time? Should I help you?"

"No, Father."

"You're sure? I can—"

"Thank you, no."

After several more offers of help and three more thank-yous, Sarah was finally able to leave. She pushed Lydia in the stroller until they were clear of the city and then, where the path angled more steeply upward, took her daughter out and let her walk, holding on to her mother's long dress with one hand.

"Nonna," the girl said at one point, as if echoing Sarah's thoughts.

"Nonna is waiting for us, yes. We'll be there soon. See our house? We'll make our legs strong, walking up the hill."

"Our house," Lydia said. *La nostra casa.*

Five

In the morning, after they'd each taken a turn at the spring—she first this time—Luca noticed that Solana couldn't look at him. They breakfasted in silence on two soft apples and some tea, and she kept her eyes averted, focusing on the food. "Tonight," he said, when they were finished, "some of our friends are going to blow up the railroad tracks again, west of Cadenabbia. Will you join them?"

"Yes."

"Are you angry at me?"

Solana shrugged. She must have washed her hair at the spring. Luca had never seen her with her hair down, and now she pulled it forward over one shoulder and ran both hands along it, tugging on the light-brown strands, a gesture from peacetime. She shrugged again, said, "I would like a man like you; that's all."

"A crippled man."

She smiled. "A woman doesn't fall in love with a man's arm, Luca. You're very naive in some ways. I hope she comes back to you, that's all. I really hope so. A month from now, a year from now, you'll be able to tell her I wanted to make love and you said no."

"A month from now—or less—we'll be able to say we liberated the country."

Solana nodded and looked away, as if, for that moment at least, the liberation of the country was a secondary matter. Then she tied her hair up behind her, pulled a wool cap over it, squared her shoulders, and was a partisan again. "Let's go."

———

Luca and Solana met with Giovanni and Eleanora in the forest west of the village of Cadenabbia and went stealthily through the trees there, following a half-overgrown path that had been trod by hunters for a thousand years. All four were experienced fighters now, well armed. They made little noise as they moved, and remained alert, wary, taking nothing for granted. At a three-meter-tall flat-topped boulder near Porlezza, they were joined by a band of fifteen other partisans, the eleven men and four women who'd taken orders from Luca for the past year and a half. They gathered in front of the stone in a copse of pines, some sitting on the ground, some standing, all the faces turned to him.

He moved his eyes from one to the next. *My family,* he thought. The people who held his life in their hands, just as he held their lives in his. They'd suffered together through two winters, sleeping in a different place almost every night, eating what they could steal from gardens, or at the candlelit tables of the few local people they trusted. Luca reported to an elderly farmer named Gennaro Masso and had no knowledge of the person or people to whom Masso reported. If Luca were captured and tortured, and if he succumbed to the torture and gave up names, the damage would be limited to members of this small group, and to Masso, too old for service, who plowed his fields on a slope west of the lake and spoke in long sentences like a professor.

"News?" was the first thing Luca said.

Bruno, standing near the rear of the group, said, "Piacenza and Cremona have been liberated. Pavia next. Genova soon."

Luca nodded. "German troop movements?"

Luisa, Bruno's lover, was seated on a stone not far from him. "There's still some fighting to the south of us and around the lake, but the big troop movements are almost exclusively northward. Our guess is

21

they're trying to preserve as much armament and as many men as possible for a defense of their Fatherland. We've seen tanks and artillery on train cars here." She pointed west of them, to the rail line that ran just inside the border with Switzerland. They knew it well: the line curled up on this side of the mountain range and then, at the northern tip of Lake Como, turned sharply east, cut across the southernmost part of Swiss territory, and ran as far as Innsbruck, Austria.

"Do we know what time the trains run?" Luca asked. "Has the schedule changed?"

"It's changed," Luisa said. "But the Nazis are still very efficient." There was a ripple of tired, mocking laughter. "The trains now leave Milan at six a.m., noon, six p.m., and midnight, exactly. Every day the same, for the past week, at least. Armed guards always. Sometimes a few patrols along the rails, but fewer over the past days. Four times in the last month we set explosives along the tracks. Three times the explosives worked, one time not. The Germans repair the tracks within a day and then station patrols along the area of sabotage. Two *partigiani* from the Garibaldi Brigade have been captured. We caught sight of them handcuffed in a lorry, but we were too far away to do anything. So probably the Nazis know a bit about our work."

"All right," Luca said. Some of it was news. None of the news surprising. "Do we know where the two partisans are being held?"

"The cells in northwest Milan, I think," Marietta said.

"Where the Sistek twins work?"

"God forbid." She shook her head. "We'd have a lot of trouble getting near where the Sisteks work. It's guarded night and day. Our men are in the cells closer to Piazza Navona."

"How do you know this?"

Marietta shrugged, said, "A friend," and Luca left it there.

He ran his eyes around the group. "Volunteers to help them?"

Four hands went up, including Marietta's.

"You have weapons? Contacts?"

Four heads nodded.

"Tonight, then. If they're still alive. If not, see if you can get close enough to kill the bastards who tortured them. If not that, see if you can destroy or damage the building and any military vehicles around it. One quick strike and gone. We can't lose anyone else now. We're too close to the end. And we can't have anyone end up with the Sisteks."

"Close to the end?" Marietta asked. "Really?"

"Really. There's still a bit of noise and flashes to the south, but the Nazis are fighting with half their mind on running. Our work is to finish the job we started. Keep as much military armor as we can from reaching Germany, make the taking of this part of Italy as easy as possible for the *Americani*. Once Milan is gone, once the Nazis can no longer use the railyards there, and no longer use the airport, they'll surrender."

"They won't surrender until Hitler dies," Bruno said.

Luca glared at him. "Then we'll kill Hitler, too."

"And Mussolini?"

"We can't get near him at this point. Eventually he'll have to move, and when he moves, we'll find out where he's moving, and we'll do what we have to do. Enough." Luca called out ten names, pointing, and said, "Bruno, take them and blow up the tracks, but farther north this time, closer to Gravedona. They won't expect us up there. Stella, you know the spot where the tracks run beside the small pond, yes?"

"I grew up hiking there with my sister."

"The bank there, on the northwest side of the lake, is very steep, yes?"

"Yes."

"Go up there and see if you can figure out how to erode enough of that bank so the tracks buckle and break. You have explosives?"

Stella pointed to her backpack and said, "More in storage, too."

"Then figure out how to cave in that section of the bank. Get the tracks to fall all the way down into the water if you can. They'll never be able to get earthmoving machinery in there to repair it, and there's no alternative for them up there, right? No parallel tracks?"

"Close by, but not there."

"Go, then. You'll need at least a day to get there, especially with what you have to carry. Go to the storage cabin, take what you need, and figure out the rest of it yourselves. Make sure four of you stand guard with the new guns. We don't want to lose anyone. Time it between the midnight and six a.m. trains, which should get there, what, an hour later?"

"Hour and fifteen minutes later."

"Good. Go. We'll meet here again in one week . . . if the war hasn't ended. If it has, we'll see you at the Duomo in Milan for the celebration. The rest of you, take care of our captured friends, then see what trouble you can cause around Como. Questions?"

"If we happen to come upon *il Duce*, should we kill him or capture him?"

"Capture only," Luca said. "Those are the orders. He's too valuable for the Allies. They won't want him killed." He could hear the uncertainty in his own voice and sense a ripple of dissent in the group. At the thought of killing Mussolini—the man he blamed for the deaths of his own mother and father, for forcing Sarah to flee—Luca felt, as he often did, a sharp-toothed serpent twisting in his belly, hungry, angry. "Capture him if the opportunity presents itself," he repeated, but he could feel the serpent slithering and hear it hissing: *Kill him! Kill him!*

Six

It was a twenty-minute walk from the Feltrinelli house, where Mussolini, Rachele, a dozen of their family members, several excitable Fascist officers, and *il Duce*'s German minders were all staying, to the villa where *il Duce* had installed his lover. Enzo had made the trip many times, sometimes by bicycle, occasionally in a car, often on foot. On this day, though he could already sense his mental clock ticking down the minutes until *il Duce* decided they must leave, he felt like walking. He needed to clear his mind, and he needed to make one final check of his conscience to decide whether or not to do what he was thinking of doing.

The day was so beautiful that Enzo felt nature was laughing at him, mocking his fears and confusion. *Look at this,* the world seemed to be saying. *Look at the cloudless sky, sunlight sparkling on the lake's ripples. Feel this soft breeze carrying the promise of another gorgeous northern Italian spring. Look at the women out sweeping their front walks, the old men sitting and gazing across the lake, the majestic gray slopes of Monte Baldo on the eastern shore, the palm trees, villas, and dormant gardens on its western side. And all you can think about is yourself?*

But here he was, walking away from the eyes of the German bodyguards, on his way to visit the lover of the man he'd idolized for two decades and was now preparing to betray.

He stepped along at a good pace, glancing from time to time south, down the expanse of cold water, half expecting to see an Allied craft there, filled with American soldiers, rifles raised. Unlikely. They were still south of Milan, and Milan lay 120 kilometers to the southwest of where he now walked. Even at the fast pace they'd been marching up the peninsula of late, it would take the Allied troops—the *Americani*, everyone called them—at least another week to reach these shores. From a comment here and there, Enzo suspected that, when he did decide to leave, *il Duce* intended to head southwest, not north. On his last visit to Milan, the great leader had been greeted by a massive, adoring throng and had talked about it for weeks afterward. Enzo guessed Mussolini wanted to have that experience again, to give one last uplifting sermon to the *fascisti* there, the loyal ones, convincing them that all hope was not lost when, in fact, *il Duce* himself had been so depressed and negative since his conversation with the Interior minister that it seemed he'd finally abandoned any thought of victory.

Enzo lifted and dropped his shoulders, long ago having given up on expecting *il Duce* to act in a logical way. He walked along almost as if there were another person beside him, a different man, someone demanding an explanation for the contradictions in his own life. He'd started out thinking Mussolini a loud fool and ended up idolizing him, sacrificing his marriage, his career, half of his friends, and perhaps his eternal soul in the name of this idolatry. And now, apparently, after all that sacrifice, it seemed he was about to betray the man. Maybe the imaginary creature walking alongside him wasn't another human being at all but the Republic of Italy, acting as a kind of mirror. Hadn't most of the country idolized Mussolini since his March on Rome in 1922? Hadn't a hundred thousand or more Italians clogged Piazza Venezia, again and again, cheering madly as *il Duce* stood on the balcony with his chest thrust forward, his chin jutting out, shouting about Italy's greatness? Hadn't children been taught to sing songs in his honor from the day they entered school?

Yes, yes, and yes to all of that. But now, didn't it seem that at least half of Italy had turned its back on the great man? Weren't Italians reported to be welcoming the Allies with bread and kisses? Weren't there hundreds of thousands of Italian partisans in the hills and forests, trying to find and kill Mussolini, and find and kill anyone who'd supported him?

For a moment, before he turned onto the walk that led to the front steps of the house where Claretta was staying, it occurred to Enzo that, if he did, in fact, betray his boss, and if that betrayal did, in fact, lead to Mussolini's execution or imprisonment, then he'd be hated by both sides of the civil war that had gripped Italy for the past two years. Where would he go then? To whom would he turn? His ex-wife, Lina, who despised him? Fascist sympathizers in Switzerland and Austria? No. Illogical as it might be, he knew he'd never leave Italy. Even if it cost him his life, he'd never abandon his homeland.

He tried to push the negative thoughts away, but they lingered there, haunting, nagging, singing lyrics of mockery in the corners of his crowded mind.

The moment Enzo knocked, Angelina, Claretta's maid, opened the door as if she'd been expecting him. Over the past two years, he'd spent many nights in Angelina's bed, and she'd spent many nights in his. Although he knew very little about her past, he trusted her, to the extent it was possible to trust another human being in these times. And she must have trusted him, too, because it was she who'd first mentioned the idea of speaking secretly to someone on the other side. A few quiet sentences after their lovemaking, some criticism of *il Duce*, at first, to see how Enzo reacted. And then, in time, a subtle suggestion. "I know someone who agrees with us," she said. "And who seems to have an endless amount of money to pay for information."

"Trustworthy?" Enzo had asked. The idea terrified him.

"Absolutely. I'd trust him with my life."

And now here she was, standing at the open door, trusting *him* with her life.

"Good morning, beautiful one," he said.

Angelina blushed, moved her head a few centimeters back and to one side to indicate that they weren't alone. "Good morning, Enzo," she said, too loudly.

"I carry a message for the *Signorina*."

Angelina stepped aside to let him pass, touching him on the hip as he did so. He turned and looked at her, the blue, blue eyes, so strange against the dark southerner's skin, and the hair as black as a burned candlewick. She mouthed one word: *"Dopo." Later.*

Claretta offered Enzo a polite *"Buon giorno."* She was sitting just to one side of the center of the plush red sofa, as if, any minute, she expected her famous lover to come and join her. Her beautiful dark eyes were fixed on him, but Enzo had no idea what she was thinking. He knew more about Claretta than he wanted to know. She was a woman with a temperament at least as mercurial as Mussolini's—fiery, fearless, and apparently unbothered by her position as the public mistress of a man whose wife still lived in the same house with him. Enzo referred to her as *Signorina—Miss*—and she seemed to welcome that title, even though she was technically still married to the man she'd long ago left behind. Her father had been a physician and an ardent Fascist, and she'd started writing to *il Duce* when she was still an adolescent, in one note telling him she wished she could strangle the woman— Violet Gibson—who'd tried to assassinate him. They'd met for the first time, near Rome, when Claretta shouted, *"Il Duce! Il Duce!"* car-to-car as Mussolini's motorcade passed their family vehicle. The leader of a nation had stopped to speak with her, and thirteen years later they were still entangled.

Odd and tumultuous as their relationship was—Claretta was twenty-eight years younger—Enzo had always believed they were perfect for each other. The screaming fights that often followed their loud lovemaking, the complete lack of concern about public disgrace in a Catholic country, and the feelings of their insulted spouses—none of it mattered. Claretta Petacci adored him, and Mussolini required adoration. On many occasions, *il Duce* had confided in Enzo about the relationship. One day it would be, "She's making me *pazzo*, she demands so much!" And the next, "What would I be, Enzo, without my Claretta?" Rachele, of course, wasn't pleased. There had been scenes in the Villa Feltrinelli. Once, Rachele herself had driven down there to try—with a great deal of fury but without any success—to convince the younger woman to leave her husband alone.

"Good morning, *Signorina*. I bring greetings from your beloved Benito, and a message, too."

"Sit, Enzo. Coffee?"

He took a cushioned chair opposite her and shook his head. "*No, grazie, Signorina. Il Duce* wants to know if you are well."

"As well as can be expected," she said. Not a glimpse, not a glimmer, of her actual feelings. She was polite, as always, but not quite friendly. Familiar in tone, but it was as if she were covered, from the top of her lustrous hair to the soles of her elegant shoes, by a shroud. Enzo thought of the way corpses were sometimes wrapped before being entombed. Claretta was watching him intently.

"*Il Duce* has decided that the time will soon come to leave Lake Garda," Enzo began, watching for a response and seeing none. Nothing. Not a flicker in the eyes, not a twitch of the facial muscles. The news meant she would be moved again, perhaps at great danger, perhaps to some unknown and unasked-for destination. Germany, Switzerland, Austria. But, hearing it, Claretta reacted as if he'd told her a geranium in the flower box on the back window had died.

"And?"

Enzo cleared his throat. "And he wants to ensure your safety, *Signorina*. He wants you to take a plane from Brescia to Switzerland, tomorrow if possible, and wait there in safety."

"And his plans?"

"Somewhat uncertain," Enzo said. "It's possible he'll join you there soon. But he may travel first to Milan to deliver an address, and then perhaps join you. But that will depend, of course, on—"

"And if I decide to remain here, in Italy? Instead of abandoning my homeland as certain others have done?"

"I don't think he will allow that, *Signorina*. It's too dangerous now. The enemy—" Enzo stopped himself there, wondering how much to tell her. He decided to lie again. "The enemy is making very slow advances, far south of Milan now, but . . . but advancing. It's impossible to know if they will reach here, or when. There's a chance the area will be bombed."

"Why haven't they bombed it before?" she asked in her neutral tone.

Because your lover isn't important enough any longer, he considered saying. *Because they save their bombs for the factories in Torino, for the port in Genova, for the rail lines in Mantova and Parma and the factories in Munich.* But he only shrugged and lied a third time: "Too dangerous for them to venture this far north. And they perhaps aren't sure where he is."

"Everyone knows where he is, Enzo. Stop lying to me. When and how will he depart?"

Enzo swallowed, drew a breath. "By car, it seems. Guarded by the Germans in a convoy of some kind. Very soon, he said. I *am* being honest, *Signorina.* He hasn't set a date or destination."

"Then I want to travel with him in the convoy."

"He won't allow it, *Signorina.* That possibility has been discussed. That would be much too dangerous for you."

And yet not for his old wife, he half expected her to say, but she only pressed her lips together and turned her eyes out the windows to her left. "Tell him I insist," she said. "Tell him to fly the other one to Switzerland. I shall travel with him."

The other one, Claretta always said, instead of using the name *Rachele.* Amazingly enough, Claretta seemed to feel *she* was the aggrieved party, that she had more right to Mussolini than did his own wife and the mother of his children. The families were entwined in nonromantic ways now, too: Claretta's brother, Marcello, profited handsomely in his business dealings by trumpeting access to *il Duce.*

"I'll tell him, of course, *Signorina,*" Enzo said, standing. "I'll convey your message exactly."

"I'll send Angelina with my answer later today. To make sure he hears it twice." She turned her eyes back to him and nearly smiled. "You'll greet her warmly, I'm sure."

For two seconds, Enzo only looked at her. Claretta must know everything. Of course she must. No doubt she had spies spying on spies, local women who saw what was going on in the Feltrinelli house and came to give her their reports; no doubt other servants told her whom Angelina was entertaining in the bedroom at the back part of this house, and where she could be found on the nights when that bedroom was empty. Spies upon spies, partisans, betrayers, Gestapo officers with their torture cells, sexual games, mistresses. This was war, a lunatic circus, a vicious celebration of madness.

Enzo performed a sort of half bow, something from the previous century; he was a servant, after all. He bade Claretta good day and left through the front door, only to find Angelina waiting for him there, standing near the sidewalk next to a large bougainvillea bush, not yet in bloom. "What was the message?" she asked, and Enzo couldn't be sure if she was asking for herself or for the two of them, wondering what future they might have. Or if she was asking for some other reason. Perhaps she, herself, reported to a partisan leader and that person checked her news against Enzo's to see if he was being truthful. Staring into those magnificent blue eyes, Enzo dropped all caution, as if he were carrying a suitcase full of protective armor and simply let it fall to the ground. He took hold of her by both shoulders and kissed her hard, almost angrily, passionately, the way they sometimes made love, casting all inhibition aside, all future possibilities, each of their tattered pasts. He kissed her for a long time that way and she kissed him back, as if neither cared any longer if they were seen. The bougainvillea bush offered only the flimsiest curtain of privacy.

When he released her, so weary of lying, he said, "He's leaving, for good. Soon. The Allies are moving closer at a rapid rate, and I'm not sure yet, but I think he's going to try to go to Milan, the fool. From there, nobody knows. Como, perhaps. Or Switzerland. He talks about making a last brave stand in the Valtellina, and asked Scavolini to summon as many loyal *fascisti* as he could. Do you know how many have shown up so far?"

31

She shook her head.

Enzo held up four fingers.

"Only four hundred?"

"Four. Not four hundred. Four. And with those four, and the others he believes are waiting for him in Milan, he's going to fight the *Americani*! He has *death wish* written across his forehead, and he's going to write it on our foreheads as well. You're coming to Feltrinelli tonight; Claretta's sending you. She knows about us."

"Silvio wants to see you."

"The one you mentioned?"

Angelina nodded. "He calls the house and speaks if I answer, quietly, secretly. He offers a lot of money for a little information. What you just told me would be worth a fortune."

"Tell him what I just told you, then. But nothing is certain."

She was shaking her head. "He wants to meet with you, not me, Enzo."

"Why me?"

She shrugged. "I don't know. We can't say much on the phone. The calls are very short. He wants to meet you in person."

"*Il Duce* or the Germans will see me. It's too risky."

"It's not, though. He has all the credentials of a good Fascist, all the right contacts. He comes to the lake often on business and doesn't pretend to hide. Everyone leaves him alone. And *il Duce* sends you to Salò on errands, doesn't he?"

"He does."

"Then it won't seem suspicious."

"You trust him?"

"You asked me that before, and I told you. Yes. Absolutely. Just have lunch with him. You can tell *il Duce* that Silvio's giving you information on the Allied troop movements. He'll pay you enough to make it so we can get away, you and I, and set up a home someplace else. *Il Duce*'s doomed anyway, isn't he? Hitler's doomed. The whole movement is breathing its last."

"Yes, okay, fine," Enzo said, though the idea of taking this next step set off a violent churning in his midsection. It wasn't the first time Angelina had tried to convince him to speak with this Silvio—she'd been after him for months, suggesting, hinting, mentioning the name over and over. Silvio, Silvio. But it was the first time Enzo had seriously considered actually meeting with the man. He felt sure now that *il Duce* would abandon him if given the chance, throw him to the Allies as he raced to save himself and his Claretta. His mind flashed on the memory of Count Galeazzo Ciano, *il Duce's* daughter's husband, condemned to the firing squad by his own father-in-law. Enzo had been ordered to witness the execution, and he could still picture Ciano, tied to a chair like the others, but, unlike the others, violently turning himself around at the last second so he could see the men who were about to shoot him. That moment, that wretched moment, had been the stake in the heart of Enzo's adulation: Benito Mussolini, he'd finally understood, would kill anyone to save himself. Anyone.

He shook the memory away. "Stay with me tonight?"

Angelina nodded fiercely, and after Enzo kissed her a last time and walked away, he had a strange thought: what they had was the opposite of marriage. *The opposite of marriage.* He pondered those words as he moved, and decided they meant that every night with Angelina now could be their last. In peacetime, at least, a married couple's future was written in fine script on a church document, as if years and years were guaranteed to them. All of that had been erased now; all futures were in doubt. The document was bare but for a smudge of ink. Anything new could be written there.

Seven

When they reached the stone cottage, Rebecca seemed to have temporarily regained her strength. Her eyes brightened. She asked to hold Lydia. The child sat beside her grandmother on the sofa, clutching her hand for a few minutes, then jumping down. Twice, Sarah lifted her back up; both times Lydia slid down again, laughing, repeating a few of the words she knew: *Nonna, triste, cibo.* Grandmother, sad, food. From a corncob, snippets of her own hair, and scraps of cloth, Sarah had fashioned for her daughter a ragged doll they'd named Principessa. Lydia fetched it, brought it over to her grandmother, held it to her face, and made kissing noises. Rebecca offered in return something resembling a smile, reached out with what seemed the last of her strength and touched Lydia on top of her head, then half leaned, half toppled over sideways. Sarah lifted stick-thin legs onto the sofa and covered her mother with a blanket.

For the rest of the day Rebecca lay there, refusing food, allowing Sarah to touch a wet washcloth to her lips, taking in one rattling breath after the next, her shoulders trembling with the effort. "Luca," she said, more than once. "Luca." As if Sarah might forget the name, or as if Rebecca were mourning the absence of her own lover. Before fleeing to the safety of neutral Switzerland with Sarah, Rebecca had spent eight months hiding from the Gestapo in a friend's attic near Lake Como. The dread she'd experienced there, the hunger and exhaustion, had nearly broken her in half.

For a time, able to be outdoors again, eating regularly, thrilled with the arrival of her only grandchild, she seemed to be gaining strength and regaining a will to live. She'd made it through the harsh Swiss winter of 1943 and the following summer, but as the weather turned cold again, it was as if a sinister force, stronger than gravity, began sucking her toward the center of the earth. Father Alessandro had kindly provided them with candles for Hanukkah, and Sarah would always remember studying her mother's face in that flickering light and seeing there the unmistakable summons of the grave.

She did what she could: gave her mother food from her own portion, even though she was nursing Lydia and almost continuously hungry; took on the larger share of the sewing work, even though she was tired from the nighttime feedings, and then, once Lydia learned to walk, from chasing her around the house and property, making sure she didn't injure herself. (For where could she take her if she injured herself? An unregistered toddler, a refugee in a country that wanted no part of refugees, and a Jew besides.) Sarah passed on to her mother what not-entirely-dependable news they received from Italy: Mussolini corralled up north in his absurd Republic of Salò; Hitler's army making a slow, bloody retreat—from Sicily, at first, then from the Mezzogiorno, and then, farther and farther north, from Rome and Tuscany. And now, if what Marlena had said was true, that German retreat had passed even beyond their home village on the western shore of Lake Como.

Week by week, through the remainder of their second Swiss winter, Sarah watched the life drain from her mother's face, and the strength from her arms and legs. Rebecca loved the outdoors—especially after those months of hiding—but she had less and less tolerance for the cold. The sunlight hurt her eyes. Her posture grew stooped. Only the steady development of her lovely granddaughter seemed to bring her any happiness, but as winter turned to spring, she became too exhausted even for Lydia's needs, spending most of the day on the sleigh-shaped antique couch, her face turned away from the window, her eyes flickering, her bony chest heaving with the effort to breathe.

"You must go back and find Luca," she told Sarah on one of those raw March days. "The father of your child—you must go back and find him!"

"I want to go so badly. I think about it every hour. But I could never leave you, Mother."

"Go, go," Rebecca persisted weakly. "You grew up without a father. Don't do that to Lydia. Please go!"

But torn though she was, Sarah couldn't possibly leave. Her mother was eating less and less, speaking in a quieter and quieter voice, already seeming to exist partly in another dimension.

At the beginning of April, Sarah had asked Father Alessandro to summon the nurse again, and he'd obliged. But the nurse only shook her head in quick signals of hopelessness, took Sarah outside and said, "Your mother's heart is failing. Even the best doctor couldn't save her now. Make her comfortable. Pray to Christ."

From time to time in those hours, Sarah would take Lydia outside into the sunshine and let her work off some energy, running at her clumsy, slow pace, lifting a pebble or handful of dirt and staring at it as if it were an exhibit in a museum of miracles. Every time they returned to the house, Sarah expected, even hoped, to find that her mother had left her heavy load of earthly suffering behind. She hoped for that now, again; prayed for it, in fact. An end of pain. An easy death.

All during that afternoon and evening the ragged breathing continued. It continued after Sarah and Lydia had eaten a meal of bread, cheese, and water, Sarah sitting in such a way that she could watch her mother, Lydia perplexed, confused, afraid at times, eventually falling asleep.

Sarah folded a towel, placed it on the cool stone floor, then sat there with her back against the sofa, holding the sleeping child across her thighs and listening to her mother breathe behind her. She wondered if, lost in a near-death delirium, her mother might be remembering the man who'd made her pregnant. One night, one incredible night several weeks earlier, before the illness had truly taken hold of her, Rebecca had waited until Lydia was asleep and said, "After all these years, I must finally tell you who your father is." And then she'd done exactly that. Sarah had been wrestling with the shock of it ever since. Her father was a Catholic priest, of all things. A desperately lonely Catholic priest— perhaps not so different from Father Alessandro. The priest had broken his vows and, no doubt, for a short while at least, salved Rebecca Zinsi's loneliness. But when she discovered she was pregnant, he'd stayed in the Church and, for two decades, pretended to be merely a close family friend. Her mother had pretended, too. All those years, each of them trapped in their societal roles, they'd played out a tragic opera along the shores of Lake Como, a masterful performance of secrets and glances, lies, imagined duty, buried love. Don Claudio, they called him in the small hillside parish where he presided over a devoted flock. Her mother's words echoed and echoed: "Don Claudio is your father."

Sarah got up and laid Lydia beneath the blankets in her tiny bed. She returned to her place, fell asleep, and awoke several times, trying— and failing—to imagine Don Claudio and her mother making love. She noticed a change in her mother's breathing. The struggle seemed to be ending. The breaths came more easily now but were pitifully shallow. At one point—it must have been three or four o'clock—Sarah thought she heard her mother say, yet again, in a hoarse, frail voice, "Go to Luca." But perhaps in her own exhaustion she was imagining it. A dozen times every hour she thought of the father of her child. Was he alive? Was he still fighting with the partisans in the northern Italian hills? Was the fighting going well? How many German soldiers and Fascist militiamen had he killed? Where was he? Had he found another woman?

On and on the thoughts went, a waterfall of images and ideas, of impossible questions.

Marlena had told her the Nazis were in full retreat, that they'd abandoned Milan and fled north toward the border. But was that rumor or fact? If the war in Italy were truly ending, would the Swiss force her to leave? Would Luca somehow find her? Maybe she'd awaken at first light, look out the window, and see him striding across the field, smiling and waving his good arm. She imagined the expression on his face when he first laid eyes upon his daughter. She imagined holding him in bed at night, listening to his stories and telling her own. She sometimes imagined her way even further into the future—more children, a house of their own, a garden, a tranquil life near the shore of the lake they both loved.

Other times Sarah imagined that Luca had fallen in love with a brave partisan woman, another fighter in the hills, and she pictured herself condemned to a life of lonely poverty like the one her mother had endured.

Rebecca's exhalations turned noisy again. Low grunts now, followed by such a long stretch of quiet Sarah was sure she'd passed on. But then her mother would suck in another breath and let it out, *unnh*. A stillness. Another breath. Another noise, louder now, more urgent, as if there were a menagerie of long-held secrets caught in her lungs and she was trying to cough them out into the room. Sarah was kneeling, leaning her face over her mother's face, watching the lips move. "Go, Mother," she said, very quietly. "Go now. Your work is finished. I love you. Lydia loves you." Tears slipping down her cheeks and into the corners of her mouth, she gently squeezed her mother's wrist and said, "Go now. Love you. Go."

Another dozen breaths, shallower and shallower. Three grunts, ugly sounds. Then her mother winced, once, squeezing her eyes and lips into tight lines, and was still.

Sarah lowered her face onto her mother's body and nestled it there between the meager flesh of her breasts. She stayed like that, sobbing quietly, until the morning's first light touched the windows.

Eight

Not long after he returned from the visit to Claretta, Enzo was summoned to the downstairs library that had been turned into *il Duce's* office. *Il Duce* sat there behind a massive desk that held a stack of papers and folders half a meter high. He gestured for Enzo to sit, then asked after his mistress.

"She seemed fine, *Duce*. Worried about you, as always."

"You told her the plan? That she should leave by tomorrow?"

"I did, *Duce*."

"And she will go?"

Enzo felt an all-too-familiar pair of knots forming, one just above the navel, one at the bottom of his throat. He'd noticed that every time he was required to deliver unpleasant news to Mussolini, he'd experience this physical reaction, and that it had become twice as strong since *il Duce* had been deposed. Two knots, his throat and stomach clenching, as if to imprison the words in the middle of his body. *Il Duce* was watching him intently, and there was no one Enzo had ever known whose eyes carried the force of *il Duce's* eyes when he focused them this way. It was useless to remain silent, dangerous to lie, perilous to keep secrets. He swallowed and said, "She refuses."

The response was a bellow: "How, refuses?"

"She says she insists on traveling with you when you leave."

Mussolini stood up abruptly and, fists on his hips in a posture Enzo had seen a thousand times, strode over to the tall windows that faced out onto the lake. Enzo could see no boats there—no sailboats, no fishing boats, no ferries moving from one side to the other. One summer before the war, he and his wife—*former* wife was the way he should think of her, he supposed; Lina had made it clear that she never wanted to see him again—had vacationed not far from where he now sat, in the village of Limone sul Garda, just to the north. They'd stayed—he would always remember it—at an inn called the Vineyards. *Le Vigne.* They'd gone out for a fine meal and, arm in arm, made a *passeggiata* along the lakeside promenade, then returned to the room and made love in a way they'd never made love before. The difference wasn't physical; it was a difference in feeling. He'd thought of it as a mutual surrender, as if they were actually one body, one spirit, as if all their desires in life had merged. When she cried out, it was almost as if the sound were coming from beneath his own breastbone. He didn't know if Lina felt the difference. They never spoke after lovemaking, and certainly never spoke *about* lovemaking—which Lina, the devout Catholic, always seemed to feel was sinful, no matter how many years they'd been married. Afterward, he lay awake for a long time, pondering the new feeling, wondering if they'd just created a child, hoping for that.

In retrospect, he marked that trip as the start of some fatal new friction between them, and it pained him terribly. The trip had been a celebration: he'd just accepted the promotion to work as *il Duce*'s chief aide, and *il Duce* had just started in on his bizarre love affair—those were the right words for it—with Adolf Hitler. For years, *il Duce* had mocked Hitler, belittled him in private, called him "that clown from the north." Everyone around Palazzo Venezia knew it. But Hitler kept courting him, pleading with him to come to Germany and see the military juggernaut he was building. Mussolini said no and no and no, and then, for reasons impossible to comprehend, suddenly changed his mind and said yes. In preparation for the trip, *il Duce* had a special uniform designed and tailored for himself, a uniform festooned with every manner of medal and decorative ribbon. No one but Mussolini knew what they meant.

Il Duce had ridden north in a special train, and Enzo, the new aide, had been invited to accompany him. Velvet seats and velour curtains, caviar, the finest wines and cheeses, *il Duce* in his uniform with the made-up decorations, Enzo feeling the thrill of his proximity to power, Mussolini's approval, the respect of those around him. In Munich, Hitler put on a parade for them, a massive demonstration complete with thousands of tanks and armored vehicles, and tens of thousands of soldiers, goose-stepping in perfectly even rows. Enzo had found it a military display of such magnificence as to be almost superhuman. Hitler—such an odd, diminutive man—had beamed with pride, thrusting out his arm in the Nazi salute and holding it there for long stretches, as if to demonstrate the power of his will. Mussolini offered the Führer a few tepid compliments and pretended to be only mildly impressed.

But he'd returned home a changed man. From that day forward there were no more mocking comments. *Il Duce* began to mimic Hitler, to speak about him daily. Hitler sent his soldiers to war in other countries; Mussolini did the same. Hitler instated the so-called racial laws; Mussolini copied him, if in somewhat milder versions. Italian Jews lost their jobs, and some were sent to camps. But the camps weren't brutal and murderous, as Hitler's were reputed to be. And though the Führer pushed and pushed, Mussolini steadfastly refused to send Italian Jews north of the border.

But he had clearly changed, and some Italians—Lina for one—grasped the significance of that change and predicted early on that *il Duce* would lead them into war. That prescience, coupled with Enzo's new position, had caused the friction. At first, it bubbled to the surface in the form of small arguments and silent hours, but it soon evolved into screaming fights. As time passed and the possibility of war grew more likely, Lina's feelings about Mussolini were distilled into the purest hatred. In the end, she'd forced her husband to choose between his marriage and his work, and he'd felt that his intestines were being torn to pieces. Their lovemaking at Le Vigne hadn't produced a child, and soon their intimate life, their entire relationship, withered to a faint memory of what it had once been.

———

Il Duce was still standing at the window, now with his hands clasped behind him at belt level. Enzo could see the short, thick fingers working, squeezing and releasing, squeezing and releasing. "The problem with marriage," Mussolini said at last, and then he fell silent, leaving the problem unidentified, unsolved. Yet again, Enzo felt that *il Duce* was reading his mind.

"She doesn't want to lose you, *Duce*, that's all."

There was such a long silence then that Enzo worried *il Duce* would fly into one of his rages—at Claretta or Rachele, or at his upstart aide who dared to put forth theories on the mental state of his boss's lover. But when *il Duce* spoke again it was in a quiet voice, shaking with anger, but quiet. "She won't fly, then, fine. I want you to arrange for her to be driven. Let her accompany us as far as Milan, but then, as we head north into the mountains to make our final stand, I want you to trick her somehow and send her on ahead. To Switzerland, if possible. If not, then Germany. *Chiaro?*"

"*Sì, Duce.*"

Without turning around, Mussolini waved a hand in dismissal.

Just as Enzo reached the door, he heard these words, spoken in a voice soaked with self-pity: "The war is over. My life is over. They'll kill me now. They'll shoot me. Sure as that mountain is made of stone." Enzo paused with his fingers on the door handle; he half turned, saw that *il Duce* hadn't moved and was still staring out over the gray lake toward Mount Baldo on the opposite shore. He tried to think of something to say, a few words of encouragement or denial, but the fleck of sympathy that might have prompted those comforting words was washed away by the memory of the man's own son-in-law, Galeazzo Ciano, whirling around to face the firing squad, hands tied. The explosion of bullets, the blood, the chair and Ciano flying over backward. Unlike the others, who'd been shot in the back, Ciano hadn't died instantly. An SS officer, inspecting the bodies, had to fire a pistol shot into Ciano's brain in order to kill him.

"Find a bucket of the proper size," Mussolini said, in that same sad tone. "Take all the papers from the desk here—I've collected them—and take the motorboat and go out into the lake and dump them. Make certain they sink, all of them. Don't read them. Simply take them and throw them overboard into the lake."

Enzo turned and looked at the papers again, gauging the size of the stack. *"Sì, Duce,"* he said, the servant again. Not an adviser, certainly not a friend. A half-trusted servant, disposable as any son-in-law, that was all.

Mussolini waved his arm again. "Go."

Enzo searched the huge villa and found a metal container large enough to hold the papers. He carried it to the office door, knocked, and when there was no answer, stepped inside and moved the tall stack from desk to container. With some effort, he carried the heavy metal bucket out of the house and down to the dock. He lifted it over the gunwale and set it on the wooden-slat seat, climbed in, started the boat's motor, and puttered a few hundred meters out into the lake. The world seemed so peaceful there, at a distance from the drama and machinations of the Villa Feltrinelli, out of sight of the German soldiers and Fascist operatives. For a time, he stared across at the mountainsides on the eastern shore and wondered if he should forget the idea of meeting with Angelina's friend, Silvio, forget about his duties, and simply dump the papers and steal the boat. Go to one of the small lakeside towns or up into the hills, concoct a story, find an elderly couple that would take him in until the war ended—how long could it be now?—and then try to make a new life somewhere with Angelina.

It was a fantasy, of course—an absurd fantasy. He'd lost his chance for a life like that when Lina gave him her ultimatum. He'd made his choice, linking his fate to *il Duce's*. The only choice left to him now was between betrayal and blind loyalty. Neither seemed to promise a happy ending.

Rather than throw only the papers and folders overboard, Enzo decided to throw the metal container as well, to follow the orders exactly, to be sure everything sank. But as he leaned down to lift the heavy load, the cover of the top folder blew open, and he couldn't keep from looking at the page it revealed. It was an official order, typed neatly on a piece of Repubblica di Salò stationery. The order instructed Colonel Dello Sallo to execute the following twelve men by firing squad. The men's names were listed in a single column at the bottom of the page, just above Mussolini's signature. Gian Galeazzo Ciano was second on the list. A pencil line had been drawn through that one name, then clumsily erased, leaving a smudge and a few tiny bits of rubber. Enzo stared at it for a time, sure it was Mussolini himself who'd drawn, then erased, the line. This was the other side of *il Duce*—the generous, dignified, sometimes sentimental side. The part of himself he almost always ignored.

Enzo was tempted to look through the other documents. But it was possible Mussolini or one of his other men was watching him through a telescope or binoculars. So, balancing himself in the boat with feet spread wide, he lifted the container, rested it on the gunwale for a moment, then shoved it over and watched it sink.

Nine

It made Sarah almost physically ill to imagine Father Alessandro saying the Christian prayers over her mother's body, but what was she to do? Once she gave him the news, the priest would have to arrange everything: find a place for the body (which no doubt wouldn't be buried, as it should be according to Jewish law, within twenty-four hours), hire men to dig the grave. Perhaps she'd have to pay for some kind of marker; she couldn't bear the thought of her mother lying forever in an unmarked grave in a foreign country.

Sarah washed her mother's body and dressed her in the cleanest clothes she could find, then wrapped her carefully in a sheet and blanket. All this before Lydia awakened. When the girl saw her grandmother lying still and wrapped from chin to toes, she laughed and walked over and tried to wake Rebecca from sleep. Exhausted beyond exhaustion, Sarah lifted Lydia away and carried her outside into the cool April sunlight.

How did you explain death to an eighteen-month-old? She held her daughter, hugged her, and said the only thing she could think of: "Nonna's spirit has gone up into the sky now." She set Lydia down so she could run about for a few minutes, then brought her inside and fed her a meal of one boiled egg with a slice of toast. Changed her soiled diaper, handed her the doll. But Lydia wanted only to stand by the sofa, run her small hands along the wrapped body, and say, "Up, up, Nonna. Up!"

At last, Sarah put her in the stroller—gift of a generous parishioner, Father Alessandro said—and walked her down the dirt road, onto the stony path, onto the paved streets, and as far as the church. The door was open, a service in progress. Sarah pushed the stroller as far as a small paved parking area out back, made circles there, humming a lullaby, and listened for the bells that always sounded near the end of the service. When the bells rang and rang and at last fell silent, she waited another ten minutes, summoned her courage, then entered through the side door. She found Father Alessandro in his back room, changing out of his robes. When she gave him the news, he walked over, wrapped her in an embrace, and held her—too long—kissed the top of Lydia's head, and insisted on accompanying them back up the hill to the stone cottage.

The priest knelt for a few minutes beside Rebecca's body, then stood and began to pray aloud. He dipped his fingers in the small container of oil he'd brought with him. He anointed Rebecca's forehead, making the cross there, and then freed her hands and dabbed a bit of oil there, too. Sarah felt she could say nothing. Father Alessandro finished his work, covered Rebecca's hands, hugged Sarah again, said, "I'll arrange everything," and walked off alone down the long hill.

It was a full twenty-four hours before two men arrived at the door in a work truck. Gently enough, but without ceremony, they loaded Rebecca's body into the back of the truck and drove off. Sarah put Lydia into the stroller and, wiping her own eyes every few steps, walked down into the city, and then across the city to the cemetery. A grave had been dug there. Father Alessandro was standing beside a plain wooden casket. There were more Christian prayers, with Lydia stepping forward so close to the edge of the hole that she nearly fell in. One of the workers stopped her, glared at Sarah as if she were a terrible mother. But she was emptied of all energy. The grief, the sleepless nights, the haunting, repetitive thoughts about Luca, Don Claudio, Father Alessandro, her illegal, uncertain future in Switzerland. She stood there, a woman cut from marble, and watched the Swiss workers lower her mother's casket into the ground. She had to turn away. She didn't want Lydia to watch strange men shoveling dirt onto her grandmother's casket. That, for a child, for both of them, would be too much.

In the days following the burial, seven difficult days, Father Alessandro visited every morning, bringing with him bread and eggs and milk and apples and sometimes a few slices of salami. They sat at the table together and ate, and at moments Sarah felt, next to the tempest of Father Alessandro's loneliness, that her grief was a small storm, a vaporous eddy above the lake. She'd sensed his loneliness before, of course, all those months in the rectory. But her mother had always been there, a buffer. Except for the occasional longer-than-necessary embrace, Father Alessandro had never touched her in an inappropriate way, never commented on her appearance, and, unlike his rich friend Gunther, never stared at her body as if imagining her naked. She wasn't afraid of the priest. But his loneliness was like another creature in the small stone house, a dragon breathing hot air against her skin. It made her wonder what Don Claudio's loneliness, and her mother's, must have been like, though she still found it almost impossible to imagine the affair that had brought her into this world, and the long dance of secrecy that had followed it. "How could you make love with someone," she'd asked her mother in that one shocking conversation, "bear his child, and then see him every few days for years and years and pretend to be merely friends?"

"You can't understand what it would have been like for him to leave the Church," her mother replied. "The disgrace he would have had to carry. You can't imagine it, Sarah."

"But what about the disgrace *you* had to carry, Mother!"

Her mother smiled in a way Sarah had seen many times and never liked. There was something smug, almost superior about that smile, as if Rebecca were saying, *Not many people are as strong as I am. Not many women could have done what I did.*

What she actually said was, "He had his faith for comfort. I had you."

Sarah sat opposite another priest now. She was eating his food, feeding her child from his parishioners' largesse.

"Life is so difficult," Father Alessandro was saying, and Sarah felt he was referring not to her situation or her mother's death, but to his own life. "The war." He waved a hand. "The suffering. All we have for comfort is each other."

"I'm so grateful, Father, for everything you've done." She had said those same words to him every day, and every day he put his hands on her shoulders as he was leaving and looked into her eyes, so close she could smell his breath, see the small patch of whiskers—already turning gray—on the part of his face he hadn't properly shaved. For one terrible moment, she worried the priest would try to kiss her. But he said only, "Tomorrow I shall come again, for Christ told us to comfort the grieving."

"You don't have to, Father. We have enough food."

"Yes, but I will." He reached down and touched the tip of Lydia's nose with one finger. "And I'll have a toy, sweet girl. I'll find a toy for you."

He forgot the toy, but didn't forget to visit, bringing Sarah some sewing work, and then, a few days later, payment for that work. Every day she wanted to tell him, *I have to leave now, Father. I have to go find Luca.* And every day, in the face of his steaming loneliness, she lost courage.

But with her mother gone, the April sun warming the air, and rumors on the Bellinzona streets that the war was surely in its final days, her longing for Luca began to fill every waking hour. At last, after one more of the priest's tender remarks, she made up her mind.

"I'm leaving, Father," she said when he visited the next day.

Father Alessandro stood perfectly still, looking like a man whose face had been slapped. *"Ma perché? Come?"* But why? How? he asked, in his Swiss-accented Italian. "You have a safe life here. Food, work. I'll make sure you and Lydia—"

Sarah shook her head. "I have to, Father. I've been trying to stay in condition. I'll make a sling for Lydia if I can buy one of these sheets from you, and I'll carry her in front of me. She can walk part of the time."

"You're not serious, Sarah. It's too far!"

Sarah shook her head in two fierce swings. "I walked here from home when I was pregnant, and my mother walked here, too, even in her condition. I've studied the map in your atlas. We're at almost five hundred meters here; the climb won't be too severe."

"But it's too much," Father Alessandro said. "The border is at fifteen hundred meters or more, even at its lowest point. I forbid it." He turned and hurried out of the house and the next day didn't come. The following day he visited again, carrying even more food this time, and remembering the toy—a small metal truck more suitable for a boy than for Lydia, but a toy all the same. "It's completely foolish of you to think of going, Sarah. It's impossible," he said, in a gentler tone. "You're going to walk over a mountain, taking your young daughter with you?"

"*Our* young daughter," Sarah said. "She's Luca's daughter as much as mine. I never knew my father, growing up. I refuse to do that to her. I've heard it's safe now. We'll be careful."

The priest looked away, something unspoken—stepchild of his loneliness—dancing across his face. "I want you to stay," he said, almost in a whisper.

"All that you've done for me, Father. I've thanked you five hundred times. I'll find a way to repay you after the war is over. We'll come back and—"

"No need, no need," he said. "I'd just like for you to stay, that's all."

Were those tears? The priest pretended to sneeze, took a handkerchief from his back pocket, and managed to wipe his nose and eyes in a single motion.

"I'll be leaving tomorrow," she said.

For a few moments Father Alessandro couldn't speak. He nodded, sadly, somberly, and met her eyes. "At least allow me to arrange for

Gunther to carry you part of the way to the border in his automobile. The town of Saint Margaret stands at eight hundred meters. From there it will be an easier climb and a somewhat shorter walk for you. Will you allow that? Can I do that for you, at least, as a parting gesture? I'll accompany you as far as Saint Margaret."

When he was gone, Sarah put clothes, diapers, food, and a blanket into a rucksack, fashioned one sheet into a sling, and having finished her preparations for the next morning, stood outside the stone house, trying to etch the view into her memory. To the south, long, smooth fields sloped gently down toward the outskirts of the city, the land broken into light-brown and pale-yellow rectangles outlined with stone walls and tree lines, the traditional white-and-brown Swiss chalets beyond, and then the church steeples and taller buildings of Bellinzona itself. She could almost see the cemetery where her mother's body lay. To her left, east, she could make out the blue mountains that marked the Swiss-Italian border, the highest sections showing strips of white in the shaded valleys. Maybe Father Alessandro was right: making that crossing with a small child was utter foolishness, no matter how many times she'd sat at the kitchen table, studying the atlas, searching for the easiest route, the lowest pass. Almost daily, she'd taken Lydia for walks into the higher hills, as if she'd known she would someday have to cross the border again, and wanted to be in condition. Yes, her child had been hardened to some degree by the life she'd led to this point. But the night or nights would be cold, and they'd have only one blanket and one sheet between them, enough food for a few small meals.

Someone had told her once that a mother's death casts a spell on a daughter, leaves her feeling adrift on a dark, enormous sea. That seemed true. Sarah felt unmoored, alone in a foreign land. If what Marlena had said was indeed true, and the war was, in fact, creeping closer to its final hours, then she wanted to be with Luca when that glorious moment arrived. Whatever wounds he'd suffered, physical and emotional, might be salved by the sight of his daughter. And her wounds might be salved as well. It terrified her to think of the other possibilities—that he might not be alive, that he might have found someone else—but those possibilities made it absolutely crucial that she return to Italy and try to find him. "Don't wait," Marlena had said. "Don't make the mistake my husband made."

Ten

A few days after the brigade meeting, according to the orders he'd received, Luca made the long walk to Masso's farm with the American automatic rifle slung over one shoulder. He avoided the roads, instead traversing the hillsides on old paths he'd walked with his father many years earlier. En route, he passed not far from the large stone behind which he'd hidden before killing the first man he'd ever slain. He didn't pause there this time—barely glanced at the stone, in fact. But he remembered, early on that same awful day, standing in Piazzale Loreto in Milan where the Nazis had left the bodies of fifteen murdered partisans to rot in the heat. Hitler's soldiers had stood guard there in the stench of decaying flesh, bored and sullen, preventing Italian family members from carrying the bodies away. That vision was etched into Luca's brain and would remain there, he knew, until he took his final breath. A plainclothes Italian policeman, one of Mussolini's OVRA dupes, had grown suspicious and followed Luca from the square, all the way into the woods and as far as that stone. There had been no choice but to kill the man, and Luca had stabbed him to death in a hateful fury, covered the body with dirt and leaves, then made this same walk, to see the old farmer, Masso.

But, as he'd learned, Gennaro Masso was much more than a simple old farmer. It had taken Luca some time to fully understand, but he knew now that Masso ran multiple bands of *partigiani*, scores of men and women who were fighting in the hills in this corner of Italy, sabotaging rail lines and roadways, blowing up trucks and armored vehicles, collecting and passing on information, shooting Nazi soldiers in twos and threes as the gray-uniformed demons made their patrols between the border with Switzerland and the shore of the lake. Masso seemed to have contacts everywhere. He received information as if he had a radio tuned to a secret war channel. It was Masso who, after that first killing, had put Luca in charge of his own brigade, Masso who fed him assignments now—though much of the time Luca was left to decide on his own what to do. The old man was wise, fearless, sly as a thief, and lived behind an armor of levity much of the time, as if the struggles to liberate their country and avoid capture, torture, and death were nothing more than arbitrary moves in a humorous chess game played out with pawns and castles carved from a chestnut tree that had fallen at the edge of his fields.

Luca trusted him; he had to. But even now, even after all these months of fulfilling assignments and risking his own life and those of his comrades, he sensed a tiny animal of doubt creeping around in his brain when he thought of Gennaro Masso. There was something so veiled about the bald old man, so mysterious, so impenetrable, that the tiny animal—a mole or baby mouse skittering here and there in the forest undergrowth—refused to die.

As he always did, Luca arrived at the edge of the woods above the westernmost of Masso's fields and waited there, crouching in the foreshortened midday shadows, studying the house. It was a ramshackle place, stone walls and tile roof supported by chestnut beams that looked as if the Romans had hewn them. A small, sagging back porch. A chimney that tilted slightly northward, two sixteen-paned windows facing west, one on each side of an unpainted back door. Luca waited and watched. Like all of them, Masso lived with the constant threat of being discovered, and so there was always the chance Luca would see a Nazi soldier relieving himself in the yard, or going outside for a smoke, waiting for other partisans to show up so he could kill them, too. Or, instead of killing them, the soldier would take them to the notorious interrogation rooms in Milan, the Sistek twins' torture cells, and the truth would be drawn out of them in the most agonizing ways before the SS officers finally heard what they wanted to hear and took the tortured partisan out back and shot him—or her—in the head.

The house seemed quiet. Luca stepped out into the light, the magical rifle in his hands now, not over his shoulder. He trotted across the field, which had been planted in a cover crop for winter. The dewy grass soaked his old worn boots. He climbed onto the porch, waited there another few seconds, listening, then tapped the door four times in a certain rhythm: *tap-tap . . . tap . . . tap.*

Masso opened it immediately. Overalls, a flannel shirt and sweater, a wool cap covering his bald head on this cool day, the old man pulled Luca tight against him in a quick embrace, then gestured to the kitchen table. Luca could smell something on the stove—there was always food at Masso's—and when the old man offered him eggs cooked with peppers and onions, Luca accepted, half guiltily. There was tea, also, and a slice of not very fresh bread with a thin line of green olive oil dribbled across it. A feast in these times.

Masso sat opposite him, and they ate for a few minutes without speaking. "We call them the *Americani*," Masso said at last, wiping the back of one gnarled hand across his mouth, "but, truly, they are the Americans and the British and the Australians and the New Zealanders and the Canadians, and others, too—some hellish Moroccans, from what I understand. Fighters of all these countries have come to liberate us. Think of it."

Luca grunted, sipped his tea, watched Masso's eyes—shimmering green marbles—in their baskets of wrinkles. The skin of the old man's face, made tough as a boar's hide after decades of working in sun and wind, looked like it would be impossible to cut with the blade of even the sharpest knife. Perhaps, Luca mused, such skin could even repel a bullet. The eyes, though, the eyes were those of a young man, alert, curious, giving off sparks in the dim light of the kitchen. And this was the way their conversations always began. There would be a little musing on the state of human life—in this case, foreign soldiers fighting to liberate Italian soil, a blessing!—then a report on the war, perhaps a personal question: *How are you feeling? How are your feet holding up? The feet are the things to worry about, Luca, remember that!* And only then would the assignment be brought out into the light. Luca almost smiled.

"Of course, in liberating our beautiful land they are also destroying huge parts of it. From what I hear, the bombing in the cities has been terrible. Milan, once a great capital, is now in places an enormous field of rubble, people living underground in shelters, or fleeing to the countryside, and Naples is the same, half the buildings destroyed. Parts of Rome have been spared—the Vatican, some of the churches, the Colosseum—so tourists can visit those places again after the war, but in order to save us, the *Americani* have had to drive us to the edge of ruin. Ironic, no?"

Luca grunted, wiped the plate clean with the last of the bread, and gave Masso his full attention.

"The war will be over soon, Luca. It's late April now, time for planting. The fighting here will last perhaps into early May, and then we'll be through with it, and like dogs after a fight, we'll lick our wounds and limp off into the trees to rest."

"And bury our dead properly," Luca said, thinking of his mother.

Masso nodded, tilting his head to one side so the flesh of his neck was pinched between chin and shirt collar. "But it's nearly over. Hitler knows it. Mussolini knows it. The *Americani* surely know it."

"Then why don't Hitler and Mussolini surrender?"

"Pride."

"Only that?"

"Don't say *only*, Luca. Pride, in its many disguises, is the source of all human misery, something that has been so since the Bible was written, since before the Bible was written. We are tiny in the world, minuscule, not even ants in the scope of the universe, and that smallness torments us. We have brains that want us to be large, to be in control. We complain about the weather, as if we should have dominion over that, too, deciding it will rain only at night, that the winters will be mild, the summers cool. We thrash and rush about to avoid dying, when every one of us knows that death awaits, certain as sunset. It's unfair, we say, as if we made the rules of human existence and know what fair and unfair must be. We're ants. Our smallness torments us."

"You should have been a priest, Masso."

The old man laughed quietly, making his gray eyebrows dance. "I thought of it, in fact. If I hadn't loved the company of women so much . . ." He paused there, lost in a memory, it seemed. He looked into his teacup, then raised his eyes. "Did you know I was in love with your mother?"

Luca shook his head. Brave beauty that she was, his mother had no doubt been part of the dreams of most local men.

A smile touched Masso's lips. "We were in school together. I knew her family, and she knew mine. A beautiful girl, she was. Brilliant, brave. For a time it seemed my interest in her might be reciprocated—I saved a friend of hers once, when the girl nearly drowned in the lake—but your father was the handsome one, not me. I always wished them well, however. Always."

"You could have been my father, then."

Masso's short laugh held little mirth in it. "I believe I would have enjoyed fatherhood. Maybe I could have had a son to take over this farm. But life turns as it must."

A small gust of wind made the windows, set loosely in their old frames, knock back and forth. Luca reached for his rifle, then relaxed. His mother had never said much about Gennaro Masso. His father even less.

"A fine weapon, that," Masso said.

"Gift from the mysterious American."

"Yes, they are here, a few of them, an advance guard. Bravest of the brave."

"You've met with them?"

Masso shrugged. "A few of them are here" was all he said, "but many thousands of them are very close now, and you can almost feel them there to the south. At night, you can imagine you hear their artillery, the grinding of their tanks' treads on the tar roads. I expect one morning to wake up and find a group of Allied soldiers in the yard, or knocking at the door. '*Signore*, can we come inside?' they'll ask politely, in terrible Italian. 'You didn't work with the Germans, did you, *Signore*? Can you cook us a meal? Do you have a beautiful daughter one of us might marry?' My imagination goes to those places."

"Mine to darker places."

"Of course, yes. We can't celebrate yet. There's still fighting around this lake, still work to be done. Still, unfortunately, lives to be lost."

"As you told me to, we're taking care of the rail lines that go to Lugano. They won't be able to retreat by that route, at least, to their damned Fatherland."

"Good, good. As of last night, the Allies have crossed the Po."

"Truly? That close?"

"Yes. The Nazis are pulling back, but they'll try to hold the rail yards and airports in Milan for as long as they can."

"And Mussolini?"

Masso bent his lips in between his teeth and hesitated a long moment. "I have word—not certain yet—that our great *Duce* will soon flee. I'm trying to get more precise information."

"When?"

"We have a person at Lake Garda, among Mussolini's people. I don't know this person's name. I've never met him or her, in fact, but I've heard we have someone there who has promised to help us learn when *il Duce* plans to leave, and perhaps by what route."

"You have a person at Garda? Really?"

"Someone there or, at least, with contacts there, that's all I know. Mussolini is guarded too heavily for even the *Americani* to reach him, but, as the fighting approaches, he won't stay there. We'll hope to know his plans a few hours, perhaps a day, before he flees."

At this news, Luca felt an electric current go through his fingers. He looked down to see if his hands were trembling, but they were perfectly still, the nails dirty, no matter how often he tried to clean them, the skin rough. For the millionth time he cursed the fact that the left hand was slightly smaller than the right; not shrunken, exactly, but obviously weaker. Worse, the left arm was weaker, too. He had to remind himself that it was the weak arm that had exempted him from military service, that he'd found a beautiful woman who loved him in spite of his deformity, that he could hold a rifle steady with that hand, and had become not just a partisan but a brigade captain. For a second, he thought of Sarah, but he forced the thought away. Masso was watching him.

"Mussolini invited the Germans here," Luca said. "The Germans killed my mother—"

"Your mother died a hero."

"Yes, and is buried in the dirt of our yard."

"I know that, Luca. You told me that. Don Claudio gave me the story in more detail. The food she was made to cook for them. The meal she poisoned, and so on. He told me everything."

"He's alive?"

"Yes. Another brigade rescued him. I can tell you that now."

"You didn't trust me before this?"

"Of course I trusted you."

"But if I'd been caught, you thought I would give that information?"

"Nobody resists torture, Luca. In real life, no one resists."

"So why tell me now?"

Masso shrugged. "Perhaps I shouldn't have. Perhaps I'm growing careless as the end nears. You, yourself, should not allow that to happen."

"My mother," Luca said. "Sarah. *Il Duce*'s to blame for what happened to them, no one else. My father was sent to the Russian front, where he no doubt also died, and where his body will never be found. Almost two years ago, you said I could have the assignment to kill Mussolini if the opportunity came. I ask for that assignment now."

"You have it," Masso said, without hesitation.

"But I thought the orders were capture, not kill. I just now passed that on to my people."

Masso shrugged. "The situation has changed. If he travels through our territory, and if the decision is up to me, I'll keep my word to you, and you will be known forever as the famous executioner." After a pause he added, "But there may very well be others there, individuals over whom I have no authority. If someone else has the opportunity, they'll no doubt take it."

"He killed my *mother*!" Luca said between clenched teeth. "My father. He chased my lover and my child from—"

"It's been impossible to get word from Switzerland. Spies are everywhere there. The authorities have put some of the refugees in prison, so we don't want to alert them to Sarah's presence. I've been trying to get news. I'll try again. Don't lose hope."

"I'll never lose hope, but I want to be the one—"

Masso held up both hands, palms forward. "I've been asked to send you to Milan, perhaps for an extremely risky assignment—I'm not sure. Perhaps to perform the work you ask for, perhaps not. These things aren't completely up to me, Luca. It may be difficult there, no matter what the assignment turns out to be, because the city is still under Fascist and German control, if barely. If Mussolini does leave via Milan—which would be foolish of him—he'll be surrounded by bodyguards, by his Nazi minders. They'll be watching everyone, every second."

"After all these months in the forests, it seems odd that I'd be sent there to kill him. That I'd be sent to Milan at all."

Masso shrugged again. "I don't know the assignment. It could very well be something else. I've been asked to send my bravest fighter to Milan, that's all. I've been asked to tell you to go to the back entrance of the Duomo at ten p.m. tonight. Someone will contact you there and you'll receive your assignment. I'll put out word that you should be the person who does the deed, but, again, I can't control that. I, personally, don't want to capture him. We captured him once before, and that didn't work out very well. But I cannot guarantee that or anything else. You understand?"

"I do."

"Good. You'll take my truck. There's enough gasoline. I've put some squash and cabbages in the back in wooden crates so it will seem you're making a delivery. Sleep here until darkness, then go. The Nazis are more concerned with their retreat now and will probably leave you alone. The road could be bombed, of course, or mined, but you can't walk from here to Milan in time, and the buses are slow and unreliable, so taking the truck is your only option. We don't know that his route north will lead along the lake, or I'd tell you to wait here and hope."

"I don't want to wait and hope."

"Fine; then sleep, rest, take the truck."

"Thank you."

"*Di niente*. If the Germans do happen to capture you, hold out for as long as you can. At this point, every hour matters."

Luca swallowed, clenched his right hand.

"Rest now, Luca. The bedroom is quiet. Sleep. I'll wake you when darkness falls, and I'll feed you again before you leave."

"Fine, good. Thank you."

"One more thing. I have word—I'm reluctant to pass it on to you because it's from an uncertain source—but I have word that your father may have survived the fighting in Russia. I have word that he's been wounded, badly perhaps, but is alive."

"Where is he?"

"That I do not know. And I won't know before you leave tonight."

Luca looked down at the empty plate, at his hands, glanced sideways at his weapon. For so long now he'd tried to put out of his mind the idea that he'd ever see his father again, that he'd ever see Sarah again, that he'd ever see his child. He'd cultivated a severe mental discipline, trained himself to keep those thoughts out of his mind. Now, it was as if Masso's words had broken open that dam and the thoughts were rushing in. He went into the dark bedroom, unlaced and removed his muddy boots, lay down, and pulled the blanket over him. Exhausted though he was, it took the better part of an hour to fall asleep, and for that hour a flood of thoughts and images washed over him. He'd trained himself not to hope; they'd all done that. In war, hope was a kind of devil. In order to fight, one had to remain always hopeless, avoiding death, but resigned to it. One had to cling to life only enough to enable one to function, but one had to set all hope in a box, lock the box, and bury it deeply in the mind's soil. Now, though, at the idea that his father might be alive, that Masso might soon have news of Sarah and their child, now the flood of possibilities had washed all the earth away, the metal box had risen to the surface, the lock had broken, the lid had popped open. He was going into occupied Milan, traveling not in the trees but in the open, driving a truck with food in the back, carrying one pistol and one automatic rifle, sent on a mysterious assignment. He'd follow the orders, of course.

But he suddenly wanted, more than anything, to live.

Eleven

Father Alessandro, it turned out, would not be accompanying her and Lydia and Gunther. On the path in front of the stone house, with Gunther waiting impatiently in his fancy automobile, the priest mumbled his excuses, held Sarah in another too-long embrace, then pressed a few coins into her hand and kissed her on each cheek. She thanked him multiple times, but he kept saying things like, "No, no, it was nothing. My Christian duty," and "May Christ care for your mother's soul and bless and protect you both here and in heaven."

As he said those words, Sarah could read a different message written on the features of his plump face. *Stay with me,* the priest's eyes seemed to be saying. *I could leave the church. We can make a life. I can help you raise your beautiful child.* The look in his eyes caused her to hear again the words her mother had spoken a few weeks earlier: "I made love with a priest, with Don Claudio. He is your father." It was a secret so deeply buried, and for so long, a surprise so astonishing to Sarah that it had crashed through the boundary between what she believed might happen in life and what fell into the category of totally impossible. Having grown up in a Catholic nation, having been surrounded by Catholic friends and neighbors, having lived with church bells on every Catholic sabbath and crucifixes on the walls of every classroom, Sarah knew a good deal about the faith. Priests were sworn to celibacy. And, for any Catholic, sex outside marriage was a sin punishable by an eternity in the flames of hell. And so on.

Don Claudio, the priest at Sant'Abbondio in Mezzegra, was her father. She simply could not imagine it.

Don Claudio had been more than just a parish priest. He'd been a kind of unofficial mayor, known and loved in the entire area. Particularly by her mother, it seemed. And now, clearly, another priest was revealing—or almost revealing—his sexual side. She believed Father Alessandro when he claimed he'd cared for them out of a devotion to his faith, but she knew, she could feel in her bones, that there was more than Christian charity involved.

Sarah thanked the priest yet again, then looked once more at the house where she'd spent the past sixteen months. Holding the squirming Lydia tightly in her arms, she went along the stone walk, placed her few belongings in the back of Gunther's Mercedes, and sat in the front seat. Gunther turned the car around and headed slowly down the wide path, onto the gravel road, then the paved road. "Would you kindly stop at my mother's grave for a few minutes?" she asked.

Gunther grunted. She guessed he was in his early fifties, but he was trim and strong, dressed in a light jacket and clean new trousers. She felt dirty beside him, as if she should have placed a towel on the seat before climbing in. He had a protruding cleft chin, thick brown eyebrows, a wide, blunt nose. Not a handsome man, not at all, but he carried himself as if he were a prince. She had no idea how he made his money and, of course, had never asked. From time to time she'd seen him around the main farmhouse. Twice, when her mother was still alive, he'd stopped by the outbuilding to bring a basket of food people at the church had put together—always seeming annoyed at having been asked to do such an errand, and always letting his gaze travel across her body. Half the time she saw Father Alessandro in the village he was walking with Gunther, the two of them talking quietly, as if engaged in a conspiracy, or an ongoing debate.

"I'll take you there, yes," Gunther said. And then, with that same tone of annoyance, "One is obliged to say a final goodbye to one's mother." He worked his lips and cheeks as if cleaning the last of breakfast from his teeth. "My own mother died giving birth to me, so I never had the pleasure of knowing her."

"I'm very sorry."

"Yes, thank you. I was raised by nannies. My father was a wealthy man and enjoyed many women friends, as have I. None of them ever seemed to rise to the level of potential mates, however." Gunther laughed in a strange way, blowing the air out through his nose in three short bursts. "*Bedroom women*, my father used to call them, a term I understand now, very well."

Sarah had no idea how to respond. After a few awkward seconds, she said, "You've never wanted to marry?" Lydia was crawling up against her shoulder and neck, as if she wanted to reach the window and climb out. Sarah kept having to pull her back down into her lap.

Gunther swung his face to her, looking through half-hooded eyes, as if the question had been impertinent. He turned to the road again but waited almost a full minute before answering. "Marriage is an impediment," he said at last. "Work matters. Pleasure matters. My friend the good priest holds higher beliefs and does many good deeds—as he did for you and your mother. I'm a more practical man."

"Why are you helping me, then?"

Gunther turned back with another superior look, the eyes angling down along the wide nose. One firm, slow blink, and he turned forward again. "For my amusement," he said, and Sarah felt a cold shiver run along the back of her neck.

She said nothing more until Gunther pulled to a stop at the cemetery's stone gates. "Don't be long," he said as she was climbing out. She set Lydia's feet on the ground, smoothed her dress, shut the car door gently, almost apologetically, and watched her daughter run with awkward steps toward the grave site. There was no real headstone, though at some point Father Alessandro must have had someone set a large round rock there on the mound of dirt. There was nothing written on the rock and never would be. He hadn't placed a cross there, Sarah thought. Not yet, at least. She watched her daughter run up to the grave and get down on all fours. Sarah hurried over and lifted the girl to standing, brushed the dirt from her knees and hands, straightened her dress. "Say something to Nonna," she said. "Say you love her. Say bye."

"Nonna," Lydia began, and then she burst into tears. "I lefted Principessa at home! When you stand up from the hole, see her, take her!"

Sarah realized it was true: they'd forgotten Principessa. "I'll get you another doll, you'll see, *carissima*. A better one. Principessa will take care of the house for us." The girl went on crying, turned and pressed her face against Sarah's knee. Sarah lifted her and held her, looked down at the mounded dirt and the pitiful stone, and said, "Thank you," and then, "Give me your strength now," and began to weep. She turned away, brushing at her eyes with one hand and bouncing Lydia up and down with the other.

"Ah, a tear fest," Gunther said when they were settled in the car again.

The remark sparked something in Sarah, a note of annoyance, or perhaps warning. For just a moment she thought of thanking him and getting out, saying she'd walk, that she didn't need a ride after all. But the truth was, with the trip now so close at hand, the reality of it terrified her. If Gunther would drive her two-thirds of the way to the edge of the forest and the start of the steepest incline, she'd be a fool not to accept the offer. She'd still have to climb to the border, holding or leading Lydia, rationing what little food and water she carried in the sack in Gunther's back seat. There was a fence at the border; she remembered it well, remembered as if it were yesterday the way Luca had snipped a kind of door in the chain link, the way he'd kissed her that final time, how it had felt to crawl through that door with her weak mother, rushing, panicked, crazed with fear. The tearing in her insides as she turned around and begged Luca to join them. How it had felt to see his face then, the torment there. How it had felt to turn and hurry down the hill into Switzerland. If she made it back to that place, she'd be able to find the doorway he'd cut and work her way back to the village they both loved, perhaps after spending a night in the cabin where Lydia had been conceived. If Marlena was right and the fighting near the lake was finished, then she could carry Lydia up and down the streets of Mezzegra, letting everyone know she was back, hoping word would reach Luca, hoping he was still alive, hoping he still wanted a life with her.

The alternative was to stay in the cold stone house and wait and hope and perhaps grow old there, with Father Alessandro becoming lonelier and bolder every month, and Lydia being raised without a father, as Sarah herself had been raised. She realized how much more she wanted for herself and her child. She wanted to garden and write poetry and have a brood of children and travel with them and Luca to Florence and Rome and Venice. She didn't need to have a fancy Mercedes, or to see Luca in clothes like the ones Gunther wore—fine shirts and vests and leather jackets. But she'd spent her childhood dreaming of a life beyond her mother's constrained and lonely existence, and she was determined not to settle for that unless she absolutely had to.

Gunther sped out of the city and into the countryside, the fields still brown and dead looking in the cool of April. The land sloped gently upward toward the border. After a few kilometers, Sarah began to see patches of snow in the shadowed areas above them. She realized she hadn't counted on it being that much colder there, and colder still as she climbed toward Italy. The day was mild, but the night would be frigid. Father Alessandro had given her a candle and matches. She'd have to make a fire, something she hadn't done since her school trips. *One night*, she told herself. *One night you can manage. Look what Mother was able to do!*

For fifteen minutes they rode in silence. Sarah alternated between trying to keep her daughter calm and studying the landscape, looking for something familiar. It seemed to her that, instead of heading due east into the mountains, the road was angling farther north. If she crossed the border too far north, it would be more difficult to find the place where the fence had been cut. It might add another day and night to the trip, and by then she'd be out of food, cold and exhausted. A persistent murmur of regret sounded in her thoughts. She ignored it.

"How do you think you're going to cross the border?" Gunther asked suddenly, as if reading her mind. "There are fences. Guards. Do you have any tools at all?"

"A small pocketknife."

"Do you have any money?"

"Twenty francs, and what Father Alessandro gave me before I left."

Gunther snorted. "Are you going to dig beneath the fence with your pocketknife? Or are you going to throw your daughter into Italy and climb over the barbed wire in your dress?"

Sarah blinked hard and pressed her lips together. The landscape was blurry.

Gunther reached his right hand from the wheel and placed it high up on her thigh. She flinched and tried to move toward the door. He laughed his snorting laugh again and took his hand away, but kept it on the seat between them like a weapon.

They passed through a tiny village—six whitewashed houses in a neat row. Sarah thought again of asking him to stop. She'd get out and walk from here, which would add perhaps another half day to the trip. But, again as if reading her thoughts, Gunther pressed down on the gas and they flew out into the countryside. The road turned slightly east, a bit closer to the border. Woods at first, and then long pastures with a few cows in the distance—silent, dark shapes. No houses to be seen. Gunther pulled to the side of the road, skidded to a stop there, and looked at her. "I have a little money for you," he said, not unkindly. "I have a small pair of shears in the trunk, the kind that can cut metal. I brought them specially for you."

"Thank you, I—"

"Don't thank me. I want something in return."

The look in his gray eyes when he said those words turned Sarah's insides to ice. "What?" she said, barely able to speak. "I have nothing."

"You have a beautiful woman's body."

She stared at him. Lydia had finally fallen asleep in her arms. Sarah thought of opening the door and running but knew she wouldn't get very far before he caught her. She and Gunther stared at each other. If Father Alessandro had given off the strong scent of loneliness, palpable as the smell of sour apples, then Gunther was giving off another scent, stronger and more acrid, burned coffee, wet hay in a field. "I can't do that," she managed to say, but the words came out in a thin, squeaking line.

"Are you sure?"

She nodded.

"You know, of course, that I could take you right here, right now, throw you down in that field and take you. Who would stop me? Your daughter? A lonely farmer's wife who happened to be out here on a cold morning?"

Sarah shook her head. Her lips had started trembling uncontrollably.

"For me, however, that would not be pleasurable. Not that I care about the morality of it. I have no morality. I act according to my whims. The priest and I argue about this constantly. He mentioned that I might help you, and I decided to do so, on a whim. Perhaps he can do me a favor one day, who knows?"

She couldn't speak. Lydia stirred in her arms.

"It wouldn't be pleasurable, that's all, if you resisted. But I want to touch you."

Sarah held out her left hand, palm up.

Gunther laughed.

"I want to touch you between your legs, under your clothing. One minute of touch in exchange for this ride, for the metal scissors and the money. Sixty seconds. I want you to count the seconds backward. Aloud."

"If . . . if . . . if I say no?"

One snort. "You can say no, of course. In which case, I'll drop you here and you can carry your child up the steep mountainside to the fence and see if your fingers are strong enough to rip it apart, or see if you can climb over the barbed wire holding her, or dig a tunnel in the stony ground."

"What if you're lying and have no metal scissors, no money?"

"You'll have to trust me, I suppose. One minute of your life in exchange for what is a rather peculiar pleasure of mine, I admit. It hardly seems like a fair trade on my end, but that is the offer. Accept or reject. You have ten seconds to decide."

———

She walked across a sloping field carrying the still-sleeping Lydia, the grass there nearly as high as her waist and brushing against her legs with cold fingers. Gunther had turned the Mercedes around and disappeared in a plume of dust. Lydia slept at her breast, in the sling Sarah had fashioned from a bedsheet. Over her shoulder she carried the small sack of food, water, and extra clothes, a pair of metal shears there now, a bit more money in the pocket of her dress. She felt as though her insides were coated in dirt, gravel in her blood, the memory of Gunther's hideous touch coursing through her, a circulatory of filth. She could feel the tears running down her cheek. When she looked down, she saw that several droplets had fallen onto her daughter's forehead. Sarah gently brushed them away.

Ahead of her she could see the place where the field ended and the trees began, and she could see, beyond a small patch of snow in the shadows there, that the ground slanted steeply upward. There were not yet any leaves on the branches of the trees, not even any buds at this altitude. Because of the outward curve of the slope, she couldn't make out the crest, the place where the border would be, the fence. She squeezed her eyes tight for a few steps, swiped at the wetness there, forced herself to think of Luca. Italy. Her mother. Home.

Lydia cried out once in her sleep.

Twelve

As he piloted his 1942 Alfa Romeo Bertone Coupe along the nearly empty Brescia Road, Silvio Merino hummed a few bars of a happy Neapolitan tune. The song was called "Comme' Facette Mammetta"— "How Your Mother Made You." He loved the melody and was amused by the lyrics, and as he steered around a long, sharp curve with one hand and shifted gears with the other, he sang a few lines:

> When your mother made you
> When your mother made you
> Wanna know how she did it?
> Wanna know how she did it?
>
> A basket full
> Of all the garden strawberries
> Honey, sugar, and cinnamon
> When your mother made you
> Wanna know how she did it?

Silvio had been told more than once that he had an excellent voice, and he loved to sing, loved driving his beautiful car, loved the feeling of the impending arrival of spring, and loved, especially, the sense that the war was nearly over.

Some important work remained to be done, however. Retreating though they were, retreating kilometer by kilometer up the Italian peninsula, the Nazis still had thousands of tanks and guns in Italy, and certain battalions were clearly being told to fight to the last man. Trapped in the ruins of his demented fantasies, Hitler was clinging to the absurd hope that some military miracle, some ingenious strategy, some imaginary new weapon, might still save the Fatherland from complete annihilation. *The fool,* Silvio thought. The cowardly fool. Instead of surrendering now and saving the lives of who knew how many of his own men, the Führer had ordered his generals to slow the Allied advance, no matter the cost. As if, with three-quarters of Italy in the hands of the *Americani,* and seven-eighths of Eastern Europe already overrun by Stalin's army, there might remain any hope at all of a German victory.

Silvio watched the road unwind and straighten. He shifted gears and pressed his foot toward the floor. In addition to the pure pleasure of driving it, the beauty of a vehicle like the Bertone lay in the fact that it marked him as someone with the highest connections. How many men could afford a Bertone Coupe these days? Very few. Even fewer would be able to find and pay for the gasoline needed for a trip like this. The Nazis, preoccupied with saving their own skins, wouldn't care what kind of car passed them on the road. And the Fascist militia and local police would assume the driver must be protected by important friends and would leave him alone. They wouldn't know, of course, who those powerful friends might be—wasn't Mussolini himself known to drive an Alfa Romeo? They wouldn't even know which side Silvio had taken in what had become Italy's civil war, a homegrown reflection of the greater conflict. Right now, for instance, he was en route to a lunch with his new acquaintance, Enzo Riccio, one of *il Duce*'s closest confidants. But only Silvio, Enzo, and their mutual friend, the lovely, sapphire-eyed Angelina, would have any idea where the lunch conversation might travel.

Silvio stopped in Sarnico, drank a quick coffee at a little place owned by a man named Lorenzo, then rejoined the main road. He turned north near Rezzato and pointed the Alfa toward Lake Garda. He and this duplicitous Enzo were to have lunch at L'Onda, in the pretty lakeside town of Salò.

He parked on a side street lined with Salò's brick townhomes and didn't bother to lock the Bertone. The same principle applied: tempting as it might be, who would dare steal a car like this? Over the past few years, human life had become very cheap in these parts. An aggrieved Alfa Romeo owner, coming upon a would-be thief, might very well shoot him right there in the street and leave the bleeding body in the gutter. Who would stand in the way? And what would another death mean?

Silvio arrived early at the restaurant, shook the hand of the owner—one freckle-faced Piero—and asked for a secluded table. A pair of large bills, passed along when they were palm-to-palm, and the agreeable Piero led him to a corner table set in an alcove, looking out on the lake. Enzo arrived ten minutes later, wearing, beneath his greatcoat, the uniform of the Fascist militia. Black tie, black shirt, black boots, olive-green trousers. Perfect.

"My friend," Silvio said, standing and vigorously shaking Enzo's sweaty hand. "How was the trip?"

"Fine, fine," Enzo said, glancing around.

When they were seated, Silvio leaned in closer and lowered his voice. "Enzo," he said, "there's no need to worry. Act as if we're friends having a casual lunch. Let out a laugh once in a while. Lavish the cook with compliments if he stops by. No one can hear what is said at this table."

Enzo nodded, but nervously, Silvio thought. An amateur.

They ate and drank for a while—a simple puttanesca; the wartime menu was limited, but the wine was quite good—Silvio knowing better than to ask about the wife who'd left Enzo behind after his embrace of *il Duce*. In addition to setting up the lunch meeting, their mutual friend,

Angelina, had given him all the background information he needed. Not long after he'd moved to Rome, Silvio and the young maid had been lovers. The relationship ended when she'd gone north to serve in the house of Mussolini's mistress, but they'd remained close, linked by pleasant bedroom memories and a shared hatred of the Fascist impulse. At one point in their wartime festival of love, Angelina had entrusted Silvio with her great secret—that her father had been a Neapolitan Jew. The man was long dead now, from natural causes, but that wouldn't matter to *il Duce*'s Blackshirts, and would matter even less to the Nazis who lorded over them. Jewish blood was Jewish blood, even on the father's side. Silvio smiled at the irony of it: after all the torment the Jews had endured, what if one of them, servant to Mussolini's mistress, ended up helping to seal the great *il Duce*'s fate!

Silvio carried Enzo through the meal on a stream of small talk and amusing anecdotes, and then, when Piero had served them a delightfully syrupy Amaro Montenegro and left them in peace, he asked, in the most casual of tones, "Any news?"

"Some," Enzo said, not turning his head this time, but swinging his eyes around the alcove as if they weren't in his control. "He's made up his mind to leave."

"Ah."

"He's not a hundred percent convinced yet that the war is lost, but Scavolini wasn't able to bring more than a handful of fighters to the lake, and *il Duce* has asked me to start making arrangements for departure."

"Particular arrangements?"

"Destroying some papers. Collecting others . . . 'for history,' he said. Gathering monies from the various places he's kept them stored. Feeling out Lieutenant Birzer to make sure he'll have protection. 'A convoy,' he called it."

"He's got a German *lieutenant* guarding him? No one of higher rank?"

"He speaks with General Wolff, or used to. The Germans don't seem to listen to him now. They just want to keep him alive. The lieutenant has orders never to let *il Duce* out of his sight, except when he goes up to the bedroom."

"They'll want him to go straight north from Garda into Austria, no?"

Enzo shook his head in small movements, took one delicate sip of his amaro, and then drank the rest in a gulp, as if he had only a few more seconds to enjoy the pleasure. "Milan is where *il Duce* wants to go," he whispered, just loudly enough for Silvio to hear. "Milan is still in our hands. He has men there, and the last time he went, some months ago, thousands of people came to hear him speak. He talked about that for weeks. He mentioned Milan to me just yesterday."

Silvio pondered this for a moment. That one piece of information was priceless. The difference between Mussolini heading southwest to Milan and *then* heading north and Mussolini heading north directly from Garda was enormous. The latter route would mean traveling in territory with little risk to him: everything north of the lake, including the mountainous terrain between Trento and the Austrian border, was still safely in German hands. If he insisted on visiting Milan first, the story could be quite different.

"Can I ask you a favor?" Silvio said. He reached into his pocket for the large wad of bills, allowed Enzo a glimpse, then passed them along beneath the table. "Can you let me know when he decides, and what he decides?"

Enzo stuffed the bills into his pants pocket. "Of course, of course," he said quietly, nervously. "But it's the Germans who might decide. Wolff and the others. They might force him to take the road to Innsbruck, for his safety."

"Yes, of course," Silvio said. "But when has he ever listened to anyone besides himself?"

The remark brought the first notes of quiet laughter from Enzo. Perfect, Silvio thought. He was about to speak when Piero came by to remove the wine bottle and to inquire if there was anything else they desired. When they were alone again, Silvio said, "What I'd like to know, what our good comrades would enjoy knowing, is exactly when he will leave his little German-guarded fortress at the Feltrinellis', and what his plans might be after his presentation in Milan."

"Soon," Enzo said, almost eagerly now, the money safely in his pocket. "He's going to leave soon."

"Ah, soon. And more specifically?"

"I'll know only the day before, maybe hours before. The Germans are getting ready. *Il Duce* asked me to throw his papers in the lake. He seemed . . . resigned."

"As well he might be." Silvio sipped the last of his amaro, set the glass down, reached up under his cashmere sweater, and took something from his shirt pocket. A small box of four cigars. "Cubans," he said, handing the box across the table. And then, more quietly: "When you receive the news that his departure is imminent, would you be kind enough to sit out on the deck that overlooks the lake and smoke one of these? It would be greatly appreciated."

Enzo slid the top of one cigar out of the box and raised it to his nose. "*Il Duce* will ask where I found such a beautiful pleasure."

"Share one with him," Silvio said happily. "Tell him Silvio, the Sicilian with the scarred face, gave it to you as a gift, along with his other gifts of information. Tell him that, due to my love of the Fascist cause, I informed you that the Allies were still a fair distance south of Milan, and the city is relatively safe at this time."

"He'll want to hear that."

"Exactly. Always tell him what he wants to hear. Folded inside the box I just gave you is a piece of paper with a phone number written on it. If you find yourself in Milan with our *Duce*, and if you have further information—what route north he'll take, for instance; what kind of protection he'll have—kindly call that number, let the phone ring three times, then hang up. It's a café in Milan. Someone will be monitoring that telephone at all times. Then, if you can slip away, go to the Duomo within an hour or two of the phone call, and you can pass on your information there in a few words. Perhaps to your good friend, Silvio the Sicilian."

"My new friend."

"Yes, exactly. You are a friend of every decent Italian. I sensed something in you immediately: that you love our country as I love it. That you want to remove from it the stain we've lived with." Silvio grew a bit more animated. He could feel blood rising into the skin of his face. "That its great beauty has been tarnished, ruined in places. That hundreds of thousands of families have been brought to misery." He drew a breath. "And for what, Enzo? Tell me. For what, exactly, has the war been brought to us? How would you answer that now?"

"For the satisfaction of one man."

Silvio was shaking his head. "Two men. One of them is our own, our own stain. Now we would like to cleanse that stain from the beautiful silk cloth of our nation. Agreed?"

Enzo could only nod.

Silvio calmed himself. He flashed his smile. "I've paid for the meal in advance, my friend, with a healthy gratuity for the owner who allowed us this privacy. Sit here for a time. I must leave and return to my beautiful Alfa Romeo Bertone. She gets lonely when I'm away too long."

"The Bertone is a gorgeous automobile."

"Indeed. Enjoy a cigar, if you wish, but save at least one for the deck and one for your boss."

"Who can see if I smoke it?" Enzo asked. "Someone's watching the villa?"

Silvio was standing by then and had a hand on Enzo's shoulder. "Ah," he said. "Fascinating question."

Silvio left him there. Walking toward the door, he complimented Piero on the wine and the lovely puttanesca, thanked him for the amaro, and hummed the same favorite tune as he walked back to his car along Salò's winding streets. He turned the last corner and saw the Bertone there, unmolested, shining in the afternoon light like a note of congratulations from God.

Thirteen

Sarah was grateful the day was mild, and grateful, too, despite the extra weight, for Father Alessandro's insistence that she carry a blanket. As she walked toward the steeper terrain, she had a clearer sense of how cold it could be once the sun went down.

Even before her mother's death, Sarah had spent hours studying the atlas in Father Alessandro's rectory, imagining, hundreds of times, how she'd make the trip to Italy, which route she'd take, which pass she'd try to cross, how she might find her way back to the place where Luca had cut through the fence. It was only about twenty kilometers from the outskirts of Bellinzona to the western edge of Lake Como, a moderate day's walk for a woman her age if the landscape had been flat and if she'd been traveling alone. But the landscape was anything but flat, and she was anything but alone.

In the early going, once she and Lydia had crossed the long corn-field and reached the edge of the forest, the slope was fairly gentle, if rocky and in some places slick. Sarah knew the border ran across the ridge of the mountainous barrier between the two countries—until two years ago she'd lived just on the other side of that border—and she also knew there were higher and lower places along the ridge, peaks and passes, all of them fenced, but some more accessible than others. But she had no map. And even if she'd had a map and could find the lowest point of crossing, that point would be some two thousand meters above sea level, at least a thousand meters above where Gunther had left her. And not particularly close to the place of her previous crossing.

It took her less than an hour of walking to realize that attempting such a journey with an eighteen-month-old child would turn out to be more difficult than she'd imagined. When Lydia awoke, she was restless, hungry, and irritable. Either she was growing heavier by the hour, or Sarah was already growing weaker, because every fifteen minutes or so she had to take Lydia out of the sling she'd made, set her down, and encourage her to walk. Lydia could walk, but not fast, not necessarily in a straight line, and not very easily uphill. It had been a mistake to try this. But, she kept reminding herself, the other option had been to wait in the stone house with Father Alessandro and his sick friend, Gunther, close by—wait there, dreaming of Luca, remembering Marlena's warning.

And that was no option at all.

To supplement their relatively meager supply of solid food, she was still nursing Lydia—that was a blessing, and a joy, a comfort for both of them: there was no feeling in the world like holding the child to her breast and letting her nourish herself. Body to body, warmth to warmth, love to love at a level so profound it sometimes brought tears to her eyes. She had some food for them in the sack, though only one canning jar filled with water. Half a loaf of bread, two apples, even a small piece of foil-wrapped chocolate Father Alessandro had pressed into her hand at the last minute when he said he wouldn't be making the first part of the trip. That, the folded blanket, five extra diapers, and now Gunther's metal scissors, too.

The worst part was when Lydia needed to be changed. At home, that was a simple task, but now it wouldn't do to return the soiled diaper to the sack, so she had to find a way to clean it. There were no streams or ponds, not even a puddle, and she didn't want to use up their meager supply of drinking water. She tried dead leaves, and sand, and she rubbed the cloth against stone, all the while watching her daughter, who toddled away in all directions. Eventually she had the cloth more or less clean.

Step by arduous step, with numerous stops to rest, they'd made it a fair distance up the slope by what Sarah guessed was early afternoon. Now, however, the path turned rocky, and, holding or leading Lydia, she had to leave the steepest parts and venture sideways into the trees, climb a few difficult meters at an angle, sometimes pulling herself upward by holding on to the trunks of saplings with one hand. She'd make a little progress, sit and rest, then get up and climb another fifty meters.

Soon, too soon, she could feel daylight fading, and she began looking for places where they might spend the night. Lydia had grown sleepy again and had to be carried, and Sarah could manage only twenty or thirty steps with the child held against her before she had to sit and breathe. Another twenty steps, another rest, the light fading around them. No rain, thank God, and it was cool but not freezing—not yet at least. She came upon a more or less flat area about the size of a large bed. The ground was carpeted with leaves, and the leaves, thank God again, were dry. She tried to make a game of it with Lydia—who was awake now—tried to pretend they were on a happy adventure, kicking and pushing the leaves into a pile to form a makeshift mattress. They sat there and unpacked the food. Sarah broke off small pieces of the bread loaf and used her pocketknife to cut slices of apple, watching her daughter carefully as the girl gnawed and swallowed. *"Mangiamo, Mami,"* Lydia said at one point, after Sarah had tipped the canning jar to her lips and let her drink.

"*Si, mangiamo.* We're eating. And soon we'll rest. It will be dark and maybe a little cold. Maybe we can see the stars between the branches of the trees." She couldn't be sure how much Lydia actually understood, but she pushed her daughter's beautiful dark curls from her face with one finger, pointed upward, and said, "*Le stelle*"—*the stars*—and her daughter looked up and laughed.

They slept huddled against each other, wrapped tightly in the blanket with the soft cushion of dead leaves beneath them. In the early-morning hours, still in darkness, Sarah was awakened by the cold. She sat up and lifted her dress above her head, took off Lydia's dress—the girl stirred, said something unintelligible—and then she pressed them together, skin to skin, and wrapped the clothes around them as best she could.

They awoke shivering. Sarah remembered the candle—which lay at the bottom of the sack with the box of matches—and together they gathered twigs and made a fire, small and smoky, but enough to warm their hands. Another few minutes of nursing, a few more sips of water, a diaper change. She threw aside the dirty diaper and saved the rest of the bread, apple, and cheese for later in the day. Determined not to spend another night in the forest, Sarah gave Lydia a corner of the chocolate and ate the rest of it herself.

"Only a little longer now, *tesoro*."

It took her four more hours to make the last part of the climb to the ridgeline. Most of the time she had to go at an angle rather than straight up, which made the ascent less steep, but longer. At last, tired and very hungry, a new, partially clean diaper and a filthy dress on her daughter's body, she saw the first warning signs for the border, and then, a quarter of an hour later, the fence itself.

The fence was just as she remembered it: chain link, four meters tall, capped with barbed wire. She was pierced again by the memory of Luca cutting a sort of door in it, of her mother bending low and passing through, of a last hurried kiss, of being on the other side, the Swiss side, and turning to see Luca gripping the chain link with one hand and waving her forward with the other, as if saying, *I hear footsteps, hurry!* She'd made one last request that he join her, and he'd stubbornly shaken his head. Go now, go! Why hadn't she paused just long enough to speak another sentence, to make a plan, to say, *After the war . . .* ? But Luca was gesturing furiously, her mother was already a few steps down the hill, and she couldn't bear to see the expression on her lover's contorted face. She turned, eyes blurry, mind awhirl, and walked downhill, into the trees, and forced herself not to glance back.

Sarah looked up and down along the fence, but guessed, because of the route Gunther had taken, that she was far north of the place where Luca had cut the door. For the better part of an hour, hiding in a copse of white birches, she watched for German patrols as her daughter napped. All was silent.

She waited, feeling the light change above and behind her. Tired as she was, she knew that spending another night in the forest would be too much to ask of her brave daughter, and she felt as though she, herself, had energy enough only to get across, to start down the Italian slope, perhaps to reach the first village and then take her chances that someone would help them.

Lydia woke from her sleep, rubbed her face with both hands, reached for a breast. Sarah nursed her quickly, cleaned her again as well as she could, then led her to the fence. The warning signs there, in German, French, and Italian, felt like sinister sentries, the letters like angry eyes: VIETATO! VERBOTEN! INTERDIT! Sarah hoped her hands were strong enough to allow her to cut through the chain link. She set the sack on the ground, told Lydia, twice, to stay still, and took the metal shears. Touching them, remembering the man who'd given them to her, she felt again the sense that her blood had been dirtied, but she shoved the thought aside and managed, using both hands, to snip through the first diamond of the chain link. The pressure of the metal handles hurt her palms and fingers, but she made another cut, then another, before she had to rest. She tried to imagine a three-sided doorway like the one Luca had cut for them, but smaller. She counted: sixteen or eighteen cuts it would require. She was able to do three at a time, and then, as her hands began to hurt more, two at a time, and then one at a time. One, a rest, a minute spent listening for footsteps, another one. She tried cutting a piece from the blanket with her knife and using that to soften the handles against her hands. It barely helped. One cut, a rest. She waited, listening. A few birds were singing in the trees, as if warning the two human females that soldiers were approaching. But there were no footsteps, no German words.

When she'd at last managed to cut three sides of the square, Sarah pulled hard on the piece of fencing and then, leaning against it with all her weight, forced it back against the uncut section. She pushed the sack and sash through, had Lydia bend down and squeeze through, and then she flattened herself on her stomach and crawled, a few centimeters at a time, until she was able to kneel and then stand up on the Italian side. The front of her dress was filthy, but she didn't have the energy to clean it.

They started downhill, and that turned out to be even harder on her leg muscles than climbing had been: with each step her thighs clenched and cramped. Even though she and Lydia had eaten most of the food and drunk most of the water, the sack seemed somehow heavier. Lydia hung in the sling against her chest like a stone. They stopped and ate the last of the food and drank the last of the water, and Sarah left the canning jar and another dirty diaper there, thought of leaving the blanket, too, but changed her mind. Lydia was crying almost continuously, raising her small arms to be lifted up. "I can't; I can't hold you now," Sarah said, but the child stood still, keeping her arms in the air, shrieking. Sarah lifted her and fell forward, caught herself with one hand against a tree trunk. She sank to the ground and rested a few minutes, then forced herself to stand again.

Another hour of torment and she came upon what seemed to be a path, angling to the right and down. The light was fading, night closing in, but soon the path turned straight down, less steep here, if barely visible. Soon, through the trees she saw a few distant lights. The far edge of Lake Como, she guessed. The trees were thinner here. She and Lydia crossed a small, square pasture—no animals, the grass ankle high. Full darkness had fallen, but a gibbous moon ducked in and out of the clouds and illuminated the way.

She tripped, fell to one knee, and cried out in pain. Lydia was moaning in a steady stream of misery, *"Mami, Mami, Mami."* But they couldn't stop. At last Sarah saw what seemed to be a church steeple, a dark triangular outline against the starry sky. Moonlight shone against it, then left it in darkness, then illuminated it again. She wondered, from the shape of the bell tower, if it might be the church of Sant'Abbondio, where Don Claudio had presided.

Don Claudio, she thought, *kindly, plump Don Claudio.* She could hear her mother's voice—"Don Claudio is your father"—and she could feel, once again, the shock of those words.

This couldn't be Sant'Abbondio. It would be too great a stroke of luck, too huge a blessing. It couldn't be. She offered up a prayer. Couldn't be. Couldn't be.

It wasn't. She was close enough now to see moonlight on a slate roof, to make out more clearly the outlines of a bell tower and a bulky building below it. Not Sant'Abbondio, but obviously a church. A small house beside it. Then a cluster of houses. In a front window of one of them, the flickering light from a candle. With the very last of her energy, Sarah lifted her moaning daughter to her chest, looped the sack over her shoulder, and shuffled toward that light.

Fourteen

It was a two-hour drive from Salò back to his apartment in Milan, and when he'd returned from the lunch meeting with Enzo, Silvio allowed himself the pleasure of a short nap. *Sonnellino* was the word in Italian—a beautiful word, he thought. The rented apartment where he enjoyed his *sonnellino* was beautiful as well: three bedrooms with high ceilings, a respectable kitchen, and a large living room complete with stone fireplace, two sofas, and elegant old molding at the tops of the walls. There was even a copy of the Bible on a side table, though he'd yet to open it. He'd been living there a few days shy of six months, having made his way north from Rome as the Allies were advancing. He wasn't afraid of the Allied advance—just the opposite, in fact: the move to this apartment was part of a larger scheme intended to make him look like the most loyal of Fascists.

Two years earlier, for reasons Silvio still couldn't quite grasp, he'd been approached by a mysterious man, half-American, half-Italian, and asked if he might be interested in aiding the Allied cause. He'd agreed, despite the danger. What kind of businessman, what kind of faithful Italian, wouldn't want to help rid the country of the northern occupiers?

He'd completed a few secret assignments, and after one of them, driving another beautiful automobile on the streets of Rome, had been severely injured in a bombing raid on that city. An American bomb, he'd later learned. Which seemed unfair, after the work he'd been doing. Couldn't they have been more careful? He'd spent three and a half months in Policlinico Celio, the city's military hospital, and except for a rakish scar on his face—it looked like an upside-down question mark—and a sometimes troublesome right ankle, he'd made a full recovery. The nurses at Celio had been kind to him in various inventive ways, and as an added bonus, during his recuperation he'd had what he liked to think of as a spiritual epiphany: he'd decided to become a good man. Not just decent, not just fairly honest, but truly good. Proximity to death could do that for a person, he supposed. After his recovery, when his half-American contact asked if he'd be willing to continue the secret work, Silvio agreed without hesitation. "Let me serve in the way that's most helpful," he'd said.

And so they'd sent him to Milan, and found for him this beautiful apartment.

The nap refreshed him. Outside the windows, darkness had long ago fallen, a particular kind of wartime darkness, unbroken by the usual urban illumination or the happy activity of the streets. He was hungry. He washed his face, changed into a slightly more formal pair of trousers, a clean pair of shoes, a white shirt, slipped his arms into a gorgeously tailored sport coat, and admired himself in the mirror. He'd long believed in the importance of cutting a *bella figura*, but it was especially important on this night, given where he was headed for dinner. He thought of it as the "Alfa Romeo principle": the richer you looked, the less likely the Nazis were to cause you any trouble. And the place he planned to dine was a veritable hornet's nest of Nazis.

Greatcoat thrown casually over his shoulders against the April chill, Silvio strode along Via Nazionale toward the Duomo, made a left onto Corso Emanuele II, another left into a narrow alley halfway down the block, and followed the alley all the way to a dark metal door at its end. He rapped twice. A few seconds' pause and the door was opened by an enormously obese man with a round face covered in a patina of sweat. Oleg.

Oleg smiled, accepted the folded twenty-lira note with a subtle readjustment of one arm, and gestured for Silvio to leave his coat.

Straightening his shoulders, running the palm of one hand back through his fine head of hair, Silvio strolled over to his usual table in the right corner, not close to the stage. He wasn't here for the entertainment—either what he could see, or what he knew lurked in the second-floor rooms. A waiter approached and greeted him by name, "Signor Merino!"

"Ciao, Mario!" Silvio asked after Mario's family, bantered with him a bit about the beauty of Italian women, the silkiness of the spring air, then ordered a small steak and a glass of champagne. Alone again, he ran his eyes casually around the room.

There were, by design, no windows in this establishment, perhaps twenty tables in all, each covered with a cream-colored cloth, some with seats for four or six, but most, like Silvio's, suitable only for a couple. At about half the tables, scattered here and there, sat a collection of German officers in uniform: Gestapo, SS, Luftwaffe, regular army. Several of them sat with lovely female companions, German and Italian both, and some of those companions were dressed in tight black dresses, the uniform of the upstairs rooms. Beyond the front row of tables stood a stage, elevated two meters above the floor. A lavender curtain covered it at the moment, but just as Mario delivered the champagne in a sparkling flute, Silvio watched the curtain split in half and slide right and left, saw a spotlight shine on a lone woman, scantily dressed in glittering silver clothes, who stood provocatively, hands on hips, in the very center. Yves. A loud cheer rose from the tables. Yves blew an appreciative kiss and began her routine, prancing back and forth, tantalizingly unsnapping a button to the side of her tiny skirt, leaning forward so her cleavage was revealed, and then coquettishly covering it with both hands, looking up as if embarrassed, letting out a teasing squeal.

Silvio had seen the act a dozen times and always appreciated Yves's skill. She was an expert at offering a not-quite-complete revelation of her intimate parts, tugging the top down just above her nipples, sliding her hands into the silvery skirt and moving them suggestively there in a way that exposed her lower belly. It occurred to him on this night that he and Yves were playing a similar game. Both of them were teasing the soldiers in the audience, she with her body, he with his presence. No Allied sympathizer would dare frequent a place like this, and yet Silvio not only frequented it, he did so brazenly, happily, applauding Yves as enthusiastically as anyone in the room. When his steak was served—medium rare, with a glaze of wild mushrooms and a few pieces of broccoli rabe to the side—Silvio sliced and chewed it and sipped his champagne as if he were among friends, as if it were peacetime, as if steak and champagne were on every menu in the city.

Yves finished her act to raucous, drunken applause, and Silvio was swallowing the last succulent bite of beef when a tall, thin colonel with a head as bald as one of the shoreline stones Silvio had dived from near his boyhood home in Sicily sauntered over and, without asking, occupied the other chair.

"Colonel Edmund Sistek," Silvio said pleasantly, as if he were overjoyed to have company, this company in particular. "Might I buy you a glass of something?"

The colonel shook his head but kept his gray eyes, the color of a knife blade, fixed on Silvio. "How are you tonight?" he asked, in his horrific Italian.

Grateful not to be in one of your cells, Silvio thought, but he said, "Rather tired, if the truth be told."

"A busy day?"

A practiced liar when the occasion called for it, Silvio knew it was always better to lie with half-truths. Better to admit to the outlines of a given action and transmute the details, rather than make up something out of whole cloth. "I drove up to Salò to see an old friend whose wife has left him. Errand of mercy."

"Ah, mercy," Sistek said, as if he'd heard the term but had no real understanding of the attribute it described. He was playing an old trick Silvio recognized from their other brief encounters: staring so fixedly across the table that Silvio either had to avert his eyes or engage in a staring contest.

Silvio drank the last of the champagne and raised his glass at the passing waiter. "Are you sure I can't offer you a beverage, Colonel?"

Sistek broke eye contact at last, but only long enough to glance at the table to his right, where one of the house women had taken up residence on the lap of a Gestapo captain. The colonel smirked and swung his eyes to Silvio again, studying him. "Will you go upstairs tonight? We never see you there."

Silvio laughed. Mario brought his second glass. "One, I don't believe in paying for sex. And two, I'm training for the priesthood, Colonel. Celibacy is apparently a requirement."

Colonel Sistek moved the corners of his lips a centimeter toward the sides of his face, then made one of his rapid swings to a different subject, as if sweeping away a thin layer of pretense and getting down to business. "Your *Duce* is up there. Salò."

"In Gargnano, actually, some kilometers to the north, but on the same side of the lake."

"Then why do they call his little kingdom there 'the Republic of Salò'?"

Silvio shrugged, smiled, sipped from his second glass. "Colonel, I have no idea. No one consults me in those matters."

"Ah." Sistek blinked, stared. "What is your work, exactly? Perhaps you've told me; I've forgotten."

"My work is making connections."

"Such as?"

"Such as when a restauranteur known to host the brave officers of the Reich needs to find a wholesome piece of beef in wartime, I connect him with a farmer in the hills of Lombardia who may know of a place to locate said piece of beef. In exchange, the farmer pays me a small sum, and the restauranteur welcomes me without charge at his establishment." Silvio grinned, as if at his own wit, and waited for the next chess move.

"The war has been bad or good for your work?"

"Bad *and* good, Colonel. The arrival of your soldiers has opened up a wealth of new opportunities, a new clientele, but the fighting and bombing has sent some of my other customers into temporary retirement. How is your work going? In logistics, aren't you?"

The question brought a terrifying smile. "I work from midnight to noon, and my brother works from noon to midnight. We deal in logistics, yes, but the logistics of information."

"Excellent. And it's going well?"

"Perfectly well. Like you, we've had to relocate northward. We both preferred working in Rome."

"Such an amazing city."

"Not Berlin, not Munich, not even Vienna, but yes, a place where one might live for a time. This is as far north as we intend to go, however."

"Good," Silvio said. "I can say the same."

"Soon, the secret weapon will be revealed and the course of the war will be radically altered. Perhaps you and I will meet in Rome again."

"So there *is* a secret weapon! For months I've been hearing rumors from my Luftwaffe friends."

Sistek nodded. "The rumors are absolutely true; though, of course, your Luftwaffe friends shouldn't be in the business of revealing such information. Our enemies have some knowledge of the weapon already, however, so it doesn't matter. They're trembling in their foxholes. You'll soon see a change in the war's trajectory."

"We'd all welcome that."

Sistek looked down at his manicured nails, examined them with what seemed to Silvio a look of intense satisfaction, then raised his eyes. "I wonder if you can do me a favor," he said, and for a few horrible seconds Silvio thought Colonel Sistek was about to ask him to stop by his "office" and answer a few questions. The building—on the corner of Roma and Santo Selvatico, a kilometer east of where they now sat—was a notorious address. People described hearing the screams as they walked past. Neighbors reported seeing bodies loaded into trucks at the building's back door, en route to the morgue or cemetery. Silvio knew certain Italians who wouldn't go within two blocks of that building, out of superstition, terror, or simple good sense.

"Anything," Silvio said, with as much confidence as he could muster.

"I and my brother, who lives and works with me as you may know, have a particular fondness for pork cheek. Our cook tells us she could make a delicious sauce for her pasta if she could find some, but apparently it's almost impossible to come by these days. Perhaps your farmer friend could oblige us?"

Silvio smiled. "Regrettably, Colonel, he cannot. Farmers in this country often specialize. He raises beef cows."

"A shame."

"Yes." Silvio pretended to be thinking. Yves's colleague, Elsa, had replaced her on the stage, and he had to wait for another raucous round of cheering and yelling to subside before he said, "But there is someone near the city of Como who raises pigs. I'd be happy to inquire."

"I'll be here again, day after tomorrow," Sistek said, and his words had the feel of an order.

"The meat will no doubt be expensive."

"Ah," the colonel said, and Silvio realized Sistek had no intention of paying for the delicacy, just as Silvio had no intention of providing it. It was a dance, a game, moves in a chess match. Sistek pushed his chair back and made as if he were about to stand. Behind him, Elsa was already naked from the waist up. The officers were pounding their tables, asking for more. Above the noise, the colonel switched subjects again, another tactic: "What do you think of your *Duce*, Silvio? I've never asked."

It was, Silvio realized, the trick question of trick questions, the chess move that anticipated checkmate. He offered his widest smile, then stole a bit of time by having a slow sip of champagne. He swallowed, ran the cloth napkin delicately across his lips, glanced up at the stage— where Elsa was already completely nude—and made his face into an approving expression. "To be perfectly honest, Colonel, I don't think he's half the general your Führer is."

Sistek didn't react and didn't respond, just kept staring. This time, Silvio stared back.

"But you wish him well, no doubt."

"I go into the Duomo three times a day and pray for his health and safety," Silvio said. "It's part of my priestly preparation."

No smile this time, either, a few more seconds of staring, then a small nod, almost as if the chess opponent were acknowledging a draw. "Day after tomorrow, then—the pork cheek. You won't forget?"

"I'll leave it with Oleg at the door."

"Perfect," the torturer said. He stood and turned away and, ignoring the visual delights on stage, made his way toward the hallway that led to the second-floor stairs . . . and other delights.

Fifteen

From Masso's house, it was an hour and a half to Milan, south along the *statale* at first, with the steep hills to Luca's right and the waters of the lake to his left. He'd driven Masso's old farm truck many times in the past, to the market in Gravedona, to buy fertilizer and seed and to pretend he was selling vegetables; to Menaggio and Dongo on other small errands. He pumped the clutch, shifted gears, the pistol beside him on the seat and the automatic weapon hidden securely beneath the bed in a box he and Masso had fashioned many months before. As Luca traveled, the road swathed in darkness now, he paid close attention to the spurts of traffic heading north: German army vehicles for the most part, Kübelwagens—their equivalent of the Americans' jeep—and armored trucks, soldiers in back staring blankly at the road. Luca hated them, of course, hated all of them. Their officers had killed his mother. Chased his lover to Switzerland. Their Führer had convinced Mussolini to send Italian troops—Luca's father among them—to the freezing steppes of Russia. At the same time, and somewhat to his surprise, he felt the smallest twinge of pity for them tonight. The smallest twinge. He chased it away. The moment for pity had not yet arrived, if it ever would.

The idea of the trip to Milan made him uneasy. Although he'd fulfilled certain assignments there, and in Como as well, he preferred doing his work in the hills and woods, dipping down into more populated areas in darkness, and just long enough to set sticks of dynamite beneath a railroad bridge, to surprise a German patrol on the outskirts of one of the lakeside villages, or, once, to meet with Caplan for a few stolen minutes in a dark fourth-floor apartment with a rear entrance and a stash of weapons.

This assignment was different. It made him feel naked, his knowledge of the terrain mediocre at best, his automatic weapon not immediately accessible, the actual work in Milan as yet unspecified. At ten p.m. he was supposed to meet Masso's contact behind the cathedral, the Duomo, a building so large, ornate, and remarkable it seemed that even the British and American bomber pilots had been given instructions not to target it. That meeting itself was an enormous risk. The Nazis still controlled Milan. Luca imagined that Masso—or Masso's unnamed boss—had calculated the enemy would be so concerned with the advancing Allied troops, with their choice to either fight another battle in the city streets or flee north and expose themselves to partisan attacks, that they wouldn't pay attention to a late-night meeting. Still, from what he'd heard—and the sources were painfully reliable—the SS torture rooms were still in operation, Jews were still being hunted down (and, since Mussolini had been deposed and the Nazis had occupied the country, the Jews were being sent north, across the border, to the work camps). What he would be asked to do in Milan, he had no idea. Assassinate Mussolini perhaps, in daylight, in the open, a suicide mission. He noticed again that, despite all the risky assignments he'd completed, the closer the end of the war came, the more insistently he wanted to stay alive, and the stronger his hopes grew of seeing Sarah, of embracing the role of father.

Masso had said that Luca's own father might be alive, but Luca didn't let himself hope for that. If it were true, if he saw his father again, he'd have to tell him how his mother had died—poisoning a houseful of SS officers with a meal she'd been forced to cook, then dying herself from the food she'd been made to share. She'd died in her own back yard, poisoned and shot, and he and Don Claudio had buried her there in darkness. If his father were alive, he might come home wounded, perhaps a broken man, certainly a widower.

Luca shook the thoughts away.

He entered Milan from the north, along Via Salaria, passing not far to the east of Piazzale Loreto, where he'd watched the Nazi soldiers refuse to let Italian mothers claim the bodies of their executed loved ones. In his mind's eye he could clearly see the fifteen dead partisans, some of them still in their teens. The mothers and sisters and little children wailing nearby, begging, being mocked. He'd sworn then that he'd take revenge for that act, and he wondered now if this assignment might be Masso's way of allowing him that bitter satisfaction.

He parked the truck three blocks from the Duomo, not worried about hungry people stealing the food, but very much worried about the weapons. What was he supposed to do with them? He decided he'd take the pistol at least, and then, depending on the assignment, return in darkness, crawl beneath the truck as if making repairs, and take the automatic weapon. But then what? Carry it through the streets in a stolen music case? Tuck it down the leg of his trousers? Who knew if the man he was meeting could be trusted? Who could ever know these days, with former Blackshirts in the south already claiming to have been *partigiani*, with Fascist mayors and school officials running away from the places the Allies had liberated, moving to a city where they weren't known, changing names and alliances the way workingmen changed a sweaty shirt for the evening meal.

Pistol tucked in his pants, Luca left the truck and found an open café, lingered over a decent *marinara* there, allowed himself a glass of wine. He wondered if the train tracks near Gravedona had been sufficiently damaged, and how long it would take for the German engineers to rebuild them, or to decide they were broken beyond repair and find another route through supposedly neutral Switzerland. He dipped his right index finger in the remains of the sauce, wrote a blood-red s-a-r-a-h on the tabletop, then wiped it away.

When he'd killed as much time in the café as he could, Luca walked to the Duomo and sat in one of the rear pews, running his eyes over the tall stained-glass windows, most of them intact, a few of them missing pieces from the concussion of nearby explosions. An elderly woman, hair tied in a kerchief, came in and sat two pews in front of him. She knelt there, face against her hands. He could hear her quietly sobbing.

She ignored him, knelt and wept for a while, then stood and walked away. Luca stayed as long as he could, marking the quarter hours by the cathedral's bells, and then he went out and around the back and waited there—not near the door, as he'd been instructed, but on a half-broken bench across a narrow street. He shifted the pistol to his right side so it didn't press against the bench's wooden slats.

In time—it wasn't even nine o'clock yet—a man more than twice his age, gray haired and stooped, came and sat on the bench an arm's length away. "Not fighting?" the man asked, and for a moment Luca thought this might be his contact. Luca raised his bad arm, a gesture he'd made countless times, even before the war, a gesture he hated almost as much as he hated admitting he was less than whole.

The man grunted in a neutral way, then gestured at the church. "What kind of God would allow this, can you tell me?"

"No."

"You can kill me if you want to. You can turn me in to the Gestapo if you're one of them, but I hate the Germans now. I despise them. And I despise the *Americani* also. Their bombs killed my wife and grandchild. How can I not despise them?"

Luca could think of nothing to say.

"You've lost people?" the man went on.

"My mother. My father was sent to Russia. The love of my life had to flee."

"Jewish girl?" the man guessed.

Luca at last turned and looked at him. "Why do you ask that?"

The man shrugged. "Why else would she have to flee? The Jews are being sent away by the thousands, even now. My closest friend was among them. Rounded up like animals, put on trains."

"Sent to the work camps?"

"Work camps, shit!" The man turned his face to the side and spat loudly. "Work camps? They're *death* camps—what's wrong with you!"

"I didn't know."

"You should know!"

"Stop yelling at me, brother. You lost a friend; I may have lost my lover, pregnant with my child."

The man stared out at the night. "Sorry," he said. "*Mi dispiace.* I've been made half-crazy. The death, the hunger, the terror. The sound of bombs fills my nightmares now. The war is almost over; everyone says so. Fine news. Magnificent news. Everything has been taken from me. What difference does it make now if the goddamned war is over? I haven't eaten in two days—what difference does it make?"

Luca was silent for a bit. "There's a truck, a farmer's truck"—he pointed—"three blocks that way. Cabbages and squash in the back. My truck. Go and take whatever you want, as much as you want. You have a place to cook?"

The man hesitated for a few seconds, as if he were processing the words, trying to believe them. Then he said, "The cabbage I'll eat without cooking. I'll eat the dirt on the cabbage." He stood up quickly, unsteady on his feet, and hurried across the street without offering any gesture of thanks.

Sixteen

In order to "gather the money," as *il Duce* had put it, Enzo needed to make another trip north along the shore of the lake to the house where Giuseppe "Pippi" Nazzacone, the republic's secretary of finance, was staying. Of all the various cabinet ministers, functionaries, Fascist operatives, and hangers-on who were part of the Republic of Salò, Enzo felt closest to Nazzacone. Pippi was a true intellectual, a high-level accountant in prewar life, but much more than simply a man who knew numbers. He possessed a deep understanding of history—military history included—and a philosophical bent that, at times, seemed to annoy the *Duce*. When Giacomo Matteotti, the only legislator brave enough to publicly confront and criticize *il Duce*, had been snatched from the streets of Rome and, a few days later, found in a ditch in the countryside, beaten to death, the public outcry was so great that Mussolini was nearly toppled. It was Nazzacone who advised *il Duce* to make a vehement denial of involvement. The members of the Fascist Grand Council, Mussolini's most trusted associates, sat around the oval table, complaining in predictable ways about the press coverage. Nazzacone stood up. Pippi was famous for speaking in short, blunt sentences, and his comments at the meeting were no exception. "I know you didn't give the order to kill Matteotti, *Duce*," Nazzacone said. "I know that well. But the public complaint is fierce. People believe you were involved. It's incumbent upon you to announce an investigation. You must say you had nothing to do with the murder. You must say it loudly and repeatedly. Otherwise, you place your entire leadership at risk."

Above all else, Mussolini hated to explain his behavior or apologize for it, and it seemed to Enzo that Nazzacone was asking him to do something very much like that. *Il Duce* fumed and fussed, a volcano sending out spumes of burning steam and rivers of lava, about to erupt. He paced in heavy-footed circles around the table where the council members sat, the heels of his boots making an ominous *bang, bang, bang* behind the now-seated Nazzacone and his colleagues. Enzo had been charged with taking notes, but since nothing was being said while Mussolini paced and muttered, no notes needed to be taken. He shifted his eyes back and forth between *il Duce*'s face and Nazzacone's, waiting for the explosion. The rest of the council members, cowards to a man, clung to a determined silence. If *il Duce* yelled at Nazzacone, they'd condemn him; if *il Duce* agreed with Nazzacone, they'd all speak up and support him enthusiastically.

After what seemed to Enzo a quarter of an hour but was more likely a matter of two or three minutes, Mussolini stopped circling and rested both hands on the back of his own chair. For a moment, Enzo watched the hands flexing and releasing, and then *il Duce* pointed a trembling finger at Nazzacone, hesitated a last second, and, to Enzo's absolute shock, said, "You're right, Pippi. I had nothing to do with the killing, and I should say so. Draft some remarks and I will present them."

Enzo suspected that Mussolini had, in fact, ordered the silencing of the brave Matteotti—if not overtly, than by suggestion or hint—but Nazzacone clearly believed in *il Duce*'s innocence. More so even than the others, loyalty seemed the chief tenet of Pippi's faith, and Enzo supposed that, if *il Duce* were ever captured and slain by the enemy, Pippi Nazzacone would die beside him.

A German private—one Enzo had often seen around the property but never spoken to—had been assigned to chauffeur him from the Villa Feltrinelli to the much more modest place where Pippi lived, a former officer's residence not far from an army barracks. As they started off, Enzo felt an urge to engage in conversation. Silence was his enemy now; he lived in an echoing cell of recrimination. One of the problems, however, was that while Mussolini's command of German was very strong, Enzo's was only fair, and you couldn't know what a given German soldier's level of Italian might be. Some were nearly fluent; others could barely manage a handful of chopped-up *grazie* and *arrivederci*. The other problem was you never knew if a soldier might make a report to his commanding officer—even a false report—incriminating an Italian in order to curry favor.

But a swelling nervousness had been pressing against Enzo since his lunch with Silvio, and so, as they pulled away from the villa, he first asked the German soldier his name—Markus—then said, "How are you feeling about going home?"

At first, Markus only shot him a worried look, afraid, perhaps, that Enzo had read his thoughts. He glanced sideways, turned his eyes back to the road, and then, after a pause, said in decent Italian, "Everyone's thinking about that now."

"It's natural," Enzo offered in a forgiving tone. At those words, he thought he saw the young soldier relax his shoulders and arms. For a while, as the car wound along the two-lane road, with the silvery water shimmering to their right, there was no conversation. Enzo tried, really for the first time, to imagine what it was like for a German to serve in Italy. The soldier beside him was not yet twenty. Chances were good he hadn't volunteered for the army but had been conscripted, then trained and sent south. Despite being some distance from the battle lines, Markus would certainly have an awareness of what was happening, his comrades being routed at every turn, chased by confident Allied troops and merciless partisans, moving northward at the fastest pace possible beneath a furious air and artillery assault. Unless he was some kind of Nazi fanatic—as many of the officers were—Markus would surely be wondering which would come first: the end of the war, or his own turn in the trenches. "Who's at home?" Enzo ventured.

The soldier glanced at him again, still wary. "Mother, sister, girlfriend."

"No dad?"

"In Russia."

"Fighting for the Fatherland," Enzo said. "Any word from him?"

The young man frowned. "I don't expect any."

Enzo decided to leave the conversation there—it was only another seven or eight minutes to Nazzacone's place—but, after stopping to let a mother and young son cross the road, Markus himself went on, in a tentative voice, as if revealing a secret to a stranger. "Have you heard of the *Volksempfänger*?"

"No."

"It was a radio. Very inexpensive. Everybody we knew had one. When I was a boy, we had the *Volksempfänger* on in our house all the time. My dad liked to listen. There was a man, Arnold Fissenwiler—have you heard of him?"

"No."

"He had a show on the radio, a famous man, an early supporter of the Führer. He'd go on and on about the Jews, the English, the Americans. About the way society was unraveling, men becoming weaker, more corrupt. About the way the world saw us only as losers of the first war. You could almost predict what he'd say, but he exaggerated, he lied, and he said everything with so much conviction, repeating the same ideas over and over, that many people were swayed by him. My father was one of those people. He became hypnotized. My mother, too, though not to the same extent. My sister joined Hitler Youth."

"She had a choice?"

"Of attitude, yes. Enthusiastic or reluctant. She chose the former. When our troops marched into Austria, my father was ecstatic. Forty-six by then, relatively old, he signed up. Went to Poland first, and then to Russia. Insisted, before leaving, that I follow in his shoes, so I enlisted, too."

"You had a choice?"

"I did, though later I wouldn't have. I ended up in Austria for a while and then here, guarding your Mussolini. Probably the safest place I could be."

I was a true believer like your father, Enzo almost said. *If I'd had a son, I, too, would have encouraged him to follow me, to serve, to fight.* But he still felt raw from his lunch with the mysterious Silvio, as if he'd peeled away a layer of skin and was sensitive to every small change in air temperature, alert to every nuance of speech, every remark, no matter how innocent. He wasn't about to reveal his true feelings to a German private, who could so easily return to the villa and make a report to Lieutenant Birzer. "I hope this assignment continues to be a safe one," Enzo said, "for both of us."

Markus grunted in a neutral way. There was another stretch of silence, Enzo studying the stony gray hillsides on the lake's opposite shore, Markus focusing on the road. But then the young soldier seemed unable to hold in the words. "I wouldn't mind dying for my country, as my father surely has done, if there was a chance of victory. But that hope is lost. Dying now would be a meaningless sacrifice."

Enzo was still facing away from Markus. He heard the words clearly, and wondered to what degree they applied to himself. If Italy had remained unconquered, if Mussolini had remained in power, if they were not now on the brink of defeat, would he have taken Angelina up on her suggestion to meet with Silvio? Would he ever have done what he did in the restaurant in Salò—pass on, in exchange for money, information that could aid the enemy, even lead to *il Duce*'s capture or death? For him, and for Markus, was it merely a question of wanting to be on the winning side, no matter the ideas for which one was fighting?

"I'd appreciate it, Major," Markus said, in another tone altogether now, a note of fear running through his words, "if you wouldn't share this conversation with my superiors."

Enzo reached across the seat and put a hand on the soldier's upper arm. Markus flinched. "*Il Duce* talks about your Führer having a secret weapon. It's almost ready, he says. It will change everything. If that's true, perhaps we have a chance of victory. If not, we both know what's imminent."

"There is no secret weapon," Markus said. "Defeat is what's imminent. I just don't know what defeat will look like."

It will look like your children learning Russian in school, Enzo thought, but Markus was pulling the Kübelwagen to the side of the road in front of a house with two small palm trees in the yard. Markus turned to face him, a question written on his face, printed there in the italics of fear.

"No worries," Enzo said. "I'm the keeper of many secrets."

———

As he went along the walk leading to the house's side door, Enzo thought, *All of us are keepers of secrets now,* and realized how easy it would be for Markus, worried about his own safety, to return to the villa and tell Lieutenant Birzer that the Italian major, Mussolini's aide, had been talking with him about the end of the war and had sounded almost as if he were rooting for the Allies. The spring air carried the scent of treachery. Treachery, terror, a constant suspicion. They were hens in a fenced-in yard, and the woman who owned the house had come outside with an ax in her hand, about to choose one of them for the evening meal. The hens would trample each other, peck each other to death, run in whichever direction they thought might let them stay alive while one of their comrades had her head chopped off.

Nazzacone answered the door with a cigarette dangling from one corner of his lips and a shot glass of something in his left hand. He blew out a ring of smoke and waved Enzo inside. They stood close to each other, face-to-face, in the stone foyer. "*Il Duce* has sent me for the money," Enzo said.

"*Bene, bene.* We're leaving?"

"Soon."

"Today?"

"I don't think so. You'll know. You'll be one of the first to know."

"*Bene.* Sit for a minute, Enzo. Your chauffeur will wait. An amaro?"

"Thank you."

Nazzacone kept all the curtains in the living room drawn—Enzo didn't ask why—and they sat opposite each other in soft chairs and shadows. Pippi offered a cigarette; Enzo declined. "How are you, my friend? How are things at the villa?"

"I'm like everyone else," Enzo said. "I spend all day and all night thinking about what's to come."

"And *il Duce*'s mood?"

"Discouraged. Zarraona told him yesterday that the war was lost. Now he's talking about arming as many loyal men as Scavolini can find and making a last stand in the Valtellina."

"I'll be beside him," Nazzacone said.

"Yes. I will also. But in the next breath he says, 'Gather the money.'"

"He called to let me know you were coming."

"But tell me, Pippi: What good will money be if we're making a last stand?"

Pippi looked down into his drink, as if the answer lay at the bottom of the glass, or as if the conversation had taken an inappropriate turn. When he looked up, instead of answering, he asked, "What have you, yourself, been up to?"

Enzo felt he'd gone too far: the question he'd just asked had the scent of doubt to it. Nazzacone was a friend, yes, but that was his second position. His first was loyal soldier in the army of Fascism, and in that battalion doubt was forbidden. "I had a meeting yesterday," he said, wondering if Nazzacone, or someone else, had followed him to Salò and filed a report. "With a contact I've been grooming for some time now. Friend of Angelina, Claretta's maid. She introduced us. He's a good man, Pippi, a Sicilian who moved north with the lines of battle. He told me the *Americani* are a few days' march from Milan. And *il Duce* wants to go to Milan. Do you think you could warn him? I've tried. He won't listen."

"Milan is the last big city we control."

"I know that."

"Hitler has a weapon. It needs another week, perhaps two, for full development, and he wants us to hold Milan for as long as possible, to give him time to use it. If the Allied bombers can fly north from there . . ."

Enzo glanced away, reminding himself, again, to be careful. "How do you know about the secret weapon?"

Pippi shrugged. "You have your contacts, I have mine."

And we're both liars, Enzo thought.

Pippi worked his lips, watching Enzo through thick glasses. "Let me tell you something," he said. "As a friend."

"Anything."

"*Il Duce* doubts your loyalty."

"How? Why? What do you mean?"

Pippi shrugged. It was a day, Enzo thought, of people revealing things they shouldn't have revealed, and then having second thoughts. "He's said nothing to me directly. I sense it in his words. He at first suggested I bring the money to the villa myself, as if there were a chance you'd abscond with it."

Enzo summoned a combination of hurt and outrage and banged a fist down on the wooden arm of the chair, toppling the half-empty glass onto the carpet. He glared at it, watched the syrupy brown liquid leak into the fibers. He banged the chair arm a second time. "After all these years! All the sacrifices I've made for him! I lost my marriage because of my loyalty to him, Pippi!"

"I know that."

"And what would I do with the money? Take it where? Bulgaria? Greece? South Africa? I'll never leave my country. Never!"

Another shrug. Pippi was watching him, appearing only half-convinced.

It occurred to Enzo that Mussolini might not doubt him at all, that Nazzacone was merely testing him, watching to see how he'd react. He tried to calm himself, but a cold hand of fear had taken hold of him. He could feel his heart galloping in his chest.

"I thought you'd appreciate my telling you," Pippi said.

"I do, I do. It's just . . . But how will I face him now, knowing this?"

"Talk to him," Pippi suggested. "Don't tell him what I said, of course. Bring the money back—the suitcases are locked—and see if you can talk to him."

"And say what? *Do you still trust me*, Duce? *Are you about to have me shot before we leave the lake?*"

Nazzacone shrugged, went into the kitchen for a sponge, and tossed it to Enzo when he returned. The servant again, Enzo knelt and sponged up most of the liqueur. "He'll be waiting for the money," he said bitterly, when he was finished.

Nazzacone stepped into the next room and returned with two suitcases. He took a folded sheet of paper from one pocket and handed it over. "A detailed list of the funds," he said. "French francs, Swiss francs, sovereigns, American dollars. Hundreds of thousands of all of them. The list is complete and accurate."

"He must be thinking of setting us up somewhere else," Enzo said, to try and cover his faux pas. "Perhaps we'll regroup and, when the weapon is deployed, make our return to Roma."

"Yes, yes, exactly," Nazzacone said, but Enzo knew they were actors in a play, feeding off each other's lines. His friend Nazzacone had been testing him—Enzo was sure of it now. He wondered if he'd failed the test. Nazzacone ran his eyes around the shaded room. "In any case, the money is all here. He'll decide what to do with it."

"Excellent. He'll be happy," Enzo said. He offered Nazzacone a hasty Fascist salute in farewell, and Nazzacone returned it gravely.

Seventeen

As she stepped out of the trees, her legs wobbling as if there were no longer any bones in them, her mind a fog-blanketed field, Sarah wondered for a few seconds whether she should angle left, toward the house with candlelight in the window, or right, toward the church. She knew that in Italy, in wartime at least, the churches were often left unlocked through the night. But she was exhausted almost beyond thinking, and the church reminded her of Father Alessandro, and Father Alessandro made her remember Gunther, and remembering Gunther was almost enough to cause her to collapse right there in the dirt, with Lydia in her arms.

In the end, the decision was a simple one: the house was ten meters closer than the church. Lydia had wrapped her frail arms around her mother's neck and was making small noises Sarah had never heard from her before: a squeaky whimpering, notes in the key of surrender. Holding the girl's limp body against her breast, Sarah shuffled across the yard toward the house, made it as far as the door, lifted her free hand, and knocked three times with as much force as she could muster. It seemed to take ten minutes for the door to open. As she waited, she put out her right hand, palm against the doorframe, arm locked straight, and held herself upright. At last the door swung inward on squealing hinges. An elderly couple stood there, the man thin and bespectacled, with a gauze bandage covering his right ear, the woman plump, gray haired, wearing a worn blue housedress and clasping her hands together in front of her as if in prayer.

"Help me," Sarah said, unable to even manage the word *please.*

The woman reached out and took Lydia into her arms. Eyes half-open, the child didn't object, didn't move. The man stood aside and, reluctantly it seemed, allowed them into a small kitchen where the floor—wide planks with grit-filled spaces between—tilted to one side. A candle shone in the middle of a wooden table. Two plates—Sarah understood that she'd interrupted the couple's evening meal. She collapsed in the chair and slumped forward, the weight of her upper body on her elbows. She was almost blind with tiredness. Holding Lydia in one arm, the woman put a plate in front of Sarah, spooned onto it from a pan the last few pieces of what appeared to be pasta and egg, then brought over water in a teacup and set it beside the plate. She sat close to Sarah, ready to catch her if she toppled sideways. The man stood opposite, studying Sarah in a way she didn't like.

She managed to lift a bit of the food to her mouth and then held out a spoonful of the pasta in Lydia's direction. The woman took the spoon from her hand, and Lydia had a small bite, then spat it onto the woman's shoulder.

"Drink," the woman said. Sarah obeyed, her hand so weak that some of the water spilled down along her chin and fell onto the front of her dress. She looked at the wet circle there and realized she was filthy. Lydia was filthy. No wonder the man wasn't happy to have them in his home. She stared at the food and started to weep.

"Where did you come from? What happened?" the woman asked. Sarah had pushed the plate to one side and lowered her head onto her hands. She couldn't answer. *"Mami,"* she heard, and that was enough to allow her to raise her head. The old woman handed Lydia to her, and Sarah set her on her lap, pushed the hair out of her face, looked up, and managed a single word. *"Grazie."* And then, *"Dove siamo?"*

"Gravedona," the man answered curtly.

Sarah knew Gravedona was twenty-five kilometers north of Mezzegra, her home. Both towns sat on Lake Como's western shore. She rocked Lydia gently side to side, took a breath, felt a tiny surge of energy. "I, we, walked," she said. "From Bellinzona."

"Impossible!" the man said. "With a child! You couldn't have. You're lying."

Sarah shook her head. "Not lying. Two days and one night. Her father, my, my husband . . . I had fled there, leaving him here to fight. I had to come back."

"Yes, yes, rest," the woman said. "Rest yourself. You had to flee, we understand. I'll heat water on the stove for you and you can bathe in our tub, and then together we can bathe your daughter. Don't worry. You're safe. The worst fighting hasn't reached here yet."

"I thought . . . I was told it was already past. Already north of here."

"Not yet, no. But soon. You're safe here, don't worry. I'm Rosa. This is Antonio, who's angry at everyone these days. They leave us alone now, the Germans. No one bothers us now if we remain here. Even if you're Jewish—I won't ask—you don't have to worry."

Sarah started to weep again; she couldn't seem to stop herself even when she felt Lydia staring up at her. She was too tired to be embarrassed, too tired even to reach up and wipe the tears from her cheeks.

"You can bathe and sleep," Rosa said. "We'll bathe the girl, you and I. We had children once, two daughters, far away now. We still have some of their clothes. You can sleep, and in the morning we have eggs and perhaps Antonio can find some bread. We have tea. You can tell us then what you want to tell us. Now bathe and sleep."

———

After the most heavenly bath she could remember, using only the slimmest disc of brown soap, drying herself as Rosa bathed Lydia and promised to wash their dresses, Sarah and her daughter lay down in a single bed in a dark back room and slept until long after the sun rose the next morning. The child woke her, squirming, diaper dirty again, crying in hunger until Sarah let her nurse on one side and then the other. The air in the room was musty, cobwebs hung in the corners, and the ceiling tilted in the same direction as the kitchen floor, as if the house would soon slide downhill into the lake. She could hear quiet voices in the next room, possibly an argument, but Rosa had put a clean dress on the bed while Sarah washed and used the toilet, and had made Lydia a clean diaper from what seemed to be an old shirt. Sarah set Lydia down on her feet and stood. She looked at her legs and saw that they were cut from ankle to knee, a forest of red scratches. Lydia had a lump on the side of her head, half the size of an egg, but she seemed almost normal again and led Sarah through the door and into the kitchen. Sarah could smell food and realized she was ravenously hungry.

"I'm sorry" was the first thing she said. "I'm sorry to bother you. I—"

Rosa waved an arm. "Sit, eat. Antonio was able to find bread. We have eggs from our own chickens. A bit of salt. Tea."

"I have money," Sarah said. "Swiss money, but—"

Antonio stepped out of the bathroom. He cleaned the lenses of his glasses on the tail of his shirt and placed them over his nose. Half his teeth were gone; his eyes were bloodshot. Sarah noticed a bright-red spot on the bandage. "Tell us what happened," he said. It was almost an order.

"I'm Jewish" was the first thing Sarah said, and she watched them carefully. No reaction. Antonio was waiting for the story; Rosa was half-turned away from the stove, listening. Sarah spent a minute giving them the outline of the past two years of her life—Luca, her mother, the Swiss priest. Rosa *tsked* in sympathy. Antonio didn't move his eyes from her and seemed to believe none of it. Lydia was still on her lap.

"I have to go to Mezzegra," Sarah said, when she'd finished. "My home is there. It's Luca's home, too. I'll try to find him. He's never seen his child."

"Antonio has a small boat," Rosa said. "He can take you."

Sarah saw a spasm of anger on the old man's face, but he said nothing. Rosa cooked the eggs and went on: "Perhaps you can pay for the gas and he can take you and your daughter to Mezzegra. It's not far by boat, twenty minutes. A few liters of gasoline, if we can find some, can get him there and back."

Antonio started to object, but Rosa glared at him. "Look at her," she said, angrily. "Look at what she's been through. Go ask Marco if he has gasoline."

Sarah offered again to pay them, but Antonio, still skeptical, said, "I don't know a young, healthy man who could have done what you did. Even without the weight of a child . . ."

"The child gave her the strength," Rosa told him. "The child. The pull of love."

Antonio snorted and glared at Sarah. "You risked your child's life to return to Italy?"

"I heard the Germans were north of the lake. I heard the war was over here. I heard the Swiss might, if the war was over, they might—"

"Not yet over," Antonio said bitterly. "The Germans are leaving, but they're taking everything they can as they go." He reached up and touched the bandage. "They did this to me, with a club. Two days ago, because I was carrying a little sack with food. Potatoes and carrots. One of them came up and clubbed me to the ground and took the food. They're crazed now, full of fear. You can see it in their faces. But they're only on the road, the lake road, the *statale*. They no longer come here in the hills. They don't bother the people in the church, though the priest was taken long ago. They don't even bother the young girls now. But they take food and gold if they can find it, silver cutlery. This morning I saw one of them carrying someone's radio on his shoulder as he climbed into his Kübelwagen."

"I didn't know," Sarah said, squeezing Lydia against her breast. "I'm sorry. I—"

"Don't mind him," Rosa said. "He thought you might be one of our own daughters, that's all. We were hoping for that when we heard the knock. The war has made all of us lose our minds. We'll keep you. Don't worry. We'll help you just as we hope people would help our girls."

Eighteen

Luca waited patiently on the bench until the bells in the cathedral sounded ten times. He had a view of the rectangle of stone pavement at the rear of the Duomo. No one was there. But orders were orders. He stood, moved the pistol to the back of his belt again, tucked it outside the shirt so he could reach it more easily. In what he hoped would look like a relaxed way, he walked toward the building, wondering about the man he was supposed to meet. Milan was under German occupation, the only large city they still controlled. If Masso had been working for the Germans all along, or for the Fascists, now would be the hour when he'd want those who'd fought for the other side to be eliminated. It would be the old farmer's parting gesture, after which his Nazi friends could spirit him away to the border, or provide him with a uniform and include him in the long lines of retreating vehicles. How simple it would be, if Masso wanted to kill one of his most important deputies, to send that deputy on an errand like this, alone, into an occupied city, late at night. Luca would be shot, his body dumped in the hills, not to be discovered for weeks, if ever.

He shook the thought away. It was rooted in fear and war craziness. Shadowy as Masso could sometimes be, he'd never done anything to feed such suspicion. They were too close to the end to waver now. He'd meet this mysterious man, he'd find out the details of his next assignment, and he'd complete it.

A person walked around the corner of the building to his left, and Luca immediately realized something by the posture and walk: the man he was supposed to meet was a woman.

He'd been in the hills so long that the sight of the woman, illuminated as she was by a hooded streetlight, came as a shock to him. The partisan women were paragons of courage and will. He had the greatest admiration for Solana and the others. But, like him, they dressed plainly, were often dirty from sleeping in the woods and in broken-down hunting cabins, their hair still tucked up beneath wool hats at this time of year, their faces smudged, eyes exhausted. This woman, tall and slim, wore good shoes and a dress with a short quilted expensive-looking jacket over it, partly open in front. Her hair—golden brown—hung over her shoulders. She walked with an air of confidence and ease, as if it weren't wartime at all, as if she were meeting a lover for a late meal.

He turned to face her fully, and she came up close and, to his complete surprise, planted a quick kiss on his lips and took him by the hand. "We're lovers meeting for a date," she said, very quietly. Her voice was silky, rich with confidence. She turned and walked and he had to do the same, their hands linked, shoulders close.

"How are you?" she asked.

"Very well," he said.

Her artificial laugh echoed out into the street and back against the wall of the church. "That's the worst-sounding *molto bene* I think I've ever heard. Just walk with me, pretend you're enjoying it. Let's swing our arms as if we're ridiculously excited to be with each other." She lifted his arm up with hers and moved it back and forth, like a child's swing. "Stop now. Turn and kiss me. If someone's watching us, if someone has been watching you, wondering what you're doing here, their questions will be answered."

She turned toward him and put her arms around his back, their faces very close. Luca guessed she could feel the pistol, and he wondered if she might lift it out of his belt and hold it to his throat. But she kissed him—a pretend kiss, a staged kiss, but a kiss all the same. He could taste tobacco on her mouth, sense the play of her tongue. The kiss lasted only a few seconds, but it was as if he hadn't tasted wine in two years and was sipping from a glass of Barolo. She turned forward again, still gripping his hand, threw back her head, and laughed happily, as if he'd made a clever joke.

As they started walking again, she said, "Use your free hand and lift your shirt up and cover the pistol. You won't need it until later. I've put something in the back left pocket of your trousers. We'll walk down the street ahead—see how dark it is? There's an apartment building there, number thirty-six. We'll go in through the front door and you can sit in the lobby. The sofa is comfortable and there are no windows, and there will be no one else coming through that door at this hour. I'll disappear. You'll be able to hear the Duomo bells from there. Stay until the first stroke of midnight, then go about your business. Use the time to read the note and decide how you'll accomplish the assignment, and when you leave, make sure no one follows you. Understood?"

"Yes. Your name?"

She laughed the stage laugh again. "Not important," she said. "Not important at all."

They walked into the mouth of the dark street, silence around them in a city that normally would have been busy at that hour, families returning home from a meal, friends gathering in the cafés. He felt the warmth of her hand and glanced at the numbers on the dark-faced buildings. Eighteen, twenty-four, thirty-two, thirty-six. They turned in unison. He held the door for her, produced a false smile, trying to play the role. In the small empty lobby, windowless, faintly lit by a single lamp on a corner table, she let go of his hand, moved her face close again, said, "That was a nice kiss. Good luck," and disappeared down a dark hallway.

Luca stood still and listened. There was the quiet closing of a door—an exterior door, he guessed. He took the folded note from his back left pocket, sat on the sofa close to the lamp, and read. The script was as elegant as the woman's posture, but strangely lacking in capital letters:

> *doctor klaus sistek is a famous nazi torturer, a man who, with his twin brother, edmund, has been doing his evil work here in milan since the nazis were forced to move north from rome. true to his people's penchant for efficiency, he leaves his "office" promptly when the cathedral bell sounds twelve midnight. he walks around the corner of the building—114 vittorio emanuele, two blocks from here—and washes his hands in the public spigot there, leans down to take a drink, then continues to his place of lodging in the vermentino hotel. always the same, always. you are to shoot him in the back of the head when he's enjoying his last sip of our water. we'll have a car pull to the curb immediately and take you away. don't worry about the truck you brought with you. there's an elevator in the lobby. after you read this, open the elevator door, tear this note to small pieces, drop them in the space between the floor and the shaft, and when you hear the bells sound midnight, go. if you walk at a normal pace, you should reach the fountain about the same time as herr sistek.*

Nineteen

Enzo rode back along the shore road with the now-silent Markus and could tell, when they were still half a kilometer away from the Feltrinelli mansion, that something had changed. There were always a few German military vehicles on the street near the front entrance—Lieutenant Birzer had strict orders never to let Mussolini out of the house without accompanying him—but while Enzo was away, their number had tripled. Cars and armored vehicles lined both sides of the street and clogged the driveway. As he and Markus drew closer, Enzo saw men—some in uniform, some not—coming out of the house carrying boxes. He thanked Markus, climbed out, and, carrying both suitcases, hurried up the front steps. Cardboard boxes and stacks of papers and folders were piled in the entranceway and along both walls of the marble hallway that led back to *il Duce's* office. Soldiers and staff were busy carrying them outside. Enzo had to push his way through, a fish swimming against the current, but he found the door to the office open, and Mussolini at his desk, signing papers. When he heard Enzo enter, *il Duce* looked up and pushed his chin forward—a gesture of annoyance. Enzo thought he looked weary.

"And you were where?"

"With Nazzacone," Enzo said, setting the suitcases on the floor and gesturing to them. "The money."

Mussolini nodded, brusquely, as if wanting to pretend the suitcases weren't there. "I meant yesterday. Where were you yesterday? I needed you, where did you go?"

"I was in Salò, meeting my contact," Enzo said, trying to speak in the voice he always used. Something had found its way into that voice, however—a vibration of guilt, a memory of Nazzacone's warning: il Duce *doubts your loyalty.* Mussolini was glaring at him, so he added, "I told you about that."

"You did not."

"I did, *Duce.* You have so much on your mind perhaps you didn't hear me. Angelina, Claretta's maid, knew the man in Roma and swears by his loyalty to the cause. He assured me Milan is safe for you. Possibly only for another few days, he said, but the city is still safely under German and Italian control."

Mussolini watched him, studied him. "*Italian and German control,* you should have said. It's still our country. You should say *Italian* first, always."

"*Sì, Duce.*"

"Sit."

Enzo obeyed, but now he could feel the vibration going back and forth along the bones of his spine. The muscles of his neck twitched in a quick rhythm.

Mussolini noticed. "You're ill?"

Enzo shook his head. "I've been outside, in the Kübelwagen. April is cold this far north."

Mussolini grunted, still studying him. "We leave before dawn tomorrow. My papers are being put into several vehicles, and I've instructed Colonel Messina to guard them as if they are a human being, as if they are his mother. He can ride with the suitcases. You'll make sure he follows that order."

"Yes, *Duce.*"

"I've arranged for Rachele to be driven to Monza with six German soldiers in three armored vehicles, one vehicle ahead, two behind.

Claretta will leave with me in the convoy, though not in the same car. I want you driving my car. You're a better driver than the Germans—any Italian is. We'll go to Milan for various meetings. I'll talk to our people there. Despite his earlier failure, Scavolini thinks he can still get three thousand Blackshirts to come to the Valtellina with us. Zarraona says that, militarily, it's hopeless, but Zarraona doesn't understand. This isn't about a military victory. It's about a final stand of loyal Fascists. It's about history. We want to leave a mark that future *fascisti* will remember and emulate. If the war is lost, it will be the generals who lost it, Hitler and his simple-minded strategy and poor decisions. Not the Fascists, *chiaro?*"

"Of course, *Duce*. Clear. I agree."

"And you'll join us? You'll fight with us? At the Valtellina?"

"You don't have to ask me that, *Duce*."

"Answer."

"Yes, I will."

"Something's wrong, Enzo. What is it? Tell me. You've been loyal to me since I first met you, and I appreciate that, but tell me now if there's something I need to hear from you."

Enzo squirmed in his seat, broke eye contact long enough to calculate the best answer. He was looking out at the lake—his eyes were often drawn there—but could feel *il Duce* watching him. He swung his head back. For one long moment, he thought of telling the truth. The truth would be something like, *I've always admired you,* Duce. *Your physical courage, your devotion to Italy, your perseverance in the face of all enemies, all obstacles. You're like a beautiful, powerful automobile, a roadster, a Bertone, that glided along the Italian roads, engine humming, in a way that made people line the streets to watch, and then follow you and cheer for you, wherever you went. But at some point you turned onto the wrong road. At the visit to Munich, I believe it was. You turned in that direction, and later, when you sensed you'd made a mistake, instead of reversing course, you only went on faster. Your incredible force of will had been set into high gear and you were reluctant to downshift, to admit an error and correct it.*

Faster and faster you went, passing laws you didn't believe in, or shouldn't have believed in, sending troops to places they shouldn't have been sent, supporting a man who was clearly mad but who somehow lit a fire inside you. You let that fire warm you as you drove, warm you and warm you, and then it started to burn you, from the inside out, and all you did was press harder on the gas pedal.

Once you made that wrong turn, I started to doubt you. Little by little, the doubt swelled inside me. Still, I was loyal. I was ecstatic when you were rescued from Campo Imperatore and we were reunited. I hoped that great moment would mark the end of your public service, a deserved retirement, but you were forced back here, to this lake. And then the fire began to consume your soul. I watched you taking revenge on the men who, with the help of the king, had pushed you from office. They, too, had sensed the wrong turn. They, too, had been loyal to you, great admirers of you, for decades, like myself. You had them murdered, and in spite of the pleas from your own daughter, your own child, you had your son-in-law, Count Ciano, sit on a stool, hands tied, and had him murdered as well. At that moment, whatever love and admiration I still had for you was killed, as if it, too, had been tied to a chair, shot, and buried.

Now, Duce, all that is over. I'll go with you now, to your death, perhaps to my own, because that's what I deserve for remaining loyal to you once you made that wrong turn. I could have gotten out of the vehicle then, dangerous as that would have been. I could have leapt out, tumbled down a hillside, swum a river, sprinted for the border. I could have done that, but I did not, and so here we are now, fleeing our own countrymen, Duce—our own people—in the company of Hitler's servants.

As that river of thoughts rushed through his mind, Enzo realized he was breathing heavily, a man about to flee, or weep. He gathered himself as quickly as he could and made himself say, "*Il Duce*, you're right, as always, to sense something in my mood. My heart is broken in two. I love this place. I have loved serving you. The thought that we have to flee before the armies of England and America is, to me, like drinking poison, that's all. I'll go with you wherever you go. Of course

I will. You're my *Duce*, my leader, my hero. Whatever happens to us, I know this: the example you've set for Italy and for the world will never expire. So I'm sad, that's all. Sad and bitter, *Duce*."

By the time Enzo finished, his neck had stopped quivering. He was able to meet Mussolini's eyes, strength to strength. But, as if she were actually with him in the room, he could hear his ex-wife's voice: *How did you turn into* this?

For a long stretch of seconds, Mussolini said nothing. The air between them seemed to tremble. And then a very thin smile appeared above the outthrust chin. The great man nodded, lifted an arm, flung his fingers up and forward in a gesture of dismissal. "I'm making you a colonel, Enzo. I should have done it long ago. A colonel in the army of the Republic of Salò."

"I'm honored, *Duce*."

"Prepare your things, my friend, my comrade. Say your final goodbyes. Angelina won't be with us in the convoy. We'll leave at five o'clock."

Enzo stood. "I'd like," he said, and then one tiny hand of hesitation seemed to take hold of him. There was a second, two seconds, three seconds, when he could feel the fingers of that hand reaching around and trying to cover his mouth, to press his lips closed. And then he said, "I'd like to sit out on the porch overlooking this beautiful Italian lake one last time. I have a cigar. I'd like to have a smoke and say my goodbyes to this place. To this life."

Mussolini grinned. "Do you have a cigar for me?"

"In fact I do, *Duce*." Enzo took the small box from his shirt pocket and was about to hand it over when he remembered the note Silvio had placed there. "They're Cuban," he said, sliding one cigar carefully out of the thin box and placing it on the desk.

Mussolini nodded, smiled, waved him away, and Enzo turned and left the room.

There were scraps of mist hanging here and there over the lake, vaporous gray cloudlets that danced above the placid surface and licked against the slopes of Mount Baldo on the eastern shore. Enzo sat alone in a metal chair, the seat bottom and back cool against his body, and watched a gull flapping ponderously from one side of the lake to the other. What call drew it, he wondered. What signal? Why didn't the wings tire, and when they did finally tire, when they eventually lost the strength needed to hold the creature aloft, what happened to it? What kind of death did it have? A spinning dive into cold water? A quiet last few moments, hidden against a rock, quivering?

He lit the cigar and sat in a swirl of sweet smoke, bringing the moist tobacco leaf to his mouth and then dropping the hand to his side. He ran his eyes over the scene—he did, in fact, love it; that part of what he'd said to *il Duce* had been perfectly true. The huge lake widening as it spread south, the hillsides close against its shores, with small clusters of stone houses decorating the slopes here and there and, even this far north, a few palm trees. He tried to spy a vantage point from which someone, some friend of Silvio's, some enemy of the Reich and the *Duce*, could be watching him. With a telescope, perhaps, or military binoculars. He turned his eyes to the top of the mountain. Someone there, perhaps, a partisan with binoculars and a radio, watching *il Duce's* aide have a last smoke and remembering the face, marking the man for revenge at another time.

Twenty

Sarah had always found it ironic and sad that, having grown up within a five-minute walk of Lake Como, she'd never learned to swim, and had never been able to overcome her fear of water. Even bathing in the spring-fed pool near the cabin had frightened her at first. The idea of sitting in a small boat while holding her restless daughter and traveling down the lake in an area still at least partly under Nazi control, just the thought of that set off a familiar churning in her stomach. She remembered a story her mother had often told her. Rebecca had been high school age, swimming in the lake with friends early in the season. The friends were better swimmers, the water still cold, and she'd followed them out to a depth that made her uncomfortable. The weather had made a sudden change—as it did around Lake Como in the first warm days. Her friends turned and headed for shore. Rebecca tried to follow, but the waves had lifted into whitecaps by then, water splashed into her mouth, and she panicked. She tried shouting for help, but her friends were far ahead and the wind carried her voice in the other direction, out over the deeper water. Small cold waves splashed against her face. "My arms and legs seemed to turn to iron, Sarah. I took in a panicked breath that was just water, and I went under."

Her mother forced herself to the surface and let out a terrible, watery scream. One of the boys heard it, turned, and swam toward her, "but by the time he reached me I'd given up. I was choking, underwater, flailing weakly, Sarah, but I'd given up. He was strong, though—Gennaro was his name. He lifted me to the surface and flipped me onto my back and hooked his arm under my chin and somehow managed to pull me that way, swimming with one hand, all the way back to the shallow water. From that day forward I never again went into the lake over my knees, and I'm sure I passed my fear on to you."

Sarah had always been ashamed of that fear, embarrassed at sitting on the shore while her friends frolicked in the lake on summer days. The fear had a life of its own, however, separate from her will, and she'd never been able to force herself to venture out a little deeper and dive in, not even once.

At Rosa and Antonio's table, partly refreshed by the long sleep, belly full, Lydia wandering around peacefully touching the spokes of the chairbacks as if counting them, Sarah felt the familiar churning. "I could take you in my small boat," Antonio repeated, as if convincing himself, or hoping she'd decline. If she traveled straight down the lakeside road, the *statale*, it would be less than thirty kilometers from Gravedona to Menaggio, half an hour's ride, then a short trip inland to Mezzegra. But, from what Rosa had said the night before, the *statale* would be busy with retreating German military vehicles. And some of the German officers, despite their haste, had not given up on capturing Jews. Who knew if, once she drew close to the place she used to live, some Fascist-sympathizing former neighbor would turn her in to save his own life or to curry favor with the police or the OVRA. Against that possibility, she considered the terror of the cold lake. Lydia toddled over to her and put her hands on Sarah's knees and said, "*Su, Mami. Su, su!*" Up, up!

Sarah lifted Lydia onto her lap, thinking about the way fear was passed down, one generation to the next. If she survived the war, if Lydia survived it, she didn't want to live a life constrained by fear and, more than anything, didn't want to pass it on to her daughter. If Luca survived, too, and if they made a life together, he'd want her as a brave partner, not a timid mother. She looked up at Antonio and said, "We could pretend to be fishing. I could just hold the fishing rod up in the air. If someone saw us, they'd think we were trying to catch something for lunch."

"I can fish on the way home," he said glumly. "That's how we've survived."

"I'll keep the child with me if you like," Rosa offered. "It would be a pleasure for me. Our own girls are far off, one with a child we haven't seen since before the war started."

Lydia was grabbing at her right breast. Sarah shook her head. "Thank you, but I want to find her father. I could never find him and not have her with me. And she's still occasionally nursing."

"You'll pay for the gas?" Antonio asked. Rosa frowned. Sarah handed him the coins Father Alessandro had given her.

———

Sarah knew that the lake's shoreline was pocked with miniature harbors, tiny inlets, sometimes at the mouth of rivers, sometimes not, where, in peacetime, local fishermen tied up their boats. Other than occasionally stealing some or all of the fishermen's catches, the Nazis and Blackshirts hadn't seemed particularly interested in the lake traffic. The northernmost end of Lake Como was still in Italy; it wasn't like someone could escape via the water; it wasn't like partisans could sabotage German warships there, or mount an assault on important garrisons or airfields. Luca had often told her that the Germans in the area had been mostly concerned with keeping train lines and roadways open between Milan and the northern border, so men and matériel could be brought south from Germany and Austria. Towns of any size were occupied, of course. Menaggio had its barracks, Mezzegra its SS house—where Luca's brave mother had been forced to cook for the officers. The Nazis loved to torment, to close churches, to rape women and girls, to capture Italian men unwilling or unable to fight and send them to the Fatherland to work in the camps and produce armaments. But before she fled, she'd never seen any German soldiers go out on the water for enjoyment, and never noticed an especially large presence of patrols near the small harbors. It was mainly the local police who bothered people there, Italians tormenting Italians to impress their German bosses . . . or their *Duce*.

Now, though, it seemed the bosses had been captured by their own fears and were leaving Italy as fast as possible.

She walked a step behind Antonio, trying to be invisible. They had to wait to cross the *statale* because a line of German army vehicles—two of them towing long cannons—were hurrying north at a pace that wouldn't allow for attention paid to Jews or anyone else. The last truck in the convoy, covered by canvas but open in back, was filled to bursting with Nazi soldiers. As the truck hurried past, one of them turned to meet her eyes. A boy, he seemed. For a moment Sarah thought he might wave to her. For a moment she wondered if she'd wave back, but then the truck curled around a bend in the road and into a tunnel, and she and Antonio were able to cross.

Antonio's boat was very small and looked unsafe, a few centimeters of water in the bottom, the paint peeling. The old man stepped in confidently, pulled the boat closer to the pier, held it there with one hand and reached out with the other. Sarah could feel her heart thumping against her ribs. She held Lydia tightly to her chest with one hand, clasped Antonio's forearm with the other, stepped into the boat, and immediately fell to one knee. There was a small sound, as if the wood had cracked. Antonio was glaring at her. She shifted her weight backward and perched on the wooden slat, then turned around so she was facing forward. Lydia started to fuss and wriggle.

Antonio untied the rope that held them and, pushing against the dock, maneuvered them out into the water. He connected the small red gas can to the engine and pulled on a handle there four or five times before the engine coughed out a puff of blue smoke and snarled to life. Lydia whirled her head around to see where the noise was coming from, and Sarah could feel the fear in both of them. Antonio turned the boat south, and Sarah kept one hand on the gunwale, fingers white. "It's fine, it's fine," she said to her daughter. "We're going for a nice ride. We'll be fine. Don't be afraid." But she, herself, was terrified, wishing desperately that someone were holding *her*, comforting *her*. *Luca, Luca, Luca,* she repeated in her mind, but she felt like she was clinging to the thinnest reed of hope. Luca could be anywhere now. Luca could be dead.

She tried not to look at the water, tried to keep her eyes up and on the shoreline as it glided past. A few elegant villas there, abandoned now by the foreign owners who'd so loved to come here in summer. Above them, carpeting the lower slopes of the hills, stood clusters of houses with red-tiled roofs. Beyond them a dirt road forked, both sides disappearing into the higher reaches. The trees were leafless still, brown and dark. Farther up, she saw the brick tower of the *rifugio*, where her mother had taken her a few times for picnics.

She concentrated on holding Lydia tightly against her and on keeping her eyes up, above the water, and she felt she was controlling the fear fairly well until she realized her feet were getting wet. She looked down: there was three times as much water in the bottom of the boat as there had been when they'd started.

"Antonio!" she cried out, over the noise of the motor. She twisted around to look at him. He had one hand on the throttle, eyes on the water ahead. He shifted them to her face. She took her hand from the gunwale for just long enough to point to her feet, then grabbed it again.

Antonio looked down. The skin of his forehead wrinkled angrily around the tops of his gray brows. "A leak now," he said. "A new leak."

"Should we stop?"

He shook his head, which caused the blood-spotted bandage on his ear to come partially loose and flap in the wind. He took an empty can from beside his feet and tossed it to her. It splashed in the slowly rising water just behind her feet. "Bail," he said, and when she didn't understand, he made a scooping motion with his free hand. "Bail. Throw the water out."

"But I have to hold on!"

"Bail, bail!"

Sarah reached down and took hold of the empty can. No longer gripping the gunwale, with the boat rocking side to side and throwing up splashes of water in front, she felt like she could topple over sideways, or worse, that Lydia would make a sudden move and fall overboard. But Lydia was holding to her like a baby monkey, arms linked behind Sarah's neck. The water was at the bottoms of her ankles now, her shoes and socks soaked. She leaned down, filled the can, and threw the water over the side. But she didn't lean over far enough; the wind caught the water and splashed it into Antonio's face and chest. He grimaced, wiped his eyes with his free hand, didn't so much as glance at her. She tried again, throwing the water closer to her. They were passing Dongo—she recognized the church—not even halfway there. She scooped and dumped, scooped and dumped a dozen times, and then Lydia did turn around suddenly, at just the wrong moment—something had caught her eye on the shore—and Sarah lost her grip on the can and watched it fly over the gunwale, splash into the water, bob there on the surface for a moment, then sink. Antonio cursed quietly, twice, and still wouldn't look at her.

The small village of Musso now. Then Griante. She saw a pier where they could pull in. "Antonio!" she called. "Antonio!" But he refused to look at her. The fishing rod lay alongside their feet. She'd forgotten about it entirely. The water covered her anklebones, and she was sure the small boat was going to capsize. Her mother's story filled her mind. It would be like that, breathing water, choking, except worse, because she'd be holding her drowning child. The boat seemed to have slowed, to have settled deeper into the lake. Antonio kept his eyes just to the right of her, scanning the water ahead. Lydia was screaming, Sarah holding her with both arms. She began to sing, in a trembling voice, an old lullaby her mother had sung to her: *"Nonnadella, nonnadella."* The words caused Antonio to look at her, then away again. "Fear brings trouble," she thought he said.

By the time she saw the large pier at Menaggio, the one where the ferries docked, the water in the boat had risen over the tops of her socks and the engine had started to sputter, but at last Antonio seemed to be turning in. He didn't steer the boat toward the large pier but went past it to a small flat one, made of concrete. She saw another boat there, two fishermen standing near it, the skin of their faces the color of rust, a red-brown painted on their cheeks, foreheads, and noses by years of sun and wind.

Antonio called out to them, and they reached down and caught the boat as it drifted close, then brought it tight against the concrete. Each of them held out an arm to her. She grabbed one arm and realized she couldn't stand. The boat was too unstable. The smaller of the two men held out both arms, and she passed Lydia over to him and was able to stand and step onto the dock. The taller man went to his boat and returned with a can similar to the one she'd lost overboard, and Antonio started to bail out his craft, leaning down and inspecting the boards for the source of the leak. Sarah's legs were trembling, shoes and feet soaked. She realized, too late, that in her fear and haste, she'd left the sack and blanket and metal shears at Rosa and Antonio's house. The spare diapers were there. Lydia's diaper felt wet, but didn't smell badly. Sarah had a knife in one pocket of her dress, the Swiss coins in the other; that was all. She started to cry. "Thank you," she said. Antonio wouldn't look at her. "Thank you," she said again, louder, through tears.

He turned just his head, nodded, said, in a flat, almost angry tone, "Go now, find him. You can come back to us if you have to."

"I left my things there."

Without actually looking at her, he reached into his pants pocket and pulled out a single bill, five lire. He handed it to her. She hesitated, took it, thanked him again. He nodded once, and kept bailing.

Twenty-One

After he'd torn the note into small pieces and pushed the pieces down into the elevator shaft, Luca sat for a while on the sofa in the apartment building's lobby and tried to gather his thoughts. He was being tested; that was obvious enough. No doubt there were good reasons to have the torturer killed: the man and his brother had terrorized half of Italy. Maybe it was personal: maybe the woman he'd met behind the Duomo knew someone who'd fallen victim to the Sisteks and she was seeking revenge. No doubt such a killing would send a message to the Nazis that remained. But it seemed to Luca that anyone could have been given the assignment, that it must be some kind of test—of his loyalty, his skill, his courage, the amount of hatred in his heart. It was entirely possible that Masso and the woman were trying to see if he was the right partisan to complete an even larger and more dangerous assignment—the killing of Mussolini himself, perhaps, or of someone close to him. But, much as he despised Mussolini and hated the Nazis for their torture and rape, Luca found that he was having to harden his heart for the task ahead, and that hardening required a massive exertion of will.

He was remembering the first time he'd ever taken the life of another human being, the plainclothes OVRA operative who'd followed him away from the horrific scene at Piazzale Loreto. Almost two years ago, that was. He remembered how he'd felt afterward, climbing up to the cabin where Sarah was hiding, seeing her, talking with her, making love with her, and then visiting with Masso later. It was as if he'd been cast to the outskirts of humanity and would never be welcomed again as a citizen of the civilized world. Even Sarah's warmth and love hadn't quite been enough to draw him back across that bloody line and end his exile. He remembered telling her what had happened, what he'd done, and he remembered how understanding she'd been, how kind, how forgiving. But the act had cut a chasm between them. He could reach across it—he often did—but it never disappeared, and in time he realized it never would.

He'd killed other men, though how many he wasn't sure. Never with a knife again, and never at such close range. Nazi soldiers, Blackshirts, two more pieces of OVRA scum—none of them deserved to stay alive. In time, he'd committed and witnessed so many killings that his heart had formed a hard crust. A crust of iron, it felt like. It seemed to him that so many important feelings had been encased inside that iron armor, songs that couldn't be sung, or wouldn't be heard, and he worried he'd never be able to cut through it and gain access to them again.

He saw clearly that this was an end-of-the-war worry: though he tried to keep himself from looking there, he knew that, not far into the future, the fighting would be over. Another few days, another week, another month. Part of him was already trying to imagine himself in the postwar world, a world that wasn't composed of days and nights in the forests, secret meetings, sabotage, murder, worrying every minute if he could trust the people around him or if they were just ordinary women and men who might lose faith at a key moment and engage in a terrible betrayal. He'd discussed this with Giovanni, his closest friend. "In a way, this is the most dangerous time," his friend had said. "A year ago, in the midst of everything, surrounded by Nazis, the *Americani* still far away, we closed off our minds to any possible future. It kept us careful, sharp. These days, we think about the end, and the life we might have after the end, and it's dangerous to do that. It can lead to a fatal mistake."

Now he'd been instructed to kill again. Not in the hot passion of a fight, but with an iciness he'd have to summon. This time it was a torturer, one of the Sistek brothers, and every single person he knew had heard about the Sisteks' methods, the cells. Sitting there alone after his odd meeting with the nameless woman, Luca felt caught between the hatred that burned in him for the people who'd killed his mother and caused Sarah to have to flee, and the love he felt for her, and wanted to feel for their child. He knew he'd have to set the softer part of himself aside for the time being. He'd have to pretend the war could go on for another year. He'd have to turn himself into a piece of machinery and do what he'd been ordered to do.

As he sensed the approach of midnight—a smaller church not far away sounded its bell on the quarter hour, and the Duomo's bell echoed a few seconds later—Luca forced himself to remember coming upon his mother's body, carrying it a few hundred meters to the far side of the house where he'd been raised, digging a grave for her with the help of Don Claudio, lowering her into the shallow hole, shoveling dirt onto her body. They'd done the deed in darkness, afraid the SS officers might discover them. He'd sworn an oath then: he would avenge her death. He brought her to mind now, but she seemed to be arguing against it, telling him to ignore the oath, to find a place to hide until the Allies reached Milan and liberated it, and then go looking for Sarah. It would mean waiting only a short while. Let God exact revenge on the torturer.

But when the smaller church, and then the Duomo bells, began to sound the midnight hour, each strike of iron echoing across the city in a measured, relentless cadence, Luca got to his feet. Three rings. Four rings. He checked his pistol to see that the mechanism was working properly—it was—six rings. Seven. He stepped out into the night and walked according to the instructions he'd been given. He turned a corner. The street was silent except for the bells. Ten rings. Eleven. There was the fountain, and there, a shadowed figure, slightly hunched, making its way toward the spigot at a brisk pace. Luca took two steps sideways so he was hidden behind the thick trunk of a eucalyptus tree. The final bell sounded. The man—what if it was the wrong man, or he had a bodyguard nearby?—was two meters from the place where he would try to wash the blood and sin from his fingers. He stopped with his back to Luca, bent forward, and lifted a hand to his mouth. Luca could hear the splash of water on pavement. He took the pistol from his pocket, stepped out from behind the tree, made three long, quick strides across the street, came up behind the man, and fired twice in short order, top of the spine and back of the head. The man fell forward and caromed off the spigot, his bald skull broken open, the ruined face turning to one side as the body hit the sidewalk in a splash of blood.

Luca hesitated just a moment, listening desperately for the sound of an automobile, but there was no sound, no auto, no rescue. He waited a few more seconds, then hurried away, staying on the same street, keeping in the shadows near the wall. Just as he was turning left, into a dark alley—still listening, still hearing nothing—he felt himself struck behind his right ear with great force. One second of amazing pain, and then nothingness.

Twenty-Two

By nightfall, the lorries were loaded with papers, boxes, and certain personal items belonging to *il Duce* and his family. The offices were mostly bare except for the shelves of books that had been there when the Feltrinellis still lived in the house. The suitcases of money had been entrusted to Colonel Messina. *Il Duce* had asked Enzo to take another load of papers out into the lake, and Enzo had done so, not even glancing at them this time, just heaving them over the side, idling there for a few minutes to savor the long, watery view and consider his options, and then bringing the boat back to the dock.

There was a last meal—*il Duce*, Scavolini, Zarraona, Nazzacone, Rachele and their son Vittorio, Enzo, and a handful of lesser Republic of Salò functionaries. The two cooks, local women, had prepared pizzas in the Neapolitan style, ordinarily something *il Duce* enjoyed, but that evening Enzo noticed he ate very little. A few bites, half a glass of wine. Mussolini seemed pensive and withdrawn. Conversation went on in spurts around him, but he said nothing until he bade them good night.

Enzo retired to his room, a suitcase open on the floor, half-packed, and was glad when Angelina tapped on his door, quite late. In the feeble moonlight slanting in through the curtains, he watched her taking off her clothes, then felt her slide in beside him under the covers. They lay there on their backs at first, touching only at the shoulder and hip, Angelina rubbing her ankle up and down against his lower leg, as she liked to do. He reached over and with one finger traced small circles on her thigh, feeling the warmth emanating from her body. The night had a strange energy to it, almost an electric charge, but also a vast spaciousness, as if they were lying together in a room separate from their normal lives, set apart in a great black box of timelessness. For once, it was as if the conversation—hanging just above them in the air, like fruit ready to be picked—was a prologue to the lovemaking instead of an epilogue.

"My brother has a friend," Angelina said at last, so quietly Enzo had to strain to hear her, "a friend from childhood. The first person I ever kissed." She laughed. "Though nothing more than that ever happened." Angelina turned onto her side, and he could feel her breasts against him, and feel her breath on the left side of his neck. "My brother's friend is a good Fascist." She laughed again, though there wasn't much joy in the sound this time. "He can get us out of Italy, he says, and I believe him, Enzo. He can get us out and get us documents. We can go to Argentina. A lot of his friends are going there, a lot of Germans have gone there already. It's supposed to be nice. No war, at least."

Enzo couldn't answer. He realized that one part of him was hoping, or had hoped, that he could do what he had to do with regard to Benito Mussolini, and then cut himself loose from the man and from his own past the way one might cut the string of a kite and watch it float up and up and disappear. His betrayal—*a shift of loyalties* was the way he preferred to think of it—was such an immense presence in his mind that he'd somehow believed it would block out the sight of his past and allow him to begin a fresh life with Angelina. Marriage, house, children, a second chance—he'd imagined all of it, but always in Italy. He wondered if millions of Italians were clinging to a similar fantasy. They would rid themselves of Mussolini and the Germans, and the past would magically evaporate. Life would blossom again, fresh, untainted by history, by all the death and blood and suffering and hunger and ruin, all the cowardice and heroism and betrayal and loyalty. Partisans would live side by side with Fascists; all would be forgiven. No one would ever remember Enzo Riccio's long service to the disgraced former dictator.

That fantasy was always particularly strong when he was lying beside Angelina.

She pushed her bent arms against his shoulder. "No answer, lover? Will you come away with me?"

He slid the edge of his hand between her thighs, not too high up yet. She opened and closed her legs, gripping his fingers, but, for once, there seemed to be no urgency in either of them. He released a long breath and stared at the ceiling. "I think," he said, and then he paused and considered his options one last time. "I think I'm going to have to go with *il Duce*. I think his fate is going to be my fate."

"But how, Enzo? But what do you mean? You talked with Silvio, didn't you?"

"I did. I have some of his money for you."

"You told him the plan, the route?"

"As far as I knew it, Angelina. Nobody knows the exact route yet, but I gave Silvio the signal that we'd be leaving tomorrow. To Milan and then . . . nobody knows after that. *Il Duce* says the Valtellina, a last stand for Fascist history. He asked me if I'd fight with him there, and I said that I would."

"That's crazy, Enzo. He can't fight the *Americani*! With what? A handful of Blackshirts with rifles, against bombers and tanks?"

"He said it was 'militarily hopeless'; those were his words. But that he wanted to leave a mark in history, to show the *fascisti* dying in glory."

"That's stupid talk, the talk of a little boy. You'll go along with that?" She moved herself slightly away from him, took his hand from between her thighs and pushed it down and away. "What's happened to you? Have you gone insane?"

Enzo shook his head. "He won't fight. It's talk. He's amassed a small fortune in various currencies—I brought it here in two suitcases from Nazzacone's—and told me to be extra careful that it was loaded into a certain vehicle, driven by Colonel Messina, but under German guard. You don't do that if you're going to make a last great stand for Fascism."

"Come with me, then. Let my brother's friend take us."

Enzo shook his head again, more forcefully now. "I don't think I could live outside Italy. I don't think you could, either."

"If we stay in Italy we'll be killed, Enzo! You're living in some crazy dream! I was Claretta Petacci's maid, for God's sake! You were Mussolini's right-hand man, his chief aide, practically a younger brother! If the Italians catch him, they'll slaughter him like a pig and leave his body to rot in the street, and you think they'll just forgive me and you? For being part of the family that dragged them into this . . . this *shit*, this *hell* that we've lived through?"

"I don't know, Angelina. If we can make a life here afterward, I'd like to make a life with you. But I can't run now. If he goes to Switzerland or Germany, I won't even run with him there. I'd hate myself if I abandoned my country."

"Even to save your own life?"

"I can't imagine my life anywhere else, Angelina."

"That's guilt. It's just stupid guilt talking."

"I've already come to hate myself. I went out on the porch and smoked a cigar Silvio gave me—that was the signal to say we're leaving for Milan tomorrow. And the whole time I was hating myself for doing that. And I would have hated myself if I hadn't done it."

Angelina rolled onto her back and was quiet.

"I'm sorry," Enzo said. "I'm going with him tomorrow. If he's killed along the route, or if he escapes and I'm not killed, I'll come back to you here unless you go with Claretta. Or with this friend."

"Claretta's not taking me. I received that news this morning. They're saving themselves, Enzo. They don't care a shit for people like us."

"I'll come back here for you, then, if I live, if you stay."

"I won't be here," Angelina said coldly. "And I don't want any money from you." She flipped the blanket and sheet off her body and sat up on the far side of the bed. "I'll let the Fascists get me out, like the loyal maid I am. And then I'll make a good life for myself in another place. I don't like the choices I've had to make here, the choices I've been forced to make. Not you, just . . . serving these people. These . . . these careless fools!"

"War does that to people," Enzo said. "No matter if you kill or if you run, if you're a hero or a coward. Win or lose, it forces you to make choices you can't live with afterwards." Angelina was sitting on the bed with her bare back to him. He reached out to touch it, ran his fingers over the bones of her spine. "I want to make a life with you."

She shook her head. "I think you've been guilty since the day Lina left you. She was right about Mussolini and you knew she was right, and now, good Catholic boy that you were, you want to be punished for your sins. You want to die with your idiot *Duce*. I don't." She took two deep, angry breaths. "I'm going now," she said, without reaching back to touch him. She stood up. Another few seconds and he could hear her putting on her clothes. "Good luck, Enzo," she said. "I was glad to know you."

The door closed with a soft *click*. Enzo lay awake for hours, until he heard the Germans knocking, calling out that it was time to leave.

Twenty-Three

Despite her soaking wet shoes and socks, and despite the fact that Lydia seemed to have grown heavier during the short boat trip, Sarah knew, as soon as her feet were on dry land, where she would go. This was familiar territory: the ramshackle house where she and her mother had lived stood only a few hundred meters away, just on the other side of a small promontory. But the chances were good that Nazi soldiers still occupied it, and from the first days of the war she and her mother had stopped trusting their neighbors, the Ontillios, who played Mussolini's speeches at top volume on their radio.

Sarah looked up at the hillside opposite her, a stretch of houses with the bell tower of Sant' Abbondio and the steeper slopes above, a landscape she knew like she knew the look of her face in a mirror. She thought of the time—another terrifying day—that she, her mother, and Luca had climbed into those hills, how arduous it had been, and how her mother, weakened by all those months hiding in an attic, had wanted to stop, to quit, how she kept saying, "Go ahead, Sarah, go. I'll stay, I'll stay here." And how Sarah had refused to let her give up. In the end, thanks to Luca, they'd made it to the top and crossed over, and she was thinking of him, and thinking about the way she'd forced her mother not to give in to her exhaustion and weakness.

She felt that way now, juggling a restless, smelly Lydia from one arm to the next: the child was keeping her from simply giving up, lying down someplace and sleeping until the war was over. Life insisted on life, Sarah thought. Young life, especially, insisted on itself. But even for the older ones, sickness and pain and every manner of misery couldn't quite quench the thirst to keep living, at least not until one reached the place her mother had reached, where the body, not unlike Antonio's damaged boat, settled deeper and deeper into the water, carrying a heavier and heavier weight of suffering, and finally succumbed and let itself sink.

She hurried across the *statale*, went along Via Campo de' Fiori, which ran, in a gentle rise, past a handful of houses, then narrowed onto a slightly steeper path. The path was well traveled at first. Sarah waited until it crossed a small stream and grew even narrower, and then she stepped a few paces into the trees, sat on a large stone, and nursed her daughter. Lydia seemed dazed, and Sarah wondered if the cold night had made her ill. But she ate eagerly and, when Sarah set her down, stood on her feet holding on to the bottom of her mother's dress.

"*Mami, casa,*" she said. *Home.*

"*Si, tesoro.* Soon you'll be home. You'll see. Not too much longer now."

Sarah rested there a bit, then joined the path again. It grew even steeper, angling this way and that up the hillside. Where it forked, at a moss-covered stone, she turned left, onto another path so overgrown there was little worry about meeting anyone coming the other way. The climb was difficult, but not long, and not nearly as difficult as the steep ascent she'd made two nights earlier.

The cabin where she'd once hidden was so dilapidated and so far back in the trees that Sarah walked a few steps past it before she looked over her shoulder, spotted the broken roof, and turned around. The stone walls were bowed and cracked, the door hung crookedly on its hinges; she had to pull hard to force it open. Inside, the one large room was more or less as she remembered it—stove, sink, bed—but thickly covered with cobwebs now and showing evidence of mice. She set Lydia down. A wave of sorrow washed over her. She hadn't really hoped to find Luca here—no doubt he was elsewhere in the hills—but she'd thought maybe he might have left something: an old shirt, a second pair of boots, even a note for her on the slim, slim chance she'd find it. She cursed herself again for not having made a plan with him. Impossible as the end of the war had seemed at the time, they should have made a plan.

Lydia toddled over to the bed and rested both hands on the sagging mattress, then laid her head on it sideways, almost as if she sensed it was the bed where her spirit had been called to earth. "We can't sleep now, *carissima*," Sarah told her. "We can't stay here." Safe as it might be, the cabin was a ruin of a place, far from any source of help or food. They couldn't stay, but then, where could they stay? She thought of going back down the hill and north a kilometer to Luca's family's house, but there, too, the Nazi soldiers could have taken refuge. It might be possible to head back to Rosa's—she had some things there, at least—but the idea of riding in a boat again, or making the long walk along a busy road, held little appeal.

Weary, wrestling with another wave of hopelessness, she sat on the edge of the bed and lifted Lydia onto it. The girl crawled around a bit and then took hold of something in the rumpled blankets. It was a cloth hair band, with a few hairs stuck to it. A woman's hair. Long and reddish brown. Sarah took the strip of cloth from Lydia and stared at it, twirling it between thumb and second finger, studying the color of the hairs.

Not hers.

She leaned her forehead into her fists, then let herself topple over backward onto the bed so she was staring through tears at the slanted roof. A streak of sunlight shone through a large crack above her. It was possible someone else knew about this cabin. Possible, but unlikely. Luca had hidden her here precisely because it was so remote, so well hidden in the dense foliage thirty meters from a path that looked as if it hadn't been traveled since the previous century.

Which meant that he'd taken a woman here, perhaps made love with her on this mattress.

Sarah squeezed her eyes tight. A quiet, logical, sensible interior voice tried to convince her she was simply caught in the grip of exhaustion and fear, and that if Luca had, in fact, made love with a partisan woman, it wouldn't mean anything to him, wouldn't matter once the war was over. That woman wasn't the mother of his child.

But a worm of jealousy had burrowed into her brain. As had been the case so often during her Swiss exile, she couldn't keep herself from picturing a life painfully similar to the life her mother had led: no man, little income, raising a daughter in a cramped apartment with rats scurrying in the cellar and never enough food on the table. She let herself weep then, a deep, shaking sorrow it seemed she'd been holding back since she'd left this cabin and climbed across the border, pregnant and afraid she'd never see her lover again.

Lydia crawled onto her chest and lay there, patting her mother's face to comfort her, and Sarah remembered Rosa's words: "The child gave her the strength." She let herself cry for another minute, then slid Lydia to one side and sat up. If that kind of life awaited her, then that was the life she'd live. She'd raise Lydia with the same kind of fierce love her mother had always given her; she'd find that same courage. Rebecca had refused to lose hope, even when she'd had to eat and shit and piss in an attic for months, hiding from the devil.

Sarah lifted Lydia and carried her up to the spring, washed her there, cleaned her diaper as well as she could without making it soaking wet. Lydia cried when Sarah put it on her, said *"Freddo!"* Cold! But there was no option. Sarah washed her own face, neck, and arms, drank from the clean pool beside the spring, and cupped some water in her hand for Lydia. And then she bit down on her sorrow, lifted her daughter again, and made her way back toward the town. She had a little money. She'd see if the buses were running to Como, see if there might be some kind of shelter there, even knock on the door of a church and beg for help. If Luca was still alive, and if she could somehow manage to get together with him after the war had finally passed, then she'd find out if he'd been with another woman, and how he felt about that, about her, about the idea of raising their daughter together. It was almost as though her mother's spirit had returned to inhabit her, to insist on going forward. To insist on love.

Twenty-Four

When Silvio drove out of Milan, heading north toward Como and the lake that bore the city's name, he was humming a Neapolitan love song he'd heard often in the years he'd lived in that city. He'd forgotten the exact words of the song, but he thought they told the story of a woman betrayed by her lover. Still, it was a happy tune, brimming with vengeance. He didn't remember if the woman in the song had killed her cheating boyfriend herself, had him killed, or only wished that he'd been killed, but the notes of the tune expressed something like triumph. She would pay him back for his sinfulness, or God would pay him back, or he'd fall in love later in life and the woman would do to him what he'd done to her.

None of that mattered; Silvio liked the tune and often hummed or sang a few bars of it when he was feeling particularly happy.

There were so many reasons to be happy. The war was coming to an end. The tank was full of gas, the engine purring like a cat whose belly was being stroked. Mussolini's departure was imminent, it seemed, if the signal had been given sincerely and passed on correctly. That item—*il Duce*'s departure—wasn't surprising, wasn't a particularly valuable piece of information. The interesting part—the part that had made the lunch with Enzo so important and the payment so worthwhile—was the idea of Mussolini heading not farther north from Lake Garda with the German retreat, as one might expect, not up through Trento, Bolzano, Merano, and toward Innsbruck, along the route the

Nazi trains took, carrying their cargo of captured Jews. No, Enzo had said that the *Duce* would be heading to Milan. West, instead of north.

It was the act of a crazed egotist. Everyone in Italy knew the Allies were growing closer by the hour, aided by what were now hundreds of thousands of partisans coming down out of the hills and killing Nazis in the open, machine-gunning their convoys, blowing up their barracks, assassinating their officers.

Humming always seemed to help Silvio solve problems. He mused as he drove. Little chance he, himself, would be bothered now, even on this road. The Germans were intent on leaving, keeping a small number of troops in place only long enough to delay an advance so they could salvage men and equipment in the hopes of making a last stand at the German border. And the *Americani* were intent on chasing them back to Berlin as quickly as possible and killing as many of them as they could in the process.

Would Mussolini actually go to Milan then, in a moment like this, instead of fleeing straight north? Was he really that addicted to adulation?

Perhaps he intended to arrange some kind of official surrender there, even though he was no longer head of the Italian state and hadn't been for almost two years. In his mind, maybe he was still the actual *Duce*, the leader. Maybe, as Enzo had hinted, the man embraced a historical perspective, focusing on his legacy, when any normal human being would be focused on saving his skin.

So, assuming Enzo was correct, and *il Duce* was headed to Milan, and assuming he wasn't planning to surrender, where would he go from there? Where would a man like that run? To the Valtellina, Enzo had said. But the Valtellina was directly north of Lago di Garda, directly between where Mussolini had been living and the German nation. If he were aiming for the Valtellina, it would have been so much easier to simply head northwest from the so-called Republic of Salò, up through Sondrio, the Valtellina's main city, then continue on into Hitler's embrace.

From Milan, of course, it was still possible to reach the Valtellina—which spread east to west across the top of Italy in the shape of a shallow bowl. But that would mean taking the route north along Lake Como, either on the east or west side. The west side would probably be safer, and would have the added advantage of bringing *il Duce* closer to Switzerland. Mussolini could claim to be going to the Valtellina to make a last stand, while in fact he was heading to Switzerland to seek exile, to save his life and that of his mistress and sycophants. Perfect sense, that made! Absolutely perfect sense! The great *il Duce* could parade his ego in front of his supporters for a while, and then, perhaps finding some convenient excuse, take the road that ran along the lake's western shore, veer off near Gravedona, and beg to be allowed to cross into Switzerland.

A wide smile split Silvio's scarred face. He loved it when he thought his way through a problem. A few bits of information from the kindly Enzo, the notes of a happy tune, all of it fed into the workings of his own analytical mind, and voilà: the answer.

He decided he would drive all the way to Como and take a little tour up the lake's western side. Why not? The Germans would pay him no heed. If he was stopped by the partisans, he had his handwritten note from Anna, one of the bosses, certifying, in code, his value to the cause of liberation. They'd understand the code and not bother him. And there was no substitute for firsthand inspection. If, in fact, Mussolini and his minders would be heading up the lakeside road, then Silvio would scout out the perfect place to stop him before he reached the pass that led toward Switzerland. Silvio Merino would end up being famous as the mastermind behind the capture of *il Duce*. As he drove north—Seveso, Mariano, Cantù—he was already imagining the women he could entertain with the story. *Yes, I admit it. I was the one. It all came from a conversation with one of* il Duce*'s aides, and then a bit of figuring, nothing too special. Let's go upstairs and I'll give you the whole wondrous story.*

When he reached the outskirts of Como, Silvio found the city eerily quiet. There was little traffic besides a few German military vehicles, hurrying, he noticed, north. He stopped only long enough for a coffee, then headed north himself, into and then through the city, which sat at the foot of one of the great lake's two legs. From there, slowed for a few kilometers by more German vehicles parked in a long line at the side of the road, he went through some of the most beautiful territory in all his magnificently beautiful country: through Cernobbio and Argegno and Cadenabbia. To his left, steep, forested hills, ready to burst into greenery, climbed and climbed; to his right the silvery-blue lake shimmered. What a place this was! What if he bought a villa here and settled down after the war? Another fantastic idea!

In Menaggio, with the promontory of Bellagio lying in all its glory just offshore, he came upon a pitiful sight: an attractive young woman sitting on a bench at the side of the road, holding a small child against her shoulder and apparently weeping. The day had been so fine that Silvio decided it was his duty to give comfort where he could. Especially where a beautiful woman was concerned.

Twenty-Five

Luca regained consciousness in a gray-walled, windowless room. He was seated in a wooden chair, and his hands were tied tightly behind the back of the chair with thin wire. The wire cut into his wrists. His shoulders ached. There was a throbbing pain behind his right ear. A terrible smell filled the room—urine and blood and something else. In front of him was another chair, empty, and beyond it a metal door, brown and dented. After a few terrible moments it squealed and opened. A tall, thin man entered the room, leaving the door slightly ajar. The man looked almost exactly like the man Luca had killed at midnight, and for a few seconds Luca thought he'd died and gone to hell and now the ghosts of the people he'd slain were going to enter the room one by one and torture him.

And then he remembered that the man he'd killed had a twin brother. This was Edmund Sistek, then, the more notorious of the two torturers. This Sistek was wearing a white knee-length jacket like those worn by doctors, but there was a German Army uniform beneath it— the gray collar was visible, and Luca could see the Gestapo insignia there. A colonel. Sistek held something in his right hand, a straight razor. He smiled and sat in the chair opposite, tapping the flat of the blade against his palm. For a few seconds he studied Luca and didn't speak.

"You know," he said at last, in a high, reedy voice, "some of my colleagues have already given up the fight. They're scurrying home like rats now, thinking only of their mothers and wives, saving themselves. For me, you understand, the situation is different. Like my late brother, I am part of a holy crusade, a righteous cause. A man of honor doesn't so easily abandon such causes. If we can remove a few more Jews from this earth, a few more sordid Italians, before we leave your country, then we are bound by duty to do so. You're not a Jew, are you?"

Luca shook his head. He could feel sweat pouring out of his armpits and down the sides of his ribs. The back of his head was throbbing, and his breath was coming in short, shallow spurts.

"Good. A partisan, though?"

Luca didn't move.

"An assassin?"

"No."

"There must be a mistake, then, because someone assassinated my brother last night, not far from where you were captured. Klaus Sistek. Do you know him?"

Luca shook his head.

"Do you happen to know who murdered him?"

"I do not."

The thin man tapped the blade against his left palm and grinned. Luca thought he heard a small noise, a metallic bump, in another part of the building. Sistek didn't turn his head. "Perhaps not. But I suspect you are lying to me, and I suspect the truth rests somewhere in your depths, and I suspect I shall be able to excavate it. What do you think?"

Luca felt his lips trembling. His legs started to shake, so he pressed his boots hard against the concrete floor. He thought he heard muted voices, a shout. Maybe the screams of other prisoners.

"What amazes me," the thin man went on, "what has always amazed me, is how well the human body can function without some of its parts. I see you have one arm that's smaller than the other, and yet it seems you've functioned fairly well to this point." He held the razor straight up in the air. "I intend to see how long you can continue to function as you lose certain parts of yourself. The tips of the fingers, for example.

The ears. The nose and lips." He grinned lewdly. "Certain other parts. What do you think?"

Luca's entire body was shaking now, his teeth tapping against each other as if the room were freezing cold. He tried to hold eye contact but found himself glancing down at the razor, then up into the man's eyes. The expression in those eyes—which were gray as the walls—was like nothing Luca had ever seen. A kind of perverted delight mixed with a cold, cold evil. "Shall we begin?" Sistek said, rising to his feet.

Although he knew it was useless, Luca couldn't stop himself from struggling to free his hands. He managed only to move the chair a few centimeters back and cut the wire deeper into the skin of his wrists. Sistek was approaching him slowly, grinning. There were new louder sounds outside the door, and in another second it flew open and slammed against the wall. Sistek whirled in time to face two men bursting through the doorway, rifles raised.

"I'm—" the torturer managed to say, before there was a deafening burst of gunfire and he flew backward, blood spraying everywhere. His body knocked against Luca's left shoulder and spun down onto the floor, his bald head striking hard against the concrete, his legs jerking madly in a death spasm, the top of the white doctor's robe already soaked red.

Luca felt blood dripping down his left cheek. One of the men was behind him. He heard a snipping noise, felt his hands freed. The man lifted him to his feet and hurried him out the door and down a grim hallway, with three other metal doors closed onto it. At the open door of a fourth room, Luca could see first a boot, then a uniformed lower leg, then a body in a German Army uniform. The men had Luca by either arm and were pushing him through a rear exit. They followed him into the cooler air of an alley. It was just dawn, gray light glancing off the metal of a motorcycle and sidecar parked there. One of the men gestured for him to sit in the sidecar, then straddled the motorcycle and started it. "Tell DaVinci," he called to the other man, who headed off, by foot, in the opposite direction.

The sidecar jerked forward and they were racing to the end of the alley, making a fast right turn, and speeding through the city in the first minutes of the day. Luca put his hands—both wrists were bleeding, but not badly—on the front of the circular seating area to brace himself. His head hurt terribly, his shoulders ached. None of it mattered. He was free, alive. He held on, one sharp turn, another. Without a second's hesitation the driver wheeled left into a narrow driveway, raced to the far end, and turned sharply right so the motorcycle went into some kind of temporary metal shelter. Parked there beneath the shelter's roof was Masso's truck. The driver stopped, killed the engine, allowed himself one deep breath, then looked at Luca and grinned. *"Tutto a posto?"* he asked. *Everything okay?*

Twenty-Six

Accustomed as he'd become to *il Duce*'s romantic life—he'd helped facilitate some of Mussolini's trysts and encounters, and was on decent terms with both Rachele and Claretta—Enzo still found certain of his boss's behaviors perplexing. One time, when a woman was visiting Mussolini, midday, in his office at Rome's Piazza Venezia, Enzo had been in the outer office and had overheard what sounded like animals copulating. From the noises, he guessed Mussolini and the woman were making love on the floor of the Mappamondo room, the main office. There was a short period of violent grunting and thumping, accompanied by the woman's exclamations, then a pause of a minute or so followed by *il Duce* serenading her on his Stradivarius. In a way, that had made a bit of sense to Enzo because he'd always believed Mussolini was something of a split personality: a wounded war veteran, the man was capable of violence, and often claimed it was necessary to remake society; but the other side of him was almost tender, easily bruised, occasionally sentimental, and even, at times, empathetic.

More bewildering was his relationship with Rachele. *Il Duce* seemed truly to care for her, and yet for years he'd carried on the affair with Claretta Petacci without making any effort to hide it. His wife knew, all of Italy knew, much of the world must know. *Il Duce* liked to drive his Alfa Romeo, but some days he'd leave the Alfa parked in front of the villa—as if to pretend to Rachele that he was in the office hard at work—and either take the Fiat or ask Enzo to take the Fiat and drive him along the lake to Claretta's place . . . with Lieutenant Birzer trailing behind. Rachele didn't turn a blind eye to her husband's betrayals: they infuriated her. The long-term, openly public relationship with Claretta particularly infuriated her. And yet, *il Duce* had never seemed inclined to break it off.

On the day they left the Villa Feltrinelli for the final time, just before dawn, *il Duce* spent a long while in the garden having an animated and, from all appearances, tender conversation with his wife. But when the convoy left the villa and headed for Milan, it was Claretta in one of the rear cars. Arrangements had been made for Rachele to travel separately to Monza and fly from there to Switzerland.

General Wolff made one last attempt to convince *il Duce* it would be vastly safer to head directly north toward Innsbruck—Enzo was present for the phone conversation—but *il Duce* stubbornly insisted on going to Milan. The man, Enzo mused, not for the first time, had a death wish.

Early in the morning they headed off in a string of private cars with German military vehicles ahead and behind.

The road from Lake Garda to Milan passed almost due west through Brescia and Bergamo, and then just south of Monza. Enzo had driven or ridden along it only twice before, once in summer and once in fall, and remembered it as a beautiful ride through low hills, with the taller mountains draped across the horizon to the north like the purple fringe of the sky's pale-blue skirt. Now, however, on this April morning at the tail end of northern Italy's harsh winter, the landscape was painted in various grays, as if announcing the onset not of a vibrant spring but of a slow, grim death.

Mussolini sat in back, as he sometimes did when he wasn't driving, Enzo at the wheel directly in front of him. Scavolini occupied the passenger seat, and Nazzacone sat beside *il Duce*. There was little conversation. In Sarnico, on Lake Iseo, they left the main road to stop for an early lunch. The restaurant was called da Cosimini, and the owner was a friend of Mussolini's son Vittorio. Enzo himself was ravenous and found the food delicious, but Mussolini ate little, twirling a glass of Nero d'Avola without taking more than a few sips, and moving pieces of penne back and forth on his plate in the blood-red sauce. "I remember," *il Duce* said at last, looking at each of them in turn, "I remember from the Bible the story of Judas betraying Christ. He was paid for the betrayal, thirty pieces of silver, but later returned the money and went out and hung himself."

Enzo stopped eating. The last bite of penne had caught in his throat, and he thought for a moment that Mussolini would point the fork across the table and announce that there was a betrayer among them, a Judas. *My Enzo, can it be true?* he imagined *il Duce* saying.

Mussolini was sadly shaking his head. "I wonder sometimes," he went on. "I've heard rumors, and I wonder sometimes if the Germans are negotiating a surrender behind my back."

"They wouldn't dare!" Nazzacone said. Enzo was able to swallow.

Mussolini tilted his head sideways, skeptically, pursed his lips, twirled his wineglass. "I've been told the war is lost now, and perhaps this is so. The point is, then, how one finishes this chapter of history. I trust myself to act with honor." He raised his fork again and circled it around the table, pointing at them one by one. "And I trust all of you. But the Germans, I'm not sure. Cardinal Schuster, not sure. If we're caught, of course, they'll try us in a fake court and hang or shoot us before the sun goes down. Who wants to end things that way?"

"No one," Nazzacone said. "Never."

The best Enzo could manage was to manufacture a confident nod to show his agreement, while looking at Nazzacone. He felt Mussolini's eyes on him for a second, and then Paolo Cosimini himself was at the table, looking worriedly at Mussolini's dish and asking if everything had been satisfactory.

"Fine, fine," *il Duce* said grandly. "The food is excellent, Paolo; it's only my mood that has dimmed my appetite. Thank you. We insist on paying."

"And I insist on not letting you pay, *Duce*," Paolo said.

Mussolini nodded approvingly and put a hand on Paolo's forearm. "I'll remember you," he said, in the grandiose tone Enzo had heard many times, and they were soon on the road again.

Twenty-Seven

Lydia was fussing, clawing for a breast, but Sarah didn't want to unbutton her dress on a bench beside the main road in Menaggio, even to feed her own child. As it was, she felt half-paralyzed with self-consciousness and fear, worried some Fascist-sympathizing ex-neighbor, hoping to curry favor with a retreating German column and earn a ride north, would recognize her and turn her in. From the moment she'd left the relative safety and comfort of the tilted house in Gravedona and Rosa's warm welcome there, the day had been an exercise in trying to hold on to a measure of sanity. The terrifying boat ride, the flood of water against her feet, Antonio's coldness and suspicion. *Luca, Luca, Luca,* she'd repeated to herself, a silent prayer. A thin snake of jealousy wrapped itself around all of it. The discovery of the headband and the woman's hair on the bed where she and Luca had made love had felt like a kick to her midsection. If she could just find her Luca, hold him, show him their child, she'd know within minutes how important his affair had been, and whether or not he could still love her, and she could still love him.

Her scratched lower legs were wet to the calves and so cold she was shaking. Lydia's diaper badly needed changing. There was no clean replacement. All Sarah could manage for the moment was to hold herself more or less upright on the bench and keep Lydia from tumbling out of her arms.

What now, though? In which direction was the urge to stay alive calling her? A friend of her mother's had owned a small store near the center of Lenno, the next village south. If it had stayed open during the war, if Philomena still owned it, if she'd been able to keep it stocked, then maybe Sarah could walk there and buy a diaper and some food with the money Antonio had given her. Lydia would be clean, at least. She could find a private place and nurse her. And then what? When the Nazis had started harassing Jews, she and her mother had been chased out of their apartment near the harbor. The last she'd heard, just before Luca convinced her to go into hiding, was that those two bedrooms, tiny bath, and kitchen were occupied by Nazi soldiers. She could take the risk of going there and seeing if the soldiers had fled, and if they had, she'd at least have a place to sleep. Or she could climb up to the house where Luca had been raised, the place where his mother had hidden Rebecca for months and months, and see if anyone lived there now, if perhaps something edible remained in the cabinets—a few stale biscuits, a jar of pickled beets.

Lydia fussed and fussed, her cries growing more urgent. Sarah stood, rocked her back and forth in her arms, and moved in the direction of the road, still not sure where to go. She'd taken a few steps, collapsed on a bench, and was frozen there, trying to decide, when a large, expensive-looking car skidded to the curb a meter in front of her. *Car* wasn't the correct word, however. The machine that pulled up so close was a magical assembly of metal, chrome, and glass. Its front end was curved, with headlights—the top halves painted black—that looked like eyes positioned on either side of the oval grille. The fenders—dusty and mud stained, painted green as a spring leaf—swept down and back from a long front hood and beneath a black roof that appeared to be made of leather or velour.

If she hadn't been holding Lydia, she would have run.

A man opened the driver's-side door and stepped out, and Sarah had the sense, immediately, that she knew him, that she'd seen him before, in school long ago, or in a dream. One side of the stranger's face was marred by an awful scar, but he was dressed as if for a wedding reception—clean dark-blue suit, white shirt open at the collar, gold watch. These were impossible things now, relics of a lost era. Since the war started, all but the fabulously rich dressed plainly; and with the scarcity of gasoline, everyone either walked, rode bicycles, or sat in buses staring out dirty windows.

"Beautiful young lady!" the man called. He seemed to be addressing her. "I have never seen anyone look so absolutely miserable, and I have seen so much misery lately. May I be of assistance?"

The man had spoken to her in Italian, but there was a lilting intonation—some kind of accent—and the words were strangely formal. A southerner, she guessed. Perhaps a factory owner, immune to the suffering around him—how else could he be driving such an automobile? He stepped closer, ignoring the fact that other vehicles had to move into the opposite lane in order to pass. She couldn't find anything to say.

"Beautiful young lady," the man repeated, "with the beautiful child. Allow me to help. What is it that you need?"

"I . . . I," she stammered. "I—" He was almost comical. A dandy. Perhaps a famous actor—that's where she'd seen him: on the screen at the cinema. "Who are you?"

"Silvio Merino!" he sang out.

"An actor?"

"Of sorts, yes. I act counter to the war. People grieve, I make them laugh. They hate, I make love to them. They suffer, I try to help."

"You have money," she said, and then realized what a stupid comment it was.

"Of course I have money! I've had money since I left my parents' farm in the dry hills of Sicily thirty years ago. Even then, even as a boy, I found ways to have money. Let me help; are you hungry? Your child is hungry. Even a man unaccustomed to children can see that! I'm hungry myself—let's find a place. Sit in my beautiful car, we'll find a restaurant that will serve us."

"I'm dirty."

Silvio laughed, waved a hand.

"My child, she . . . needs a diaper."

"Then we'll find a diaper, or make one. Sit, sit in." He was opening the door. Sarah hesitated a moment, wondering if he could be another Gunther, if there would be a price to be paid for soiling the leather seat of his elegant car, for accepting his help. But there was simply no place else for her to go. She stood, walked over to the car, and sat in the front seat. He closed the door gently, then marched around past the grille and headlights and arranged himself, with a shifting of shoulders and hips, behind the wheel. "Oof," he said, squeezing his lips up against the bottom of a large nose. "Yes, a diaper is needed. Very soon."

"My mother's friend had a store, in Lenno." Sarah pointed back over her shoulder. "I don't know if it's open. They might have a diaper for sale there."

Silvio glanced in the mirror, glanced out the side window, and made a risky U-turn right in the middle of the road, with a farm truck bearing down on him in the opposite lane and three German lorries hurrying up behind. Someone yelled out a curse in German. Silvio laughed loudly out the open window. "Your name?"

"Sarah. And this is Lydia."

"A beautiful woman and her beautiful child."

At that comment, delivered innocently enough, but with what seemed to her a certain intention, Sarah felt the middle of her body turn hard. Silvio was speeding down the road, smiling, humming. They reached Lenno in three minutes. She pointed left, toward the store, and he waited for a bus to trundle past, then turned in. "It's open," he said. "Let us see what we can find."

Philomena perched on a high stool behind the counter, gray haired now and shrunken, but with the same ferocity in her face Sarah remembered from childhood visits to this store. The older woman stepped out from behind the counter, wrapped Sarah in her arms, kissed Lydia on top of her head, and said how beautiful she was, how perfect.

"She needs a diaper. I'm sorry."

"Of course, of course. I have two left. You can have them both. And I have a dress for you. No stockings, of course, but"—she looked down at Sarah's wet feet—"clean socks, and possibly shoes that will fit."

Sarah reached into her pocket and pulled out the bill Antonio had given her. "I have only—"

"Later, later," Philomena said. "After this is over. I'll be here. Pay me then. No one is buying anything now, it doesn't matter. I only keep the store open out of habit."

Silvio had lingered near the entrance, perusing the shelves of clothing and tools, fingering a piece of fabric, or lifting a hoe from its place and fondling the handle as if he were trying to understand what it was used for. In a small back room where Philomena said she took her lunches, Sarah was able to clean and nurse Lydia, wash her own arms and face, and change into the new clothes, too. She realized how hungry she was, a steady gnawing in her midsection, as if there were four or five children living there, crying out to be fed.

When she emerged, in the new but simple dress, Silvio smiled at her. She let Lydia walk along the aisles to release some energy, her small legs working well for a few steps, then collapsing under her. The girl fell forward on her face, and Silvio laughed and lifted her up. She reached out her arms to him. "What's this, what's this now?" he said happily. He held her against him and juggled her up and down as if he'd been practicing for years. "A new feeling!" he exclaimed, beaming a smile in Sarah's direction, then handing Lydia over.

Sarah thanked Philomena profusely and, embarrassed, said she'd left the soiled clothes in a wastebasket. She promised to pay as soon as she could, then saw Silvio take out a leather wallet and remove several bills. "I'm a friend," he said. "A friend of the family. Fine, fine, that's fine. No change. My birthday is coming in a few days, and I like to give people gifts on my birthday! We're going to eat now. Where do you recommend?"

It was a simple question, but it changed Philomena's face like a slap. "Orlando's bar is open," she said.

Sarah was watching her closely. "How is Orlando?"

Philomena's face changed again, another slap. "You don't know?"

"I had to leave," Sarah said. "My mother and I had to leave. What happened?"

"A German soldier was killed by the partisans not far up the lake, near Dongo. One of their officers forced Orlando and all his customers out into the street, and his soldiers grabbed several others who were walking there. Women, children, elderly men. The priest."

"Don Claudio?"

"*Sì*. The officer lined them up and asked them if they knew who had killed the soldier. No one knew anything. How could they know? He said if one person volunteered to go to the work camps, he'd set the rest free. Don Claudio stepped forward, the brave man. But instead of setting the others free, the officer had his men shoot them, all of them. With machine guns. Right there in the street. Orlando and all the others. Orlando's wife, Violeta, runs the bar now and we try to eat there when we can, to help her."

"Don Claudio was killed, too?"

Philomena shook her head. "He was taken away, to the work camps. There was a rumor that he escaped, that the partisans freed him as he was being taken to the train station in Milan. But no one has heard from him or seen him since that day."

He's my father, Sarah nearly said, but she felt it would be somehow unfair to the man and to her mother to spread that news widely. And what difference would it make now, to Philomena or anyone else? She was the product of a brief liaison between a Catholic priest and an unmarried Jewish woman, a transgression from every angle, and the shame of that pregnancy had haunted her mother until her last day. It occurred to her that she'd repeated the pattern—the unmarried part, not lovemaking with a priest—and she realized Philomena was the first person from what she thought of as her "old life" who knew that about her. She wondered, if she stayed here when the war was over, and if she wasn't able to be with Luca, if she'd feel the weight of an unmarried mother's shame on her shoulders, too.

———

Orlando's bar—a five-minute drive back up the lake—was indeed open. Biscuits, wine, and tea were available, stale panini made with the strange combination of potatoes and vinegar peppers. Four men sat at a table against the wall, playing cards. One of them looked over at her and nodded in a neutral way; she nodded back. All of them eyed Silvio.

"So," Silvio said, when he'd paid for the food and carried it to her table, "tell me your story."

"I'm searching for . . . my husband. Luca. Lydia's father." Sarah felt the card player glance over at her again, and she lowered her voice. "He grew up here, near me, but I haven't seen him since I had to leave."

"Of course, of course. How could a beautiful woman like yourself have remained unmarried? But you're not wearing a ring."

"He's not exactly my husband," she said, very quietly now. "We intended to be married. We were lovers. He was excused from military service because he was born with a weak left arm. We . . . I . . . when the Germans came, I had to flee." She looked around the empty room. "I'm Jewish. Half Jewish, really."

"Of course, of course." Silvio sipped his tea, nodded five or six times, glanced at the men at the other table, kept his voice low. "You were wise to leave. You're probably safe now, from the savages. But be cautious. There are still a few of them who remain crazed by their Führer, and no one can say what they'll do."

Sarah decided to take a risk. "And a few who are crazed by our *Duce*, no?"

Silvio nodded agreeably. "It's strange now, isn't it? We're not yet quite liberated, and already we're trying to live as we lived before, to say things we haven't been saying for years. I hope you find your husband."

"My . . . Luca is his name. Lydia's father." Sarah leaned in closer, risking another remark. "He's been fighting with the partisans. I don't know if he's still alive. He led me and my mother to the border with Switzerland and helped us cross. I had to come back to find out if he's alive. I had to."

"I'll help you find out!" Silvio said. "It will be my honor."

"You're kind," Sarah said. "And also—I'm sorry—very strange."

Silvio threw back his head and laughed. "That strangeness has saved my life so far," he said, very quietly. "No one knows what to make of me, which side I'm on, if I happen to have connections in the exalted realms of the Mafia, the Republic of Salò, the Vatican, or the Allied high command."

"Do you?"

"All of the above," he said. "All of the above, and others, as well."

"I trust you for some reason—I don't know why."

"Because I am a man to be trusted, that's why! I feel now that we are within days of the end of this torment. I've been driving on this road." He gestured out the window. "What do you see, heading north? German army vehicles, Nazi soldiers. Fleeing for their lives, leaving behind only the most fanatical and obedient, to be killed or captured."

"And *il Duce*?"

Silvio shrugged. "Ask me in three days and perhaps I'll have an answer. Now we have to help you find your man. Now I serve the nation of Sarah and Lydia and Luca. Where should we look first?"

Tears came to her eyes. "I have no idea. I've had no word from him, nothing."

"Do you know anyone he worked with?"

"He'd never tell me a name."

"Of course not. Of course he wouldn't. That's correct." Silvio broke off a small piece of biscuit and offered it to Lydia, who took it in her hand and crushed it, then licked her palm. His happy laugh filled the room. "You know, I'm thirty-six years old now—tomorrow, in fact. For as long as I can remember I've told myself I didn't want to have children. I live a life of, well"—he spun two fingers in a circle above his head—"an adventurous life. In some ways the opposite of the domestic life. But perhaps the war has changed me. I look at you with this beautiful creature and I admit to feeling a stab of envy."

"She likes you. She's not so at ease with most men."

"I'm flattered, Lydia," Silvio said to her, and he made a clownish face that drew a laugh.

"Will you watch her for a moment while I use the toilet?"

"Of course! I'll teach her my Sicilian dialect!"

Sarah left the table with only the slightest doubt circling in her thoughts. Either Silvio was the nicest man she'd ever met, or the best actor, but there were others in the bar, and Orlando's wife sitting beside the coffee machine with her rosary. She'd be quick. Nothing would happen.

When she asked for the toilet, Orlando's wife pointed to the stairs, and Sarah followed them down into a poorly lit basement with a dirt floor and a toilet behind a door with peeling paint. When she'd finished and opened the door again, she saw that one of the men who'd been playing cards upstairs was standing there, blocking her way. She was about to yell for help when he put his hands up, palms forward, a gentle gesture. "You're Sarah," he said, "yes?"

She backed away half a step and nodded, watching him.

"Luca's Sarah?"

"Why do you say it that way?"

The man, old, bald, and stockily built, with the face of someone who'd worked in the sun all his life, moved closer and glanced over his shoulder at the top of the stairs. "He works for me, do you understand? Tell no one, even now, do you understand?"

She couldn't speak.

"Listen." He reached out and put a hand on her shoulder. She flinched. "I sent him to Milan, with my truck. A farmer's truck. The cab is green. One of the slats on the side is missing. The number is CO445."

"Is he coming back?"

"Perhaps, but I cannot say when. It depends on . . ." He lifted a hand from her shoulder in a gesture that seemed to say, *It depends on the fates, on God, on luck.* "You can stay with me, if you like. I have food. I think it will be safe. You can wait there for him."

"You're not lying?"

"I wouldn't lie."

"Where in Milan, can you tell me?"

"Yes, if you tell no one. Near the Duomo. More than that I don't know."

"A dangerous job?"

"All the jobs are dangerous now, but yes."

"Then I'll go there and find him."

"*Signorina*, Milan is a large city. I can't say exactly where he is now. He could be coming back with the truck. He could remain there. And—"

"And he could have been killed. Say it."

"He could have been killed, yes."

"What is your name?"

"Masso. The farmer Masso. Gennaro is my first name."

"Then I'm going. I'll find him."

The old man seemed about to try to dissuade her, but something in her voice or face stopped him. "Let me pass," she said. "I'm going to Milan. My friend will take me."

Twenty-Eight

In Milan, *il Duce* set up an office on the first floor of the prefecture at Palazzo Diotti, a grand building of ochre stucco above two stories of gray Apuan Alps granite. Claretta and her family had been lodged in a nearby house, *il Duce*'s son Vittorio in another. Rachele was still in Monza, awaiting a flight. Mussolini had a large map of Europe tacked up on one wall of the office, and on the morning after their arrival, he started in on what would be several days of receiving visitors. Everyone, it seemed, wanted to see the *Duce*—local officials of every stripe, elderly supporters, members of the Fascist militia (*il Duce* himself wore the green-and-black militia uniform, trousers tucked into the top of tall black boots), even a pair of eighty-year-old sisters who brought him a loaf of bread and asked for an embrace. Late into the evening, Enzo remained in the anteroom to the office, allowing visitors in to *il Duce*'s presence singly and in small groups, stepping inside if they seemed to be overstaying their welcome, dealing with a journalist whom he didn't trust and who pestered for an interview.

Enzo noticed how much the attention lifted *il Duce*'s mood. Attention, praise, adulation—those things were like medicine to him, like food. After the meal at Cosimini's and the last stretch of the ride from Lake Garda, *il Duce* had sunk into a silent depression, but now his voice could be heard through the office door, a confident bellowing at moments, a short, satisfied laugh at others.

On the second morning, however, a rainy Friday, *il Duce*'s speech, scheduled after High Mass in the Duomo, was canceled, and the news from the front could hardly have been worse. Bologna had fallen to the Allies. The stream of visitors continued unabated, but, sensitive to *il Duce*'s moods as always, Enzo could sense a slight downward trajectory. He, himself, was a tormented man; his eyes kept going to the telephone from which he was supposed to give his signal about the route of escape, and he awoke each morning to such an assault of guilt it was as if there were another person in the room, and that person followed him through the day, pointing a finger, mocking, accusing. He kept worrying that someone, somewhere in the mysterious underground world of resistance fighters would have found out from Silvio the name of Mussolini's betrayer and passed it on as a kind of twisted revenge. Every time he went into the prefecture office to announce another arrival, to suggest that a talkative visitor's time was up, to bring *il Duce* something to eat or drink, he worried Mussolini would throw him onto the floor, take hold of him by the throat, and keep him there until the German torturers came to carry him away.

Il Duce still seemed pleased with the visitors and the attention, but also atypically distracted. At one point, so tormented by what Enzo thought of now as his own "moral predicament," so unsure of the decision he'd explained to Angelina, and so eager to set things up in case he had to meet Silvio's contact at the Duomo, Enzo asked if he could steal away for an hour and attend Mass at the cathedral. Mussolini looked at him as if he'd asked to borrow the *Duce*'s private plane and fly it to Rome for coffee. *Il Duce* studied him, smiled ironically, said, "You haven't been to Mass in years, Enzo. What is it? Fear of eternal judgment? Fear of death?"

Enzo shook his head. "No, *Duce*. This is the anniversary of my father's passing. I thought I'd go to Mass and say a prayer for him."

"The cardinal will be saying Mass today. We're supposed to meet later on. Let me know if you feel I should trust him."

"I will, *Duce*."

"Go, then," *il Duce* said, waving both hands. "Nazzacone can handle the visitors for a while. Go."

It was true that Enzo hadn't been to Mass in many years, and true, also, that in his earlier visits to Milan he hadn't had much interest in seeing the Duomo's interior. Stepping into the massive nave now after the two-block walk from the office, he found himself disappointed. Except for the stained-glass windows, set high up in the walls, the building seemed rather plain in comparison with its stylized exterior. He walked most of the way up the center aisle and sat in a pew on the left. In his years of absence, the ritual of the Catholic Mass hadn't changed at all. For a thousand years or more, it hadn't changed. It wasn't true that his father had died on this date, but it *was* true that his parents had taken him to Mass in the Basilica di Santa Maria Assunta in Castel di Sangro every Sunday and holy day for the first fifteen years of his life. The Latin prayers, the cardinal's garments and gestures, the Bible readings—all of it was perfectly familiar to him, a kind of dance performed around the golden chalice for the benefit, today, of a few dozen worshippers.

Only the topic of the cardinal's sermon surprised him, as it seemed, so eerily, to echo what *il Duce* had said at Cosimini's, and seemed to be aimed, not so much at the collection of elderly women who made up most of the sparse congregation, but at the man near the center aisle, the most senior aide to the most famous Fascist in history. "We all remember," the cardinal intoned, in a voice that echoed against the high ceiling and startled a pair of pigeons who'd taken refuge there, "that Judas Iscariot betrayed Christ. We all remember what became of him, how he took his own life in regret and shame and guilt. What we don't always remember, however, is that Peter, Christ's favorite, also betrayed Our Lord. Not once, but three times. Out of fear. And yet, Peter did *not* take his own life. Why was that?" The cardinal ran his eyes over the worshippers as if one of them might raise a hand and offer an answer. When no answer was forthcoming, he went on, "Because, unlike the evil Judas, the holy Peter retained his faith in Christ's mercy. He knew he had sinned, yes, perhaps the most grievous sin in human history, and he felt the searing pain that always accompanies sin in the soul of a good man. But he also had faith in Christ's limitless forgiveness. 'Ask, and you shall receive,' the Bible tells us. 'Knock, and the door shall be opened to you.' The question is not, Have we sinned? Of course we've sinned, all of us, to one degree or another, in one way or another, many, many times. The question is: Do we have faith in our Lord's forgiveness? And do we have the humility to ask for it?"

Enzo didn't walk up to the altar rail and receive the host, but during that part of the Mass, he did slip forward onto his knees, elbows on the pew in front of him, face lowered against his knuckles, and whispered, "If I take justice into my own hands now instead of letting it be administered by you, my God, then forgive me."

Leaving the church and stepping out onto the Duomo's grand stone patio, he remembered the way he'd felt as a boy, stepping out of Santa Assunta's after having made his confession and said the prayers of penance. He'd felt clean. The inside of his torso, the place he imagined as the home of his soul, had been washed and dried, like a shirt his mother had laundered at the local fountain, then hung on the clothesline behind their house. Whatever sins he'd committed the week before—a minor theft, a disobedience, disrespect for his parents—had been made, by God's miraculous powers, to disappear. It was almost as if he'd been given a new life.

The feeling outside the Duomo wasn't as pure and simple as that, but thanks to the cardinal's words, the specter of guilt had at least been set at some distance; the haunting creature was smaller now, trailing him, perhaps, and speaking in softer tones. It occurred to him, belatedly, that the cardinal—he seemed a decent man—might have been preparing his flock for the time after the war ended. Italians had been fighting against Italians for almost two years now, since the invasion of Sicily. Brothers had killed brothers, cousins had killed cousins, neighbors had turned in neighbors—Jews and Christians, both—to the dreaded Gestapo. How were they going to form one country again after the fighting ceased? *How,* he thought, *are we going to live with each other?*

Twenty-Nine

The motorcycle driver who'd rescued him from the torture cell accompanied Luca up a rear set of stairs to the third floor of the building, pointed to a small corner bedroom, and said, "You can sleep here. There's a bath in the hallway on the other side of the kitchen. Clean yourself there and leave your clothes. There's blood on them. We'll have something else for you to wear when you wake up. Sleep now. Good work."

"What happened to the car that was supposed to be there?"

The man shrugged. "Not even a *grazie* to me for saving you?"

"*Grazie* . . . But there was supposed to be a car. If there had been a car, you wouldn't have needed to save me."

The man shrugged and said, "Ask the boss tomorrow. You're here now. You're safe. Sleep."

Luca peeled off his clothes—they stank of sweat and were stained with Sistek's blood—opened the faucet, and lay in the tub a long time, until the water went from hot to tepid to cool. There was no soap. He washed his hands again and again, cleaning the nails and fingers. Again and again. He finally realized what he was doing and stopped and lay back, afraid to close his eyes and let the images grow even sharper. The man he'd killed, one of the Sistek twins, toppling forward. The other twin's icy eyes, the gleaming razor, the satanic grin, the blood. As he always did after an engagement during which someone had been killed or wounded—one of their soldiers, one of his people—Luca tried to bring to mind a picture of Sarah, tried to imagine them living in the house where he'd been raised, with its fertile garden in back and magnificent view down over the lake from the front side: the shimmering blue water stretching to the green hills on the far shore; the houses of the small towns there; then the tall gray peaks beyond and above them. He imagined children in the rooms of the house, imagined all of them hiking up to the *rifugio* for a picnic, or walking downhill, across the *statale*, and along the alleyway next to Orlando's bar to the little gravel beach where the locals swam in summer. Sarah, he remembered, was afraid of water. In her first days there, even just dipping her body into the cool spring near the cabin where he'd hidden her had been terrifying. He lowered himself deeper into the tub, letting the cool water rise to his bottom lip, imagining how he'd help her overcome that fear, take her by hand out into the lake, knee deep at first, then waist deep, then encouraging her to dunk her head under for a few seconds at a time— the way his father had done for him so many years ago.

He stood up and dried himself with a worn white towel hanging from a hook, then wrapped it halfway around him—as if there might be women in the hallway or kitchen at that hour—made his way to the bedroom, and fell into a dreamless sleep.

When the morning light woke him, he heard voices outside the bedroom door, a woman and a man, speaking quietly. A full set of clothes had been laid out on the chair beside the bed: underwear, pants, shirt, sweatshirt, socks. A size too large, but clean. There was a single drop of blood on his left boot, a bright red star. He spat on his finger and cleaned it away.

In the kitchen he saw the motorcycle driver from the night before and, next to him, cooking something on the stove, the woman who'd kissed him outside the Duomo. She was dressed plainly now. She turned and studied the fit of his clothing, said, "A little too large for you," and laughed. "Sit. We have eggs and even some coffee. A miracle. We can use names now. I'm Anna. This is the man who saved you, Giacomo."

Luca sat. Giacomo poured the coffee. "No sugar, sorry," he said, grinning. Anna brought three plates of fried eggs to the table and joined them.

"The car never came," Luca said.

She looked up from her plate. "We know the car never came, Luca. There was a problem with the car."

"You could have taken the truck to get me—someone brought it here."

"*I* brought it here, yes."

He tapped a pocket of the pants. "But I have the keys!"

She smirked. "There are things one learns in wartime," she said, and then, sarcastically, "Even women can learn them. Giacomo here saved you from a horrible fate; I'm feeding you eggs. Stop complaining."

"Who are you?"

She fixed her eyes on him, two circles of cool blue. "Who is it that gives you orders? The old bald farmer. You can say his name now."

"Masso."

"Exactly. And, make a guess: Who gives Masso orders?"

"You?"

"Excellent guess. Now eat, and when you've finished eating, we'll discuss what happens next."

For a little while they ate without speaking, leaving not a scrap of egg on the plates or a drop of coffee in the cups. Anna sat back in her chair and studied him. "The Allies crossed the Po yesterday," she said after a moment. "They've taken Bologna and Modena and Reggio. Parma and Genoa have been liberated. But some idiot Nazis are still fighting for their madman leader. And some idiot *fascisti* still want to fight for *their* madman leader. The war is coming to an end; I imagine you realize that."

"I do."

"But now there are disagreements among the various partisan groups about what will happen afterward. One group—not ours—is trying to get our famous *il Duce* to sign a treaty of surrender. He's here, in Milan. You knew that, I suppose."

Luca shook his head.

"He's here. Representatives of that group have arranged a meeting with him tonight or tomorrow. The saner German generals are negotiating secretly with the Allies. If those two treaties are signed—one between the *partigiani* and Mussolini, the other between the Allies and Hitler's generals—we can stop the fighting and prevent the last of our people, and the last of the Allied soldiers, from being killed." She paused again, as if deciding how much more to tell him. "We're happy to have the war end, naturally, but we're not as lenient as some of our comrades. We're not interested in capturing *il Duce* or letting him escape without paying for what he's brought upon us. He could run off to Switzerland or back to his Führer friend, as he did last time. He could take his own life. The Allies could capture him and put him on trial. We don't want any of that, as you might understand."

"I do. He killed my mother. He—"

"We know that. We've all lost people. We could have let you remain up in the hills with your fighters. In fact, we almost did that. Masso and I discussed it at length. The other faction wants to receive his surrender and arrest him, and right now they're in charge. But that's not good enough for us." She studied Luca for another moment. "We want to kill him. We've been looking for the right person to commit the final grand deed of the war, and Masso believes you are that person."

Luca watched the blue steel in her eyes as she said those words. He looked at Giacomo, who seemed about to grin and shrug again, as if to say, *I just do what I'm told.*

He looked back at Anna and said, "I'm your killer, then. An assassin now."

"Exactly."

"Since when?"

She tilted her head to one side. "Definitively, since last night. But really, since the day you killed the OVRA plainclothesman with a knife on the trail leading north from here. Not everyone could have done that, or done what you did last night. Your mother killed, too, we understand. She deprived a houseful of SS officers of their beautiful lives."

Luca nodded.

"And your father?"

"Sent to Russia."

"And your lover sent to Switzerland, yes?"

"Yes."

"Your farmer friend and I discussed all this. All of it makes you the right person for the job."

Luca nodded, studied her eyes for a moment, then looked away. *That's fine,* he almost said, but the words caught in his throat.

Thirty

Lydia slept most of the way to Milan, and Sarah was glad for the respite. She felt worn to the bone, physically and mentally. The image of herself that came to mind was that of a dry tomato stalk that had survived the winter with one miraculous red fruit, ripe, not rotten, clinging to its branches. The roots were weakened in the cold soil, the stalk was brown and thin. At any minute, the weight of that single tomato could topple the whole plant over sideways into the dirt. The strange man, sitting a meter to her left and piloting his beautiful car with one hand, was a solid stake in the ground beside her. She'd allowed herself and her daughter to be tied to him, just enough to remain upright, just enough to keep her from giving up.

But what would giving up look like now? What would the future look like? Even if she managed to find Luca, who knew how the neighbors would react to the Jewish girl who'd fled while they stayed and suffered for their *Duce*? Who could know that Mussolini wouldn't flee to Austria or Germany, sew together an army from the remnants of forces loyal to him, and try another invasion? Or set himself up in Zurich, Vienna, or Berlin, spewing hatred for the Jews and socialists and anyone who opposed him? Despite all the troubles she'd endured over the past two years, she'd learned to accept help, and she'd learned to trust. True, those two lessons had led to the putrid minute with Gunther, another well-dressed man with a fine car, but she knew other women had suffered things a thousand times worse, and, so far at least, this strange Silvio had given her no reason to be afraid.

But then he said, "I have a large apartment. You can stay with me," and Sarah felt her insides go hard and cold again. You could trust until you could no longer trust. He could be kind until he was no longer kind. But she couldn't make herself refuse the offer. Where else could she go? Find a place for herself and her child to sleep on the streets of Milan? Beg in front of the Duomo like the Gypsy women she used to see there on school outings to that city, those reverent church tours with her Christian friends making the sign of the cross and genuflecting? Hitchhike back to Menaggio and see if the Nazis had abandoned her mother's house, hope it hadn't been taken over by rats, sleep on the floor there, with her daughter, on an infested mattress? Go back to Rosa and Antonio?

What were her other options?

"I can feel," Silvio said—he reached out his open window and waved happily at a line of German military cars, heading north—"that you worry I will take advantage of you. In the way a man can take advantage of a woman. Am I wrong?"

She shook her head. Lydia stirred in her lap.

"Please don't entertain such thoughts. You're a beautiful woman, and I'm tremendously attracted to you, but please believe me: I've been with scores of beautiful women, and it's not so much that my appetite for such pleasure has been quenched, as that my pleasure has always come from the mutual enjoyment. A woman's discomfort, for me, would ruin the joy of the act."

It was close to what Gunther had said. Close enough to freeze Sarah in silence. She remembered the feeling of Gunther's fingers on her body and waited for what Silvio would say next.

"Stay as long as you like. Eat, feed your child, look for your child's father. I have a few small remaining tasks to accomplish, and then perhaps you and I and Luca and Lydia will celebrate the end of the war together. I have a friend who can secure us some champagne. Another few days, a week perhaps, and we can all celebrate."

"I'd like that," Sarah said, without much enthusiasm. "But what matters to me is finding Luca."

"Of course, of course," Silvio said, in a tone Sarah couldn't quite read. "We'll find him. I'm sure we will."

"But Milan is enormous."

"It is a large city. Yes. Another few minutes and we'll begin to see the outskirts. You gave me a description of the truck. We'll drive the streets near the Duomo. Or we'll park and walk around there. We'll find it; I'm sure we will."

But the closer they came to the city center, the less likely that seemed. Sarah started to cry, and hated herself for it. She turned her face out the window and swiped at her cheeks. Lydia awoke, fussing, overflowing with energy, twisting this way and that, reaching for the door handle, kicking her feet. "*Mami*. Home. Now!"

"Another few minutes, Lydia," Silvio said, as if he were speaking to an adult. "Then we'll let you walk all you want. We'll find some food for you and let you walk and run."

They entered the city center to the sound of wailing sirens.

"A bombardment?" Sarah asked.

Silvio shook his head, driving with both hands now, concentrating on the turns. "Those are factory sirens. I suspect the partisans are calling for a general strike, a stake in the heart of the last German occupiers. Look at the streets! Empty of people. Perhaps the Allies are very close."

"Then we'll never find Luca."

"We'll find him, we'll find him. Here, I'll park here. We're two blocks from the Duomo and two blocks in the other direction from my place. There's a café just fifty meters away. I know the owners. It's open, I'm sure it is. This noise is deafening. Let's get out. You can change Lydia's diaper again and let her move, we'll have a coffee, and then we'll begin our search."

Thirty-One

The parade of visitors had slowed to a trickle, so Enzo wasn't as busy as he had been during their first few days in Milan. In quieter moments, *il Duce* asked him to help with the complicated task of organizing the large amount of papers he'd brought with him from Lake Garda. "The great truths of life are enshrined in history, Enzo," he said on one of those occasions, using the flowery language he resorted to in times of triumph or great stress. Again and again Enzo had been impressed by those flights of lyricism, whether he heard them in a quiet office or from the balcony on Piazza Venezia. *Il Duce*, it seemed to him at those moments, was demonstrating that ordinary language was for ordinary people, and that someone at his level needed to push the gorgeous *lingua italiana* to its highest reaches in order to express the most profound truths. "History," *il Duce* went on, "distills the human predicament to its essence, leaving the mundane and the weak behind, and trafficking in glory and tragedy."

To Enzo, though he couldn't say it, the papers they were sorting seemed terribly mundane: records of the meeting of the Republic of Salò's ministers, plans for changes to the postal service and the system of taxation. He wondered if *il Duce* believed the documents would help him in case he was ever brought to trial. Many of the folders were marked with the years XXII and XXIII, as if *il Duce* wanted to throw the Christian calendar aside and measure human time not from Christ's birth but from the March on Rome and *il Duce*'s rise to power.

He thought again of the documents he'd thrown into Lake Garda and wished, for a few seconds, that he had the courage and the kind of relationship with his *Duce* that would have enabled him to raise the subject of the execution of Count Galeazzo Ciano. *How could you have killed your own son-in-law,* he would have asked, *when family means so much to you? How could you cause your daughter such pain?*

But he'd always felt that a force field of energy surrounded Mussolini. It was that field, that *aura,* that had catapulted *il Duce* to the pinnacle of Italian politics, given him a place on the world stage, a place in the history of humankind. Guiltily—there was so much guilt in him these days—Enzo wondered, as he closed box after box and set them in a stack in a corner, what would happen if the Italian people saw through that aura to the ordinary, flawed man behind. What would they think of their *Duce* then? What would they think of themselves? And how would they manifest their disappointment, shame, and self-hatred?

As the hours passed in the prefecture, terrible news—terrible to *il Duce,* at least, and to the loyal Fascists gathered around him— continued to arrive. Parma had fallen. Genoa had been occupied by the partisans. Allied troops were said to be marching toward Brescia, less than a hundred kilometers from Milan. *Il Duce* was given this news, of course. First thing in the morning, Nazzacone and Defense Minister Grazanini spent hours with him in the prefecture, passing on their depressing reports. They knew what was happening better than anyone. Only Scavolini, it seemed, was still talking about fleeing to the Valtellina and making a last stand. But *il Duce* appeared to value his opinion above everyone else's.

Il Duce's mood grew more and more sullen. He was barely eating— always a bad sign—and kept staring at the large map on the wall as if searching for another place, as yet undiscovered, where he might take over the government and lead a nation. He left for an hour in midafternoon, saying he was going to visit Claretta at the house where she was staying, and asking Nazzacone if he'd drive him there.

Alone in the office, Enzo looked at the telephone on the desk and thought of the way he was supposed to contact Silvio when and if he had news of the route north. He'd memorized the number, but there was no news, no certainty as to when and how they'd leave the city. He lifted the receiver and set it against his ear, as if rehearsing for the moment when he might make the call. "Tomorrow," he said quietly, to no one. And then he realized the instructions had been to let the phone ring three times and hang up—not to speak a word—then go to the Duomo. He replaced the receiver and waited for *il Duce*'s return, thinking that, if he did go to the Duomo with his secret information, he might just keep going, turn himself into the Allies and beg for mercy.

———

Another day. More bad news arrived. With each passing hour, Enzo grew more and more nervous and confused. He had his own office, right next to *il Duce*'s, his own phone there. But he spent as much time as possible with the *fascisti*, trying to sense what the plan might be. Everyone seemed to have a different idea. Over the past week, at one time or another, in one way or another, each of the loyal ones had advised *il Duce* to abandon the idea of fighting in the Valtellina. *Fly to Switzerland,* they said. *Get to Austria as quickly as you can by the safest route. Have Hitler arrange for the Luftwaffe to fly you to Berlin when the skies are safest. Go now. No, wait until the Allies are closer. Flee to Switzerland by car. Go by plane with Rachele.*

From Scavolini, and only from Scavolini: *Head to the mountains with all the men available and the Germans, too, and prepare for a last battle.*

No one was suggesting an official surrender, but Enzo felt the idea swirling around the building like wind before a storm.

When, late afternoon on the twenty-fifth, *il Duce* abruptly announced he'd be meeting with Cardinal Schuster in an hour, Enzo sensed from his demeanor that despite Scavolini's urgings, Mussolini might actually be intending to use the cardinal as an intermediary and sign a document ending the war. Over the past hours, *il Duce* had spoken more and more about "sparing our soldiers further trouble" and "ending the pain," but then Scavolini would swing by, and the mood would shift. There would be talk of the Valtellina, the last stand, glory, heroism; there would be more soaring flights of language. It had always been difficult to keep up with Mussolini's moods. Now, it seemed, they changed by the minute.

At quarter to five, *il Duce* marched out of the prefecture with Grazanini and Nazzacone at his side, and a coterie of armed guards in loose formation around them. Enzo followed close behind, listening to the Duomo's bells, hoping against hope. If *il Duce* did, in fact, agree to a surrender, and if he were arrested, treated like a head of state and not killed, and if Silvio could be trusted not ever to name his secret sources, then it was possible Enzo Riccio would survive, perhaps even find Angelina, if she hadn't yet been spirited off to South America, and see what the future held for them. Maybe, if no one knew of it, or spoke of it, his guilt would slowly recede into the past, along with the guilt of the millions of *fascisti* who'd brought war to Italian soil. Perhaps some form of peace—internal and external—might still be part of God's plan for him and for Italy.

When they arrived at the archdiocesan building, they were greeted by the cardinal's aide—a corpulent priest—and led to a room with gilded trim and velour curtains. Enzo was allowed into the meeting. "This is a moment for history," *il Duce* said to him. "I want you to take notes."

No longer presiding over the Duomo altar in his robes, Cardinal Schuster seemed, to Enzo's eyes at least, a smaller man, thin, dignified, and deferential in the way he treated *il Duce*. They sat at a table, biscuits and liqueurs there, and the cardinal carried the conversation. Enzo copied down a few of his words, but he was speaking mostly in platitudes, the vernacular of the Church. *The good Lord is asking us now to make peace,* and so on. *Il Duce* looked distracted, his face painted in shades of anguish, as if it had taken time for the horrible news from Parma, Genoa, and Brescia to pierce his depths. Enzo sat two meters away from the table, notebook on his knees, trying to be invisible. Now the cardinal was speaking to *il Duce* about Christ's mercy, repeating some of what he'd said in his sermon. When Mussolini mentioned Scavolini's idea of making a last stand with thousands of loyal Fascists in the mountains to the north, the cardinal said, in the most delicate way and yet pointedly, "*Il Duce*, I fear you are being misled."

After a time, a small delegation from the National Committee of Liberation arrived, and all of them moved to a larger oval table—Mussolini, Nazzacone, Grazanini, Scavolini, Cardinal Schuster, and three of the partisans. There were bottles of wine, and some food, all of which remained untouched. Enzo sat quietly, ostensibly taking notes, but in actuality too shocked at the sight of *il Duce* in a room with partisan leaders, too hopeful, too excited, too worried to make more than a few scratches on the pages of his notebook.

"I want my men protected," *il Duce* began, and even Enzo thought his tone was incorrect. He was acting the part of boss, of *il Duce*, when in fact, he'd come with hat in hand. The partisans—hefty men in mustaches and workers' jackets, the shine of victory already on their faces—tolerated him at first, saying they wanted only his surrender, not to quibble over details.

"Fine, fine," *il Duce* said, but it obviously wasn't fine at all. Enzo could tell he was reaching for any last scrap of authority, of dignity. His pride lay on the room's magnificent carpet like a meal that had been spilled there, a delicious chicken cacciatore with the onions and peppers and tomato sauce seeping into the carpet's woolen pile. Mussolini was reaching down, proudly trying to salvage a piece of meat that hadn't yet been dirtied, a bit of pepper or onion that might still be eaten and enjoyed. "My men and their families, I want no harm to come to them. The ministers of the Republic of Salò are diplomats. I demand that they be treated as such."

"You're not in a position to demand anything, Mussolini," one of the partisan representatives snarled, and *il Duce*'s head jerked backward as if he'd been slapped. "But we're human beings. What we care about now is the surrender, the end. We agree to the treatment of diplomats and family members."

"Fine, then," Mussolini said proudly. He seemed ready to ask for a drafting of the surrender, something he could sign, when Marshal Grazanini, who'd been fidgeting and angrily shaking his head the whole time, leapt to his feet. "Our allies, the Germans!" he shouted, so loudly that the cardinal leaned away from him and winced. "We cannot and will not agree to a surrender behind their backs!"

The elder of the three partisans smirked. "Your German friends have been negotiating with us for weeks," he said calmly, the way an experienced butcher slaughtering a sow might calmly wield his blade. Once, right there, into the heart. Mussolini's head jerked backward again, more violently. "A treaty is ready," the mustachioed partisan went on. "It will be signed later today. Apparently they weren't as concerned as you are about loyalty."

Mussolini turned and glared at Nazzacone. "True?" he demanded.

Nazzacone nodded, as if he'd known about this all along, but before he could say anything, *il Duce* exploded. Enzo had seen such explosions hundreds of times over the years, but this one had vastly more force to it, the difference between a few smoky puffs from Vesuvius and the eruption that buried Pompeii. *Il Duce* made a fist and slammed it so hard against the table that the dish of biscuits in front of him jumped two centimeters into the air. "Betrayed!" he shouted. "Betrayed by them again!"

The partisans sat calmly—almost, it seemed to Enzo, amused. Triumphant. Deadly. Grazanini looked as if he'd been kicked in the throat. He sat with his head lowered, hands clasped and flexing in front of him. Enzo wrote *German betrayal* in shaky script on the page, but could add no more.

He thought they'd reached the bottom then; nothing worse could happen. But at that moment, another partisan—a short, wide man with dark stubble on his cheeks and hands like massive paws—burst into the room and, as if he'd been listening through the door, started shouting about "summary justice." "To hell with these details!" he screamed. He flung an arm in *il Duce*'s direction and pointed a shaking finger. "Justice, now!" And then, to the other partisans, "How many of us has he killed? How many wives and daughters have been raped by his Nazi friends? Your group is too weak. Arrest him now. My people will try him within the hour and—"

"Be quiet, Maurizio," the elder partisan said, wielding the knife of his steady voice more delicately now. "Our 'group,' as you call it, is about to take over this city, as we've taken over others. We're fighting for the same cause as you are. Calm yourself."

Maurizio sputtered and stomped and eventually strode over to the wall and flung himself down in the chair, but he glared at Mussolini with absolute hatred.

The interruption had given *il Duce* time to consider his options. "Cardinal," he said, "given the German betrayal, I request an hour to consider my position."

The cardinal looked to the other end of the table. One of the partisans shrugged and nodded, as if Mussolini's position mattered little now. *Il Duce* stood and marched out of the room, and Enzo and the others followed.

Thirty-Two

Luca sat as if pinned in place by Anna's eyes. A minute earlier, Giacomo had walked out the apartment's rear door. Luca heard his footsteps in the stairway, and then the sound of the motorcycle engine coming to life.

"Everybody's tired of the killing," Anna said, and now that they were alone in the apartment, Luca thought he detected a slightly softer person behind the steely manner. "Even the Germans—with a few exceptions, like the two devils whose lives were ended in the past twenty-four hours—even they must be tired of it. Probably even Mussolini's men are weary."

"He's here, you said."

She nodded, lifted the coffee cup, noticed it was empty, and set it down again. "We've been watching him for weeks, waiting for the right moment. We have someone . . . close to him. And we have someone else—maybe you'll see him in a little while—who's been in contact with that source. But our *Duce* has been surrounded by Nazi soldiers every minute of every day. They even constructed a defensive bunker in front of the villa where he was staying. Concrete and steel. The SS, we understand, were literally given orders not to let him out of their sight. I wouldn't be surprised if one of them sits outside the room at night while *il Duce* entertains his Claretta. We always expected him to run at some point, but we thought he'd head directly north from Garda—that's the route most of the retreating Nazi troops are taking.

North through Bolzano and Innsbruck. I don't know what we would have done then. Imagine how surprised and pleased we were when we learned that his pride was drawing him back here, farther into Italy, one last time to Milan. You know the map. There's nothing of any size between here and the northern border."

"Monza, Como, Varese."

"Small places, in comparison. Not suitable for a grand last speech to rally what remains of the glorious Fascist cause."

"You want him to be killed here?"

Anna shook her head. She reached up and loosened her golden hair from its clasp, let it fall around her shoulders, and shook her head again, swinging it side to side. "He can't stay here, he knows that. The other partisan group I mentioned is within a few hours of taking over the city. You heard the sirens. There's a general strike going on. The Allies are a day or two away. There are scores of houses in this city and the surrounding areas filled with armed partisans. They're coming down out of the hills."

"My group?"

"Your group is still near the lake. *Il Duce* won't stay here unless he turns himself in, which I doubt very much will happen. If he does that, he does it. We'll take the city and celebrate. Our more merciful comrades will hand him over to the Allies and put him on trial, and we'll have to be satisfied with that. But his men killed my brother—who was our leader then—and that planted in me a seed of the most terrible hatred. Can you understand?"

"Of course. I have the same seed."

"And that seed has only grown over the past fifteen months as I've lost more men and women, as I learned of their torture, as we heard reports of the Nazis lining up twenty or fifty or a hundred Italians in the street and shooting them because one Nazi soldier had been killed. One! The raped women, the traumatized children, the old men killed or beaten for nothing. The seed has grown inside me like a cancer, and

I've come to the conclusion there's only one cure for that cancer. Some of my colleagues disagree, but I imagine you understand."

"I do."

"So now we have to wait." She pointed at the window. "It's dark now. While you were sleeping, I learned that Mussolini is having an important meeting. My comrades from the other group are there, our contact may be there. Even if he isn't, we're expecting he'll get the news and pass it on, and then we'll have a visitor here, you and I, and we'll find out if *il Duce* is, in fact, going to surrender, or if he's going to flee. If he's going to flee, we may very well know the route. It has to be to one side of Lake Como or the other—there are no other options left to him. Once we know that, if things work out just so, I'll be able to put you in a position to cure our cancer, if you still want to do that."

"I do."

It was the first time Luca had seen her smile. The smile seemed to change, not just the expression on her face, but the posture of her whole body. He felt a spark of attraction. "We have to wait, then," she said. "An hour, a few hours. How should you and I entertain each other in the meantime?"

Thirty-Three

Before they stepped into the café, Sarah set Lydia's small feet on the sidewalk and held one of her hands. The girl toddled along happily in her tattered shoes, tugging at her mother's grip. Sarah released her, but followed closely behind. Silvio stood between the two of them and the curb, though there was no traffic in the street now, only a few pedestrians, all hurrying, it seemed. The sirens had fallen silent, but there was a certain tension in the air, a sense that something monumental was about to descend upon the city—something terrible or wonderful, Sarah wasn't sure. Oblivious to all of it, Lydia trotted awkwardly along, lifting her feet and waving her arms for balance, falling once onto her knees, but leaning forward, placing both palms on the sidewalk, and pushing herself up again, legs straight, body hinging to vertical. They let her go as far as the end of the block, and then Sarah turned her and let her walk back, until she slowed and stopped not far from a door with the words CAFÉ NICOLINA above it in unlit letters.

Inside, eight tables covered with red-and-white checked cloths stood empty. Sarah sat at one while Silvio walked up to the counter, ordered, conversed quietly with the woman there for a moment, and carried back the food: there was coffee, which surprised Sarah, and a not-quite-fresh *cornetto*, small pieces of which she broke off for her daughter. Seeing that Lydia had nothing to drink, Silvio got up again and returned with two glasses of water, almost the way a father would, laughing happily when some of it ran down Lydia's cheeks, then reaching out with a finger and brushing it away.

"The city feels silently electrified," Sarah said.

Silvio's wide smile stretched the scar on his face and lit his eyes. Sarah realized how handsome he must have been before the skin of his left cheek had been sliced open. Green eyes, thick black hair with a few streaks of gray, beautiful cheekbones and jaw. She tried to remember the details of Luca's face—also handsome—but all she could seem to picture with any degree of accuracy was the *spirit* of him, a fierce insistence and self-discipline that permeated every aspect of his life. His love for her, his devotion to his parents, the way he had of forcing himself to do everything a man with two healthy arms could do—all of it was colored by that same fierceness. Even before the war, she'd felt he was living at twice the pace of everyone around him, squeezing everything out of every day, as if he had an intuition he'd die young.

Silvio was older than Luca. The first premature signs of gray were contradicted by the way he moved, the energy, the poise. "What happened to your face?" she asked.

Silvio laughed his gentle, infectious laugh. "The good Lord decided I was too handsome!"

"No. Really. What happened?"

He broke off a piece of his own *cornetto* and reached it across to a delighted Lydia. She took it from him but, instead of eating it, threw it on the floor and laughed. Silvio laughed with her. Sarah bent down and retrieved it, blew the dust from it, and ate it herself.

"An unfortunate accident," Silvio said. "I had a *macchina* even more beautiful than the one you see me in now. I was driving through Roma, performing a holy errand for the cause, and a bomb fell a bit too close. The Allies missed me! But the car was overturned, and I was caught under it for a time. One broken leg, one damaged face, three months in hospital with the most gorgeous Roman nurses imaginable."

"Was the errand . . . like the work you do now?"

"My work has always been the same. In Sicily, in Napoli, in Roma. Here. Do you know the Sicilian dialect at all? The term *facciatu*?"

Sarah shook her head. Lydia was clutching at her breast.

"A *doer* might be the translation. A facilitator. I connect people and take a small piece of the profits they make for each other."

"And now?"

He kept the pleasant expression on his face but ran his eyes over the empty room before answering. "Now, the same, really. Though, instead of olive oil or oranges or motorcycle parts, I traffic in information."

"For which side?"

"You don't need to ask that, my dear Sarah," he said.

"But you waved to the Nazi soldiers as if you were a friend, as if you wished them well."

"Let them think I'm a friend," he said. "Nothing would be better than to have them think Silvio Merino is their friend."

Lydia kept pawing the front of Sarah's dress, more urgently now. *"Mami. Mangio!"*

"Do you think there's a room in back where I could feed her? It's just comfort she wants; she's not very hungry."

"Of course, of course!" Silvio told her, in the same cheerful tone in which he said almost everything, as if there were no boundaries in life, as if everything were possible, everything arrangeable for a *facciatu*. "I'm best of friends with the couple who owns this place. Beatrice is behind the counter there. Let me ask, but I'm sure it's possible."

Another few seconds and Silvio was back at the table again, beaming. "Come, come." He put a hand gently on Sarah's back, and she followed him past the counter, down a short hallway, to a small room with two chairs and piles of boxes. "Sit as long as you want, and when you come out, there will be a surprise."

When Silvio left them, Sarah opened the front of her dress and made herself comfortable, and while Lydia suckled happily on first one side and then the other, she closed her eyes and tried to magically sense where Luca might be. There had been times, before the war, before she'd had to hide in the mountain cabin, before she'd had to flee, when she believed she could will him to come to her, or will him to look at her if he was on the other side of a room. She knew it was only a little game she played with herself, but at times she did seem to be able to sense whether he was at his stonemason's job, at his parents' house, or out on the lake fishing with friends, and now she pressed her eyelids tight and focused her thoughts on him. Nothing came to her, no sense of him, and for a terrible few minutes she was sure he was no longer alive.

There were what sounded like two sets of footsteps on the other side of the door. She heard Silvio's happy laugh and the footsteps fading. Lydia finished eating. Sarah buttoned her dress, checked her daughter's diaper, kissed her on the forehead, and went back out and toward the front entrance.

Silvio was waiting for them on the sidewalk just outside the door, beaming his wonderful smile. The fingers of his right hand were resting on the handle of a stroller. "From my friend Beatrice!" he said. "Not new—she used it for her own children—but as you go around looking for Luca, you won't have to carry the sweet little bundle every minute. Please allow me the pleasure of placing her inside." He reached out both arms, and Lydia reached out her arms in response. Silvio lifted her with a small grunt, kissed one cheek, and set her carefully in the stroller's seat. *"Ti piace?"* he said. *Do you like it?*

"Piace," Lydia repeated, bouncing herself hard against the back of the seat and giggling.

Silvio reached into the pocket of his suit jacket and pulled out a set of keys. "I'm at 422 Via Trieste, ground floor. Number three." He handed the keys to Sarah. "It's a short walk in that direction, two blocks. The Duomo is there." He pointed in the other direction. "When you are tired of searching for the truck, you can go to the apartment and rest—422 Via Trieste. Please make yourself at home. There are three bedrooms, and some food in the kitchen. Please do not worry. I'll be looking for the truck, too, but I have to return to the apartment now, briefly I hope—I have another key—and wait for a phone call. And then, perhaps, if the call arrives, I'll have another meeting. Come and go as you please."

"Why are you so kind to me?" Sarah asked.

A shrug, the smile. "Because I have traveled in the territory close to death," Silvio said. "When I was pinned beneath my car, I ventured into that territory and heard the Lord whisper to me. 'Silvio,' he said, 'be good.' And so now I do that as part of my life's work."

"I can't pay you anything. I might never be able to pay you anything."

"One question, my lovely Sarah."

She waited, confused, hoping it was one kind of question and not another.

"Do I look like a man who has need of money?"

He put one hand on top of her shoulder and squeezed, blew a kiss to Lydia, and sauntered off like someone on his way to a splendid dinner with friends.

———

For two hours, Sarah walked the dark streets, asking directions to the Duomo first, starting there, and then moving in widening circles around it. Just as it had in Bellinzona, the gentle bouncing of the stroller on the sidewalk cobblestones soon put Lydia to sleep; the city remained eerily silent. At every corner, she paused and looked down the side streets, sometimes walking along them, peering into alleys. There were a few parked vehicles, but nothing remotely resembling the truck the strange old farmer at Orlando's bar had described to her.

Thirty-Four

Leaving the cardinal's residence, *il Duce* set a fast pace. Enzo, Grazanini, Scavolini, and Nazzacone marched slightly behind him, with Lieutenant Birzer and his men ahead and to the sides. It was only two blocks from the Duomo to the prefecture, but even at that pace, it seemed to Enzo like two kilometers. The streets were empty, poorly lit, and quiet, but rumor had it a general strike had been called—he'd heard the sirens—and he had the sense that something vital was happening just on the far side of the buildings they passed, just on the edges of the city. He listened closely, half expecting to hear the staccato reports of machine guns, or the muted *thump* of artillery. But all was quiet. They passed a place called the Café Nicolina, and Enzo couldn't help but notice a magnificent car parked out front. He glanced at it as casually as he could manage. An Alfa Romeo Bertone. The same car Silvio had told him he drove. The world was mocking him.

The guilt had its talons in him again. Marching along with the most loyal of *il Duce*'s associates, Enzo felt he belonged to a different race than these men, held a different passport, prayed to a different God. *Il Duce* had his head up, chest and chin thrust forward, an aggrieved man, a martyr for the great cause. Scavolini hurried up beside him. "They'll kill you if you go back there, *Duce*," Enzo heard him say. But the great *Duce* said nothing in return.

Once they'd entered the prefecture—one or two lights glowing faintly behind shades in the upstairs windows—Mussolini went straight to his office and slammed the door behind him. Enzo heard the loud *click* of the lock, and then he and the others were stranded in the ante-room, milling about. Scavolini was feverishly trying to argue that they must fight, but a palpable scent of uncertainty hung over the rest of them. They paced back and forth in different directions, like prisoners in a fenced yard, quiet side conversations taking place in the corners, the words sounding urgent, angry, fearful. "He has a pistol in there," Nazzacone said. "He could take his own life."

"Never!" Scavolini retorted. "The *Duce* would never do such a thing!"

After a tense quarter of an hour, the door was thrown open and Mussolini called them in. Enzo could see that his mood hadn't eased. *Il Duce* stood at the map like a teacher. "I've decided," he said, and nearly punched a hole in the map with one thick finger. "We'll go to Como. We leave in an hour." He pointed at Grazanini. "Tell Messina to guard the papers with his life." And then, to Scavolini: "I'll drive my own car this time. Ride with me."

"I can have a thousand fighters in Como by the time we arrive," Scavolini promised.

Il Duce nodded forcefully, but before they were dismissed to their duties, Enzo detected a splash of skepticism on the famous face.

Enzo slipped into his own office and closed the door. He dialed the number and let it ring three times, then set the receiver back in place very gently.

He found a mostly empty box, carried it into the hallway, and was headed for the exit when Grazanini stopped him.

"Where are you going?"

"To put this in the car, and then to the church to say a quick prayer for *il Duce*'s safety."

Grazanini sent him a mean, suspicious look, then laughed and waved a hand. "Go then, pray to your imaginary God, while an actual god sits in that room behind us. We won't wait for your return."

Enzo hurried out the door, placed the box in *il Duce*'s car, then looped around the block, not at all in the direction of the Duomo at first. He heard no one following him. He walked halfway up the next block, ducked into an alley, and waited there for another few minutes. No one. He made it to the Duomo and stepped inside. A few candles were burning in a neat row on the altar. Here and there a worshipper knelt in prayer.

By his watch, he'd used up eighteen minutes walking his circuitous route. He estimated he'd need to leave at least fifteen in order to get back to the prefecture in a direct route. But what if he didn't go back? What if he let them leave without him?

He took a seat at the far end of the last pew, in the church's darkest corner, and waited, pondering, figuring. Every half minute he checked his watch, tapping one foot, glancing around, then pretending to kneel and pray. No one. Eighteen minutes until he had to leave. Fifteen minutes. Eight. Six. At last, he gave up, made the sign of the cross for show, and was headed toward the doors when he spotted Silvio standing in the shadows beside a confessional, hands clasped in front of him. As he walked past, Enzo slowed and whispered three words, "Como, fifteen minutes." Silvio slipped him another thick fold of bills and was gone.

Enzo stepped out into the city. He paused at the edge of the piazza, squeezing the money in his pocket, considering his options one last time. The *Americani* were only hours away, bands of partisans even closer. Some Italians, at least, would recognize him as Mussolini's aide, the most loyal of Fascists, and that would be the end of him. Safer to head out of the city with the Germans. Safer for a while, at least. He'd travel with them as far as the border, at least, and then, perhaps . . .

At the prefecture, he was happy to see a commotion. No one seemed to have missed him. Scavolini must have summoned the fighters; others must have heard about the plan. Perhaps thirty men were crowded around the front step. There were military cars, *il Duce*'s Alfa Romeo. He was introduced to a new German officer, Lieutenant Fallmeyer, who appeared to be in charge of a dozen or so Luftwaffe soldiers. Enzo saw

Claretta hurrying into the building. Just inside the door, Grazanini and Scavolini were having a heated exchange. No one paid attention to his return. He'd been in the anteroom less than ten minutes when *il Duce* emerged from his office, Claretta trailing behind, her hair wild, her face a wet map of fear.

"To the Valtellina!" Mussolini shouted, and they poured out the doors like water through an opened floodgate.

Lieutenant Birzer led the procession of several armored vehicles, then Mussolini and Scavolini in the Alfa Romeo, then Enzo, Grazanini, and Nazzacone in a Fiat, then Claretta and her family in a car with Spanish diplomatic plates, then *il Duce's* son Vittorio, then Fallmeyer and another half dozen armored German vehicles with mounted guns.

It took them an hour to reach Como, and just as the entourage stopped, Enzo thought he did hear the distant *thump, thump* of artillery rounds. At the front steps of another prefecture they were greeted by the city's mayor, who practically bowed to *il Duce* and said, in an utterly unconvincing, trembling voice, "What a historical moment this is for me, for my city!"

Inside, there was no crowd of fighters waiting to go to the mountains. Scavolini threw a fit, stomping around the room and yelling, "Betrayers! Cowards!" as if to cloak his own embarrassment. *Il Duce*, Enzo noticed, was quiet on the subject. He sat on a leather sofa in the lobby of the second floor and asked the mayor to find places for his men to sleep. Alone again, he summoned Enzo with one hand, and Enzo sat in a chair opposite him.

"Where's the money and the papers?" *il Duce* asked quietly.

"With Messina, as you ordered. Two suitcases."

"I don't see Messina and his men."

"They were in Milan with us, and left just a few cars behind us. Perhaps they had to stop for a minute."

Il Duce nodded and looked out of the tops of his eyes. "We made the correct decision, not returning to the cardinal's. They would have killed me."

"I agree."

"But now?"

Enzo shrugged. "Now," he said, guardedly, "now I think we have to go up the western side of the lake—the east is too close to Allied forces—and see if we can get into Switzerland. Once there, with Hitler's help, you can form a government in exile and attract a large following. Our people will be fleeing Italy and Germany by the thousands."

Mussolini watched him through tired eyes. "Not fight, then?"

"I don't see how we can, *Duce*"—Enzo waved an arm—"with this small number of men. But I believe Fascism will grow well in another soil and then will come the hour to fight."

Il Duce had his hands resting on the tops of his thighs. He looked down at his thick fingers, pressed his lips together, nodded once. "Thank you for your loyalty, my friend," he said. He reached out and squeezed Enzo's forearm. "Thank you for never abandoning me."

"It has been an honor," Enzo replied. "I say that to you with all my soul, *Duce*. An honor."

Thirty-Five

Luca stood on the balcony of the apartment, elbows on the railing, enjoying the cigarette Anna had given him. He was staring down into the alley, and she was standing so close beside him he could smell her sweat.

"Well," she said, "I'm surprised, but not offended."

"I don't mean to offend you."

"Whatever our own personal agreements and arrangements, given all that we've been through in the past two years, I'd think we'd be allowed some moral flexibility."

"You're beautiful," he said. "I'm sorry."

"Was it what you did last night—the killing—or are you always so . . . loyal?"

Luca pulled a breath of the sweet tobacco into his mouth and slowly blew it out into the night. "At certain moments, I've kept myself sane," he said, "by thinking about the time when all this is over."

"Some people I know do exactly the opposite. They don't allow themselves to imagine their way one minute into the future."

"I think about Sarah. She was pregnant when I last saw her. I think about the child I've never seen, my child, who must be, now, walking and talking. I think about a different Italy. No *il Duce*. No Fascists. No bands of people in the hills with filthy clothes and stolen rifles. No soldiers in German uniforms on the streets. No more poverty existing next to obscene wealth."

"You sound like a communist."

"I'm not."

"A lot of the *partigiani* are communists, or think they are. That's going to be the problem after the war is over: instead of Fascism, we'll have Marxism."

"I joined for personal reasons, and to liberate my country. Afterward, I want to be left alone to live an ordinary life, that's all. Love, family, work, a free Italy, that's all I want."

"I'll be shocked if anyone leaves us alone," Anna said. "It's not human nature. Human nature requires a boss. Certain people are more than happy to fill that role, and millions of others are more than happy to follow."

"Our *Duce* was that boss for a very long time."

She nodded. "His people killed my brother. His invited guests, the Nazi soldiers, raped my best friend. I think about killing him. That's all I think about now. Later, I'll think about other things. Now I just want him to pay."

Luca grunted sympathetically, watched a skeletal gray cat make its way down the alley, creeping from one side to the other, searching for a meal. "How many people do you lead?"

"A hundred and four."

"Five times the size of my brigade."

"Every brigade matters. Masso leads yours and one other about the same size, on the east side of the lake. I pass orders on to them, and I have another larger group, too, around Lecco. I suspect the Allies will be there very soon. Today, maybe."

"And who gives you your orders?"

"I can't say."

"Even now?"

"Even now."

"What's next, then? For me, I mean?"

"I'm expecting a visitor, as I said. He's in touch with our contact who's close to Mussolini, and he's been scouting out the western side of the lake. If he brings word that Mussolini and his minders are definitely headed up that side, you'll take the truck and meet your people at the church in Dongo, and you can decide how to act depending on the circumstances. Most of us are letting the German soldiers go home. There are different views on what should happen to *il Duce*. There could be other *partigiani* there, beside your people. I can't guarantee anything."

"Then I want to go now."

"Wait until we know which route he's taking. You might end up going there for nothing."

"You have other killers, then, at the ready."

"Four of you. A woman and three men. The woman is the best shot. By the way, can you shoot a rifle, given, you know, the arm?"

Luca snorted, drew a last drag from the cigarette, and flipped it out into the air. He watched it somersault into the alley, landing a meter in front of the starving cat. The cat sniffed at it and walked away. "Remember when I asked you how you got the truck here without the keys? A stupid question, yes?"

"Yes."

"The question you just asked was even more stupid."

Anna said nothing else. She finished her cigarette and tossed the last tiny scrap of it down into the alley. They'd just stepped out of the cold when a single knock sounded at the rear door. Anna took the pistol from the counter, held it in her right hand, and opened the door with her left. Across the threshold came a strange man, someone Luca thought must have stepped out of the pages of a fashion magazine, out of the future, out of the luxurious past. He had an oddly shaped scar on the left side of his face and was wearing a cashmere topcoat and holding a felt hat in his hands. He leaned across and kissed Anna once on each cheek, frowned when he saw the pistol, and then turned his eyes to Luca. Anna said, "He's fine, no worries." And then, "Sinless, in fact."

"Good, sinless is good," the man said, smiling so that the scar was pinched up into a shiny curlicue.

Luca studied the man, trying to understand where he might have seen him. There were a couple of strands of gray in his hair—which he wore swept back from his forehead—but he seemed too young for gray hair. Something in his posture and the way he moved, something about him was vaguely familiar. "One piece of news," the visitor said, in the same lighthearted tone he seemed to say everything, "and then I shall be going. I have a woman and a little child waiting for me at home."

"I didn't know."

"Borrowed," the man joked, and then, with another look at Luca, he turned slightly more serious and said, "He's going via Como. Leaving right away." He glanced at his watch. "Probably already left, in fact. From there, I'm almost certain he'll go up along the western shore."

"You're sure about Como?"

"Unless our contact has changed sides."

"Good work. You'll stay here?"

"The aforementioned woman."

"Enjoy her."

The man set the fedora on his head, tipped it once in Luca's direction, kissed Anna again on each cheek, then turned and went quietly out the door.

"He looks familiar," Luca said. "A film star?"

Anna laughed. "He's a film star only in his own mind, but quite brave. I think you should go. If they're heading to Como, there are only two routes from there that lead north, up the east side of the lake or up the west side. He's right: the west is the more likely choice. The Allies are coming in from the east, from Brescia. And Como is closer to the west side anyway, and that route would be closer to Switzerland. Do you still have the keys to the truck?"

Luca reached into his pocket and held them up.

"Good, I won't have to start it a second time, then, or show you how. Go. Meet your people at Dongo, and if you see *il Duce*, and if you have a shot, kill the cancer inside both of us."

Luca stood up, not knowing quite how to say goodbye.

"One small kiss," Anna said, pointing to her lips. "And if things don't work out with your woman, Masso will know where I am. Come find me."

Luca touched his lips to hers for two seconds, then went through the door and trotted down the back steps. He checked first to see that the submachine gun was still where he'd hidden it, in the box beneath the truck bed. He took it out and set it on the seat beside him. Masso's truck started on the second try. Luca backed it out into the alley, headed through the center of Milan, and then took the Como road north.

Thirty-Six

As she scoured the city center, block by block, pushing the stroller in front of her, Sarah felt a heavier and heavier weight of hopelessness on her shoulders. Milan was enormous, with countless piazzas, alleys, and side streets, some of them closed off by landslides of rubble from bombed buildings. Luca could have driven the truck here to deliver weapons, then disappeared into the suburbs, the forests, the hills. She believed she'd have a better chance of finding him there, above Menaggio, than encountering him here on these city streets. But she kept on, walking in wider circles, finding routes through the rubble, searching and searching until she could feel the exhaustion taking hold of her, and Lydia losing patience.

Near a wide avenue called Via Napoli, the quiet of the dark evening was broken suddenly by the sound of tires and engines, far off at first, then moving closer. She listened for a moment and, on instinct, turned the carriage into a narrow alley between two apartment buildings. As the sounds drew closer—cars or trucks and motorcycles—she stepped farther back into the shadows, lifted Lydia from the stroller, and pressed herself against the wall. A line of German vehicles passed on the avenue; she caught only quick glimpses of them. Military vehicles with mounted guns, then several passenger cars. And then a long line of other vehicles, twenty or thirty in all, with German military lorries, an open Kübelwagen with officers inside, and three motorcycles with sidecars bringing up the rear. When they were safely past, she waited, listening to the noise fade, then stepped out of the alley and watched the red lights snaking off into the distance. A German retreat, perhaps, or a last-minute military maneuver. But why the civilian cars?

She went on, making her way slowly down an entire block that had been reduced to rubble, and then another block of storefronts, their large front windows covered haphazardly with boards. A solitary figure appeared out of the shadows ahead of her, a man of late middle age, walking with the help of a cane. She asked him where she might find Via Trieste, and he pointed. "Take this next right, and then go always straight, *sempre diritto*. Twenty minutes from here, you'll see it."

"Is there any danger?"

"Not now, I think, young woman. Not anymore. I believe the last of the Germans are gone now."

———

She found Silvio's building without trouble, an old five-story classical townhouse in a neighborhood completely untouched by the bombing. The door to his apartment led off a tile foyer. When she opened it, she stepped into a small entranceway and stood facing a grand parlor. A chandelier, two sofas, an oriental carpet, floor-to-ceiling windows covered by purple drapes. She left the carriage in the entranceway, lifted Lydia up and out, and followed her daughter as she walked the rooms, making sure she didn't track dirt onto the carpet, knock into a table holding silver candlesticks, or disturb the quilts in any of the bedrooms. The place seemed absolutely untouched by war. The kitchen faucet worked; the cabinets were full. She poured herself a glass of water and tilted it to Lydia's mouth. Other than that, she felt as though she couldn't touch anything, couldn't lie on the beds—one room was obviously Silvio's—couldn't even sit on the damask sofas for fear she might have gotten some dirt on her new dress and would stain them.

There was a sitting room lined with shelves of books, and, overcome with tiredness, she allowed herself to rest in one of the leather armchairs there, rocking Lydia against her bosom and humming a lullaby. She felt as though she were living minute to minute now, keeping her daughter alive, drawing, from some deep well, just enough energy to stay upright and remain sane. Luca could be anywhere. Probably it had been foolish to come to Milan and try to find him in such a huge city. But at least she could hope that he was still alive. She concentrated on one thing: the thought of seeing him, of showing him their child.

By the time she heard the door open, her daughter was asleep and Sarah was having a difficult time keeping her own eyes open. She shook her head, stood up, laid Lydia gently on the seat of the chair, and went to greet Silvio.

He was wearing a felt hat and carrying bags in each hand, looking like nothing so much as a prewar husband arriving home from work and errands. He set the bags on the sofa, took off his hat and coat, and said, "First of all, two new diapers are not nearly enough. I managed to find another six and some pins for them. And, secondly, one dress isn't enough." He opened the top of one of the bags and lifted out a beautiful blue-and-green dress—not formal, exactly, but like nothing Sarah had worn since she began hiding in the mountains.

"I can't" was the first thing she said. "It's beautiful, but I can't."

"Please," he said, "let us be plain with each other. You may stay here as long as you like, but we may never see each other again after tomorrow morning. I can't bear pretense with my close friends. Please just accept the dress, wear it if you like, and let me help you now. I have food." He reached into the other bag and, with a magician's flourish, brought out a bottle of wine, a loaf of bread, and what seemed to be a large piece of wrapped cheese. "Not the best cheese," he said. "Not the best bread. And not the best wine."

"It's been so long since I had Italian wine with Italian cheese."

"There are plates in the cupboard, knives on the counter. I can see that you're tired, but would you prepare something for us? I'll open the wine. Lydia's sleeping?"

Sarah nodded, and in the kitchen, slicing the bread and cheese and setting them on two plates, she had the strangest memory: a scene from a forgotten dream. In the dream, she'd been preparing food for dinner with a man, in a fine house. She shook the image away, but it persisted, a colorful butterfly floating around her on a summer day.

They sat opposite each other at the kitchen table. Silvio filled their glasses. "To the end of the war," he said, and they drank. "Tell me about your life, Sarah. I'm curious. When I saw you, you seemed, forgive me, you seemed dirty and ragged, almost a peasant woman. But I can tell now by the way you talk and the way you think that you come from a cultured family, am I correct?"

"Not really. I'm the illegitimate child of a priest. My mother was Jewish. She raised me in Menaggio, in a three-room apartment close to the water. We could hear the rats beneath our bedroom floor. She was an intelligent woman, she'd been educated, and perhaps she passed some of that on to me. I did well in school. I spent a year at university. And then the war came, and a friend—Luca's mother, actually—hid her, and Luca found a hiding place for me. Other things happened, terrible things. Luca's mother was killed, and he helped my mother and me escape to Switzerland, but he stayed . . . to fight. My mother was very weak. Another priest cared for us there, near Bellinzona, and as she was growing sicker, my mother told me about her life, her loneliness, the way she met and started taking walks with the priest. Father Claudio was his name. How his loneliness matched her own, how they gradually confided in each other, how they ended up making love—one time, she said. Almost by accident, she said. And the shame and terror she felt when she discovered she was pregnant."

"He didn't leave the Church for her? When he found out?"

"She told him not to. But he helped us for the rest of our lives, bringing food, coming by for meals. I never imagined he was anything other than a caring priest, trying to help the poorest family in his parish. No one suspected. I think my mother and Don Claudio somehow managed, after I was born, to playact for all their days, to put on a show for the townspeople. And perhaps for each other."

"A definition of hell, it seems to me. The priest should have married her instead of allowing her to carry the shame on her own."

"My mother was adamant about that. He offered, more than once, she said. She refused."

"Strange, the things people do."

"Yes. And your life?"

"Less interesting. Youngest child of a poor Sicilian farmer and his wife. They envisioned me having the life they had there, plowing the fields, living in dust, eating olives and sardines. I left as soon as I could, first to Palermo, then to Naples, and then to Rome, a city I adore. I discovered early on that I had a talent for connecting people, as I mentioned. In Naples, for instance, I'd make friends with a man who had a grove of lemons, and I'd make friends with another man, in the city center, who sold lemons from his store. Instead of the farmer having to sell his product himself, I made the connection, even delivered the lemons, at first. It wasn't always holy work; I'm not sinless—to use a word I recently heard. If there was a mafioso who had a truck of stolen goods to sell, I found a buyer, and then, if someone was bothering a fisherman friend of mine, I'd mention it to the mafioso and he'd step in. Then the fisherman owed me, the lemon farmer owed me, the mafioso trusted me. Did I ever hurt anyone, physically? No, never. Did I sleep with women promised to other men? Yes, I confess that I did, but only when the men weren't behaving well, only to make the women feel beloved."

"And you never married?"

"Not yet, no. I never felt it would suit my style of life. And then the war arrived and a hundred new opportunities came my way. Professionally, I mean."

"You worked for the Germans?"

"*Mai!* Never! Once or twice for the local Fascists, but not military information. Then, one fine day, as my reputation had grown and I was living a . . . what's the way to say it? A *conspicuous* life in the finest

Roman neighborhood with a forged certificate attesting to a nonexistent heart ailment—I didn't want to fight for the *Duce*, and I'm not as brave as your Luca—I was asked to speak, very discreetly, with a certain American. This American needed a particular favor. I didn't appreciate the German presence—among other reasons because it wasn't beneficial to my business interests—so I obliged. That favor led to another; small things at first, and then not small. That has been my contribution. I took certain risks, but I've always been blessed by the saints, and nothing ever happened to me . . . until the bombing I told you about. And even that was a blessing. The months in the hospital were difficult—"

"But the nurses!"

"That's the first time I've seen any humor from you! Yes, the nurses, but something else as well. An epiphany. Since then, I've used precisely the same talents I've always used, an understanding of people and their needs, but I've used them exclusively in the service of the liberation of my country."

"And you've been paid for that?"

"No. I'm not paid for that. All this, the car and so on, is the result of earlier, what's the word, *investments*."

"And after the war, what will you do? More of the same?"

Silvio shrugged and smiled in a humble way, a way Sarah liked. "I don't know any other work. I have no trade. Except . . ." He paused there, and for the first time she thought he seemed uncomfortable.

"Speak," she said. "Be plain, as you asked me to be."

The bright smile, an adjustment of his pant legs, a sip of wine. "You've done me a great favor," he said. "You'll never know what a great favor you've done me, Sarah. You've given me the smallest taste of the domestic life. Buying diapers! Being around a little child! These are things I have not only never done, I've never imagined doing! And the favor you've done me is to make me understand that I'm capable of doing them, even of enjoying them. I feel, in fact—and this may sound odd—I feel that my life to this point, with all its risks and lack of commitment to anyone but myself, has been preparing me to marry and perhaps have children of my own."

At that moment, almost as if she'd been awakened by the word *children*, Lydia cried and called out in the other room. Sarah changed and fed her, then realized how tired she was.

"That middle bedroom is for you," Silvio called. "You have your own bath. If you feel hungry, even in the middle of the night, please come and eat. Nothing awakens me. In the morning, what will you do?"

"Keep looking for Luca, for the truck."

"I'll help you. We'll scour the city."

"Didn't you say tomorrow is your birthday?"

"It is, it is. We'll find a way to celebrate."

Sarah heard a noise in the street outside the windows. Screaming, it sounded like at first. She wondered if the lame man she'd seen on the street had been wrong, and the Germans hadn't yet abandoned the city. But Silvio cocked his head, listened for a moment, then stretched his lips into a wide smile. "Ah," he said, "perhaps the celebration will be tonight *and* tomorrow! Tired as you are, I want you to come outside with me for a moment. Bring Lydia. History is being made. She'll perhaps remember what she sees."

They stood outside on the stoop and heard a cacophony of singing and shouting. What appeared to be a wild parade came pouring down the street, with all kinds of people, some in uniform, some not, many of them carrying weapons. An elderly woman had stepped out of the house next door. "The *partigiani*," she called over to them. "The partigiani have taken Milano. The war for us is over!"

"Bravo! *Bravissimo!*" Silvio yelled to the throng. He made his hands into fists and raised them above his head in triumph.

Sarah only watched, feeling the great thrill envelop her, but at the same time searching the crowd for a man with a weak left arm and beautiful shoulders, looking and looking, and not seeing him. She held her daughter up in front of her. "A parade," she said. "A happy parade, Lydia!" But there was something besides happiness in her voice.

Thirty-Seven

From the moment he and *il Duce* finished their conversation at the prefecture in Como, Enzo noticed that everything started happening at a tremendous speed. It was as if all of them—*il Duce*, his ministers, the Blackshirts, the German chaperones—were glued together in an enormous ball, and that ball had rolled north from Milan to Como on more or less flat territory, then gone over the edge of a hill and was now hurtling down a ski slope. People rushed into and out of the building, and with every new arrival, another piece of news or another rumor filled the air. *A secret weapon has been deployed!* someone shouted. *The Allies are three kilometers away*, said someone else. *Hitler is dead! Milan has been retaken!*

Il Duce seemed deaf to all of it, almost as if he no longer cared.

They waited and waited for Scavolini's reinforcements, but the men failed to appear. The prefect's wife cooked them a late supper. *Il Duce* couldn't eat. "Where is the car with the papers?" he asked Enzo at least four times. "Where is Messina with the papers?"

As Enzo well knew, the car didn't contain merely papers, important as they may have been to Mussolini, but gold bars, American dollars, and millions of French and Swiss francs. Enzo made a show of asking everyone in and around the house, but no one seemed to know until Gatti and Casalinuovo, who'd been sent back to find it, reported that the car had been stopped by partisans and was lost to them now.

When he heard that piece of news, Mussolini turned away. Enzo watched him stride to the nearest window, neck muscles trembling. No cache of funds. No papers that might earn him some mercy in a postwar trial. Everything was falling apart.

Over the next few hours, *il Duce* tried three times to call Rachele, who, instead of flying from Monza—the airport was deemed unsafe—had been driven to a villa in Cernobbio with the couple's youngest children, but he hadn't been able to get through. Late at night the phone rang; Enzo answered, heard Rachele's voice, and immediately handed the receiver to *il Duce*. Enzo could hear him advising her to flee without him. He went silent, listening, phone pressed to his ear, his face pinched tight. And then: "No, Rachele. No, not now. It's too late for me now. No, don't come here. It's dangerous here. Save yourself. Save our children. Nothing matters now except that."

When *il Duce* hung up, he went and sat in an armchair in the building's spacious second-floor lobby again, eyes open but head down, hands working in his lap as if he were knitting something in a dream. A new life, he was knitting, Enzo thought. A different future to place on top of the same turbulent past.

Enzo lay on a leather sofa nearby and drifted into and out of sleep, glancing over at Mussolini whenever he awoke. *Il Duce* hadn't moved. Before dawn Enzo was awakened by Nazzacone. The armchair was empty. They were leaving.

Up the west side of the lake they went in a convoy of some thirty vehicles, Mussolini driving his Alfa Romeo, Enzo just behind in the Fiat, Claretta and her family in another car, farther behind, Vittorio, the ministers, the loyal volunteers, the Nazi soldiers, Lieutenant Birzer and the other German officer, Fallmeyer, bracketing them back and front. From what Enzo had heard in the daily reports delivered to *il Duce* by his military people, countless German patrols had been ambushed in those hills, hundreds of soldiers lost. Gestapo commanders had killed ten Italians for each one of those soldiers, often lining up men, women, and children in the lakeside towns, tormenting them for an hour, and then ordering them to be machine-gunned in retribution. The tactic hadn't worked. Instead of intimidating the locals, the massacres had only embittered them: all over the north, people had given shelter and food to the roving bands of partisans.

The convoy stopped near the town of Menaggio, where a side road curled west from the lake, toward the Swiss border. Enzo could see animated conversations going on around the car in front of him. Nazzacone walked back and said, "The hills here are crawling with partisans. *Il Duce* told me to send some of the vehicles onto the side road, or back to Como, so we don't attract too much attention."

And what about the last stand? Enzo almost said, but overnight the few remaining wispy clouds of uncertainty had blown away: there would be no last stand. Mussolini was fleeing for his life. "That seems crazy," he said. "The Germans are our protection."

Nazzacone shrugged, started to argue, then stopped himself. "*Some* of them are to go onto the other road, not *all* of them. That's what he wants, so that's what we'll do," he said, and he marched off to tell Birzer.

That's what he wants, so that's what we'll do, Enzo thought. It had always been that way, but now, it seemed, what *il Duce* wanted was looking more and more like self-immolation. Going to Milan instead of fleeing straight north. Staying in that city for five days instead of leaving sooner. Sending half the armed escort away *so as not to attract attention!*

Still, when their now-smaller convoy started forward again, he followed dutifully, foolishly, blindly, lost in an old dream. They turned away from the lake and climbed the winding mountain road toward the border. After only another kilometer, the cars in front of him stopped again, and Enzo could see another animated conversation going on beside *il Duce*'s Alfa. Raised voices. Waving arms.

He felt now that he was on a kind of crazed carnival ride, the convoy being turned this way and that, stopping, going forward, stopping again. Here came Nazzacone with another message. "The border's closed ahead. We'll spend the night at a hotel." He gestured up the hill.

"Miravalle, it's called. Another few minutes and you'll see the turn, and then we'll try going north tomorrow."

"Every hour we wait makes it more dangerous, Pippi—doesn't he realize that?"

Nazzacone looked down at him from his place beside the car. *Don't you understand yet?* the look seemed to say. *There's no logic anymore. It's all show, pomp, the final act of a great opera.* "It's Fallmeyer," Nazzacone said. "I don't trust the traitor. He's overruling Birzer and Mussolini both. He says his men are exhausted. If we're going to fight the partisans up ahead, he says he wants his soldiers to be rested."

"That's *pazzo!* Crazy! Rested for what? The partisans will probably let the Germans go through. It's *us* they want. It's *il Duce.*"

"You go talk to him, then," Nazzacone said.

"He's got a death wish."

"Then it's our death wish, also, Enzo. We supported him all this time—are we going to abandon him now?"

Yes! Enzo almost shouted, but the eternally loyal Nazzacone glared at him for another few seconds, then turned and walked away.

At the Miravalle Hotel there was another obsequious host, honored, he said, to have the *Duce* in his establishment. No doubt, Enzo thought, honored to have his hotel assaulted by partisans or demolished by Allied bombers if they found out who was staying there. There was more bad news, more confusion. Word reached them that the people of the north were rising up en masse. No city was safe for the regular Italian Army now; the partisans were everywhere, the Allies closing in on Milan, perhaps in the southern suburbs already. Rachele had tried to cross into Switzerland at Chiasso and been refused. *Il Duce* knew that much, but had otherwise lost touch with her. Claretta could be heard weeping loudly in one of the parlors. *Il Duce* paced the lobby—it had started to rain, a pouring, cold rain—with a dozen panicked advisers all suggesting the same things they'd been suggesting for days: flee to Switzerland; shoot their way through the roadblocks ahead; wait for Scavolini, who was back in Como, gathering, someone said, three thousand Blackshirts. Enzo felt as though a giant hand were tightening around all of them, thick iron fingers squeezing them together like a bunch of grapes. Except it would be blood that flowed, not juice.

At one point, Mussolini called Lieutenant Fallmeyer to his suite and started shouting at him, saying it was foolish to wait. They were going to fight their way through whatever they'd find on the lake road heading north.

"My men are exhausted, *Duce*," Fallmeyer told him. "You're asking them to engage in a battle on next to no sleep. I must refuse."

They argued, Enzo watched. Fallmeyer was standing stiffly at attention and kept repeating one phrase: "I have to think of my men!"

"And *my* men!" *il Duce* thundered. "You have 11-millimeter machine guns mounted on your lorries. We have rifles!"

"My men and I will leave at first light, *Duce*," Fallmeyer said, and Enzo wondered if the German was, in fact, a traitor, if he'd made some kind of a deal, another betrayal. He'd delay Mussolini's trip north, which would give the partisans time to gather more men and arrange for a blockade. The Germans would be allowed to pass through; the Italians would be slaughtered.

"*Il Duce*," Enzo said when Fallmeyer strode out of the room. His conscience was whipsawing him this way and that. "Larracú and Zarraona have left us."

"They didn't inform me."

"They're trying for the border on their own. If you wait here another night, there will be no one left except me and a few others . . . unless Scavolini brings his men from Como."

"He'll bring them, he'll bring them," *il Duce* told him, but Enzo was sure even Mussolini himself didn't believe what he was saying.

Enzo returned to his room but lay on the bed without even taking off his boots. It was the worst night of his life. Every half hour he got up and looked out the window, but all he saw was the dark, slanting rain and the parked vehicles. His mind whirled and skittered, jumping from thought to thought. *Leave, leave now! Run!* a voice seemed to be shouting in the midst of those thoughts. But something, some iron chain of guilt or frayed harness of loyalty, kept him from leaving. East and below them was the lake, west and above them the closed border, south the advancing Allies and rampaging partisans, and north . . . ambushes from the hills, blockades, betrayal, treachery. *I couldn't live outside Italy,* he'd told Angelina, and maybe that was the root cause of his confusion. Even if everything worked and they survived, he'd follow the rest of them to Germany, and then . . . ?

Late that night, Scavolini did, in fact, appear, in an armored car that had traveled in the rain from Como. He knocked timidly on the door of Enzo's room and delivered the final blow. "We had three thousand Blackshirts in Como," he said, practically in tears. "They have surrendered to the partisans." Scavolini looked as if he were about to collapse. "I couldn't stop them, Enzo. I was fortunate to escape, and able to bring only the bravest ones with me."

"How many?" Enzo asked.

Scavolini looked away, pretending not to hear. Enzo thought his face was empty of blood. His hands hung at his side, and a vein in his neck bulged and shrank in a fast rhythm.

"How many, Ottavio?"

Scavolini met his eyes and said one word: "Twelve."

Thirty-Eight

Luca went as fast as the old truck would carry him out of Milan, through the suburbs, and onto the Como road. It had started to rain. In an hour, he'd passed that city and reached Cernobbio, near the bottom of the lake's western leg. He turned onto the *statale* there, and, leaving the window slightly open so the cold spray would keep him awake, he shot up past Argegno and Lecco and then slowed slightly where the road curved through Menaggio. He noticed only one small group of German vehicles, pulled over to the side in the deluge. He passed them carefully, anxious not to be stopped, checking to see if they appeared to be accompanying an important passenger. They did not. From what he could tell, the soldiers were sleeping on the seats, sitting upright. The one officer still awake turned his face as the truck was passing but made no move to stop it: just another Italian farmer on the way to a market in Gravedona; what difference did that make now to men intent on getting home alive?

Anna had told him that his brigade was concentrated near the church at Dongo and might be joined by another. Luca knew the place well: a small stone building with a modest bell tower, perched on a narrow piece of land between the road and the lake. By the time he reached it, the rain had stopped and the rising sun was visible through gray clouds over the mountains on the eastern shore. His body was practically vibrating with exhaustion.

Just before he reached the church, he passed through one of the many tunnels on that side of the lake, a two-hundred-meter stretch of pure darkness, broken only by the truck's feeble, half-lidded headlights. When he emerged from the tunnel—perfect place for a roadblock—the church was there on his right. No *partigiani* to be seen. No vehicles. No activity of any kind.

Thirty-Nine

Sarah lay down in the guest room of Silvio's apartment and let Lydia, wearing one of her new diapers, sleep close beside her. She could feel her daughter's quiet breathing against her own body—a gentle rise and fall—but couldn't turn the corner into sleep. From time to time she'd hear a shout from the street, and she understood exactly what emotion it expressed: a relief so profound that every cell in her body seemed to be celebrating. Perhaps the war wasn't truly over yet in every corner of Europe, but it appeared to be over for her, and she hoped, wherever he was, that it was over for Luca, too. She worried he'd been killed, or grievously wounded, or that he'd found a woman he loved more than he loved her.

But in the past few hours a new worry had crept into her interior landscape, another wolf slipping into the barnyard in the dark: no doubt Luca had killed people, and seen his closest friends killed or wounded. How could someone so sensitive experience such things, witness such things, and remain the tender soul he'd always been? That quality was the one for which she loved him most of all. What if he emerged from the war whole in body but horribly changed in soul? She'd try to heal him, of course she would, and love could heal many things. But what if he couldn't be healed? What if she and Lydia were condemned to live with someone so scarred by his battles that he couldn't be the kind of father or husband they needed?

She rolled onto her side, cradling against her belly the warm, sleeping bundle that was her precious child. She wondered if she'd ever have other children, and wondered, too, if her mother had wanted more. Late in her life, when she was already confined to the sofa, her mother had opened up to her in new ways, including one conversation in which she'd used the term *sexual loneliness*. Sex was a subject her mother had never broached with her, but in a conversation about Sarah's father, Don Claudio, she said, "I think it was sexual loneliness that brought us together, Sarah. The thought of living for years, of possibly living the rest of our lives without the feeling of another body against our own, the pure joy and intimacy of that. All my friends were married. I imagined them at night, sleeping beside their husbands, kissing, making love. I saw them in the day, walking hand in hand. Don Claudio must have felt that, too, looking at all the married couples in Sant'Abbondio."

Sarah felt it now. It had been more than twenty months since she'd last made love—in Switzerland there had been no chance for that and, on her part, no interest. It was as if the war had to be gotten out of the way in order for her to think about lovemaking again. Through the curtained windows she could still hear cheering and singing in the street, someone playing a trumpet, a *bang-ba-bang bang* that sounded like fireworks. She couldn't keep herself from thinking of Silvio in bed in the other room, and though, obviously, of course, it went without saying, she wouldn't make love with him even if he appeared at her door right now or called her into his room, still, she admitted to herself that she was lonely in the way her mother had been. Tomorrow, she'd redouble her efforts to find Luca. She'd search again the streets she'd searched. The old man in Orlando's bar had said Luca was in Milan, that he'd been sent here on a job. Why would he leave? Now, of all times, when he could be celebrating with his fellow resistance fighters, why would he leave the city?

In the morning, after a breakfast of bread, cheese, and coffee, she and Silvio set out—with Lydia in the stroller she already loved—on another search. The streets were alive. There were people everywhere, the cafés were full, a few cars passed along the main avenues around the Duomo, burning gasoline, as if the drivers had no particular destination but were simply trying to remember what it felt like to be behind the wheel. Before dawn, the American army had marched into the city. They'd found it already liberated, and Sarah could read on their faces the deep sense of relief. No one wanted to fight any longer. Women young and old were approaching the military vehicles and hugging and kissing the soldiers, bringing them flowers, thanking them. After a heavy rain, the sun appeared behind the last of the clouds. The blue sky felt to her almost like a song; the joy of the streets infected her, lifted her. Walking across the Duomo square, she let go of the stroller for a moment and twirled in a long-forgotten dance move, feeling the hem of the new dress spread out from her legs, her clean hair swinging free.

Everyone else seemed to be moving as well, walking, talking, singing, the children leaping and running in circles. *Normal life again,* she thought. And then, a few steps in front and to the right of the Duomo's main entrance, she saw a portly, late-middle-aged man dressed all in black. His face was turned to one side. She kept looking at that profile, studying it. The man turned and met Sarah's eyes, and she let out a tiny sound and stopped and stood perfectly still. Silvio had taken two steps beyond her. He turned and looked back. "What is it?"

"My father," she said, the words sounding absolutely alien in her ears. She let Silvio take the carriage and she hurried toward the man in black, who was still staring at her. "Father?" she said, realizing immediately that the word had a double meaning.

"Sarah? My beautiful Sarah, could it be?"

She wrapped him in a strong embrace, and felt him embracing her in return, swinging her left and right, almost lifting her off the ground.

"Your mother?" he said, when they'd separated, and Sarah told him that her mother was gone, and watched the grief and regret cross his face like the shadow of a windblown cloud.

"In heaven at last," he said.

Silvio pushed the stroller up to them.

"This is my daughter, Lydia, Father. Luca's child. And this is my friend Silvio, who's been so kind to us."

The men shook hands. The priest leaned down and tickled Lydia's chin with one finger. The girl made a face and started crying. For a moment, Sarah wasn't sure, and then she recalled what Silvio had said about plainness with his friends, and so she said, "Your grandchild."

The priest turned his face to her, and she could see the loose cheeks trembling. "I—" he said, and then he struggled and struggled but couldn't manage another word.

Sarah put a hand on his arm. "They told me in Menaggio that you'd been captured."

Don Claudio swallowed, took a breath, glanced at Lydia, then back into Sarah's eyes. It was another moment before he could speak. "I was. I was being taken to the train station in a German truck, on my way to the camps. The partisans ambushed the truck in Cadenabbia and shot them all and helped me get away. I hid for several months, and then the good cardinal here took me in. I stayed here, sleeping and eating in a back room of this beautiful church. This is the first day in all those months that I've stood outside in the sun. And who do I see on one of the very best days of my life? A person I've loved for as long as I can remember. And her glorious child!" His eyes shifted to Silvio and back again, clearly wondering. "Is your Luca alive, can I ask?"

"We're searching for him. He's supposed to be in Milan. I haven't seen him in so long, my soul aches for him."

"Ah, yes," the priest said. "It's safe now, for me, for us. If you don't mind, I'll help you search as well."

Forty

At first light, Enzo awoke from his restless sleep, thinking: *This is craziness! We should have left in darkness!* The rain had stopped. He dressed quickly and searched the hotel lobby and wet grounds, looking for Lieutenant Birzer. The man had disappeared. That seemed exceedingly strange and worrisome: for over a year, Birzer had been charged—by Hitler himself, apparently—with keeping *il Duce* safe. Now he, and the well-armed contingent of SS men he supervised, were gone. *Saving themselves,* Enzo thought. *Everyone's saving themselves now.*

The stubborn Lieutenant Fallmeyer, who seemed perpetually at attention, was still with them, speaking to *il Duce* near the entrance. Nazzacone paced back and forth there with Scavolini, their heads bent close, words inaudible. Claretta Petacci was sitting in a chair just inside the door, sliding both hands up and down the tops of her thighs. The Luftwaffe men and Scavolini's twelve *fascisti* were climbing into vehicles. *Il Duce* waved him over.

"We're leaving finally, Enzo. Has the news about Messina changed? Has he been located?"

Enzo shook his head.

"The documents are lost, then. There's no hope, is there?"

Enzo shook his head a second time.

"I heard from Rachele," Mussolini went on. "The border guards won't let her into Switzerland. They won't let any of us in. We're going to have to fight our way through and somehow get to Austria. You drive me in the Alfa with Grazanini and Nazzacone. Claretta and her brother have Spanish diplomatic plates. They'll ride at the tail end, for safety."

———

They drove away from the hotel and descended the snaking dirt road to the lakeside, turned left onto pavement, and started north. The convoy stretched for only two hundred meters now but moved slowly. Just north of Menaggio, it stopped, and Lieutenant Fallmeyer walked back, came up to the passenger side, saluted stiffly, and said, "Come into the lorry with my men, *Duce*. You're in the open here, exposed. You'll be safer with us."

Il Duce resisted at first, then agreed with a show of reluctance and stepped out of the car without a word of farewell or encouragement. Enzo watched him walk over to one of the armored cars and reach out for the helping hands of German soldiers. *Il Duce* climbed inside without a backward glance. Despite all the brave talk about making a last stand in the Valtellina and dying for the Fascist cause, when the opportunity arose, *il Duce* had allowed himself to be moved to the safer vehicle, leaving his loyal followers—along with his young mistress— exposed to the possibility of partisan fire. *Save yourself,* Enzo thought bitterly. *Save your glorious self and let the rest of us perish.* The convoy started forward again, but now Enzo followed grudgingly, searching the road to either side, crouching a bit lower in the seat as they drove through the tunnels and in the open air.

What made him particularly uncomfortable was the topography. The *statale* ran within a hundred meters of the shoreline to the right, even closer in places. Stone and concrete houses lined the road there, along with the occasional bakery or bar or store selling household goods. To their left, hillsides angled up steeply toward the Swiss border. There were clusters of houses in the small towns, but more often that side of the road consisted only of dense Alpine woodland. Perfect cover for bands of *partigiani*.

Chances were excellent that some of those partisans were lurking in the trees, observing the orderly German retreat, the columns of vehicles rolling north, the soldiers exhausted, finished with war, thinking only of getting home.

Easy targets.

To complicate matters, there was a series of tunnels along this stretch of road, places where the hills sloped down close to the water. These tunnels ranged in length from a hundred meters to several kilometers, and except near either end, at this time of morning they were still completely dark.

Riding slowly along in stop-and-go fashion, looking anxiously to his left at every opportunity, it occurred to Enzo that, in giving the information to Silvio, he'd put not only *il Duce*'s life in danger, but his own. That was so obvious now. Earlier he'd somehow imagined the information would be used only to capture *il Duce* before he could slip away to exile, not kill him. Now, that kind of thinking seemed incredibly foolish. After all, Mussolini had been arrested before, by the king, and sent to Campo Imperatore in the highest part of the Apennines, the last place in Italy he could expect to be rescued. But he *had* been rescued, and flown to Germany. So why would the partisans want simply to arrest him again? Hand him over to the Allies and eventually try him in court? What kind of revenge was that for the massacre of the partisans' relatives and the torture and killing of their comrades? And even if they did kill Mussolini, who was to say they'd kill him with an assassin's bullet? More likely they'd blow up one of these many tunnels, and Mussolini, his cabinet members, his loyal Blackshirts, his son, and his mistress would be crushed to death beneath a million kilos of soil and concrete.

In the cool morning, Enzo could feel his hands sweating on the wheel. Beneath his army coat, he was wearing the uniform of the Fascist militia. All of them were. If they were stopped, what were the chances the partisans might mistake him for a German soldier and let him head for home? Zero.

But the convoy trundled along, and, held in the grip of the same strange inertia, Enzo trundled along with it. Except for the drone of tires on damp pavement, there was only silence inside the Alfa. Grazanini and Nazzacone sat stoically, one in front, the other in back, both of them gripped by the same inertia. *As if being chauffeured to their deaths,* Enzo thought. Because the road twisted back and forth, he couldn't always see the front of the line, so every time they stopped—for a slow-moving bus, a parked delivery truck, a fallen tree branch—he wondered if the convoy had encountered a roadblock or an ambush.

Finally, after the long tunnel at Zennala, Grazanini spoke up. "He's not going to fight. He's going to save himself. He's going to hope the Swiss will let him cross the border at some point north of here, and he doesn't particularly care if we're allowed to cross with him."

To Enzo's surprise, the always-loyal Nazzacone grunted his agreement.

"What are we doing, then?" Enzo asked after a moment, but there was no response. What they were doing was clinging to a thin, frayed rope dangling over a great abyss, believing against all reason and logic that they might somehow be rewarded for their loyalty. At the bottom of the abyss, hundreds of thousands of partisans and ordinary Italians waited, clubs and knives in hand, for the rope to finally break and Mussolini and his men to fall into their arms. He thought of Angelina's offer to get them to Argentina and wished now, too late, that he'd tried to convince her to escape somewhere in Italy. Down south, perhaps, where the fighting had long ago ended. He hoped she was safe. Maybe *il Duce* had made arrangements for Claretta's staff, but Enzo didn't think so. The Mussolinis were going to take care of themselves. No wonder the three thousand Blackshirts assembled in Como had surrendered rather than follow *il Duce* to their deaths. No wonder.

The convoy entered another tunnel and stopped just after Enzo had pulled the Alfa inside its shadowy mouth. After two full terrible minutes, he heard a single rifle shot up ahead. He listened for more, but there was only silence, a bird chirping in the trees, its lonely voice echoing in the tunnel.

"This is madness," Grazanini said, in a panicked voice, and then, as if those were the words that broke their hypnosis, all three of them opened their doors and jumped out. Enzo didn't care, at that point, who was watching from the vehicles behind—German soldiers wouldn't stop him—or what was happening to *il Duce* in one of the lorries ahead. He was running behind Grazanini and Nazzacone, propelled by one force: the overwhelming urge to stay alive. In twenty steps they were out of the tunnel. The two others turned toward the water, but Enzo went in the opposite direction. He heard a shout behind him, in Italian. Scavolini's voice, perhaps. He no longer cared. If the Germans were going to betray their allies by signing a treaty without notifying Mussolini, if Mussolini was going to betray his followers by sitting in an armored vehicle with the Germans while his men sat in unarmored automobiles, if *il Duce* was going to beg his way into Switzerland and leave the rest of them to fend for themselves, then the entire structure of loyalty was collapsing like a poorly constructed ten-story apartment building in an earthquake. Only a fool would remain inside it. He was a betrayer, yes, but surrounded by betrayers now, all of them with the fire of loyalty overtaken by a larger blaze: they were out to save themselves.

Heaving for breath, expecting a bullet in the back at any second, wishing for a weapon, Enzo climbed into the forest, the trees still bare but the leaves in the lower bushes damp from the previous night's rain. Once he'd gone deep enough into the forest, he stopped and listened. No one was following.

He climbed a little farther, then began to move southward, parallel to the road, which was hidden from his gaze by thick growth. He stopped again, listening, catching his breath, his lower body soaked, heart slamming in its cage. He had the acute sense then of a kind of loneliness he'd never experienced, as if he were the sole inhabitant of a land that issued no passports, a dark, damp world drenched in the blood of war but silent and empty. No comrades, no loyalties, no leader. It was a nation bordered by the Fascists on one side, partisans on another. And he was its only citizen.

Forty-One

Just as the first bands of gray light were appearing over the mountains on the eastern side of the lake, Luca pulled Masso's truck around to the rear of the Dongo church, grabbed his submachine gun, and climbed out. In the muddy soil near the stone back step, he could see a crowd of boot prints. So much for stealth, he thought, though stealth no longer really mattered. It no longer mattered that he and the other partisans didn't introduce each other by their real names, that they didn't discuss their families, that each band of fighters was linked to another band by only a single leader, and sometimes not linked at all. Victory, paid for in blood, was assured now. One task remained.

He tapped twice on the green-painted wooden door and waited. No answer. He tapped twice again and it was opened by Giovanni, his friend and first assistant. Instead of inviting him in, Giovanni moved out onto the wide step. "Most of the men are sleeping," he said. "My radio's dead."

"Wake them. *Il Duce* is being escorted up this road, unless he's already passed."

"He hasn't. There was one German convoy, late last night. We searched it and let them pass. I've stayed awake since then with Solana and a few others."

"The convoy stopped for you?"

"They did. We had men on both sides of the road, and if it had come to a battle, we would have been slaughtered. But they didn't know that. And, in any case, they no longer want to fight, Luca. They're going home."

"And taking Mussolini with them. Wake them all up. We need to block the road near the end of the tunnel."

In ten minutes Luca's fighters were outside. He ordered them to push as many large stones into the road as they could, and when that didn't seem enough, ordered them to fell a tree across it. One of the women went to a nearby house and returned with a long saw. Giovanni and one of the others went to work on a tree twenty meters from the opening of the tunnel. Ten minutes passed, the saw blade gnawing through the wood, before Giovanni shouted for them to clear the way. The tree leaned and then toppled with a tremendous crash, splinters of wood flying everywhere and small branches skidding across the pavement. It had fallen at an angle, however. They pushed until it was perpendicular to the road, then arranged stones and smaller branches around the sides so no vehicle, not even a motorcycle, could slip past.

Two elderly women appeared from a nearby house carrying baskets of bread, apples, and canning jars filled with water. Luca and his fighters ate and drank, and then he arranged them in positions on either side of the tunnel entrance, some hiding above on the slope, two at the corner of the church. Thanks to their American contacts and pilfered weapons, they were well armed. Two machine guns, rifles, pistols, and ammunition, not enough perhaps to do battle with the Germans, but enough to force the officers to consider whether or not they wanted to bring all their men home alive.

Suddenly wide awake, Luca checked every detail—the blockade, the fighters in different locations. Then he stood with Giovanni, half-hidden behind a tree, and waited, waving back the two vehicles that were heading south. The drivers didn't ask questions, but turned around and disappeared back toward Gravedona.

Less than half an hour passed before they heard the first vehicles entering the far end of the tunnel. Soon a Nazi Kübelwagen appeared, followed by a line of armored lorries. They came to a halt in a fusillade of German curses, but no bullets. Luca stepped in front of the lead vehicle and asked the driver to summon his commanding officer.

The commanding officer, only a lieutenant, came up and saluted.

"I'm not used to being saluted," Luca told him, finger on the trigger of his weapon.

In passable Italian, the officer said, "The war is finished. I ask you to let my men pass."

"Germans, we'll let pass," Luca said. "Italians, no."

"There are no Italians with us. I give you my word as an officer. We're heading home."

"You killed my mother," Luca said. "You ruined my country. Your word as an officer means shit to me. We'll search the vehicles, and if what you say is true, we'll let you pass."

"You must take my word for it," the lieutenant said.

"Or what?"

"How many men do you have here?" The lieutenant waved an arm in a wide circle, dismissively. "We have trained soldiers."

"Yes, the finest soldiers in the world," Luca said. "I know about that. Which must be the reason the war has turned out so well for you." He lifted the automatic weapon until its tip was a hand's length in front of the lieutenant's throat. "How many of your glorious soldiers do you want to lose in the last days of the war in order to save the life of *il Duce* and please your Führer? If there are no Fascists in the convoy, we'll let you pass."

"There are none."

"We'll see." Luca waved a hand, and his fighters started to go down the line of vehicles, searching them one by one. They'd gone through only the first few lorries when a man in a Fascist militia uniform came running up to him and said, "He's here, in the back. Mussolini!" He pointed. "Will you let me go?"

Before Luca could stop her, he saw Solana step around from behind him, raise her pistol, and shoot the Italian in the heart. The man toppled over backward, his body making a hard *slap* on the damp pavement and then, two seconds later, blood leaking out from beneath him, spilling toward the lieutenant's boots. "You're still sure he's not there?" Luca asked the German officer.

The lieutenant stood rigidly at attention, shaking now, not meeting Luca's eyes. The search went on. A few minutes later, three of Luca's men came walking out of the tunnel with grim smiles on their faces, one in front with two rifles in his hands; the others, a pace behind, each holding one arm of their prisoner. The prisoner was Benito Mussolini.

Luca kept his weapon against the lieutenant's neck. "On your honor as a soldier," Luca said bitterly, and he spat on the bloody street. "I should kill you. But I've killed enough of you. And it seems you've delivered us our prize."

Il Duce was dressed in a green militia uniform, but he was wearing a German greatcoat and helmet. He seemed much smaller than Luca had imagined—not old, but feeble, eyes cast down, back slightly bent in a posture of defeat. "Kill him now," Solana said behind him, but Luca didn't want that. Not yet. The great *Duce*, founder of the Fascist state, was standing two meters in front of him, exhaustion on his face, but no fear there, no apology. Two of the women in Luca's brigade appeared at the tunnel's mouth. They were leading Claretta Petacci. She was weeping, reaching out for *il Duce* the way a small child reaches for her father. Mussolini stood calmly and quietly, not looking at his lover. "I will meet my fate," he said, as if giving an order to the forest.

"Yes," Luca told him. "Yes, you will." He turned to Giovanni. "Take them both into the church. Arrest the other Italians, if there are any."

"There are."

"Don't shoot them. Hold them in the church, bury this man, and let the honorable officer and his magnificent soldiers go on their way."

"Thank you, sir," the lieutenant said, but Luca had already turned away.

Mussolini and Petacci and seventeen other Italians were brought into the church under guard. The road was cleared and the convoy allowed to move on. Anna had told Luca he was the appointed killer, handpicked, but though a deep hatred seethed and roiled in him now, Luca didn't want Mussolini to have the exact fate of the Italian that Solana had killed. Though he'd imagined it many times, even put himself to sleep imagining it, a summary execution seemed somehow wrong. Not too cruel, just not monumental enough, not a suitable punishment for Mussolini's years of terror.

Once the convoy moved on, his fighters cleared the roadway. A few cars passed, heading south, and Luca suspected none of the drivers or passengers had any idea who was being held in the church. He wondered what would happen if he simply did what Solana had done—walked inside, took the pistol from his belt, and shot Mussolini in the heart. What could anyone do to him then? What could Masso or Anna do? It would be over.

But something, some whispering internal voice, held him back. He walked up to the nearest house, knocked, and asked the woman who answered if she had a telephone that worked. "It works some of the time," she said. "You're welcome to use it. But tell me, who do you have there in the church?"

"We have the man who ruined Italy."

"Then kill him," the old woman said. "Don't wait. Kill him."

Luca dialed Masso's number, hoping the farmer would answer before Luca's people in the church decided on their own to do what the woman wanted them to do, what at least half of them were more than eager to do.

On the fifth ring, Masso answered. "It's Luca. The radio's down. We're at the church in Dongo and we have a certain prisoner."

Masso answered with one word: "Wait."

And Luca promised that he would.

Forty-Two

The next day, in the midst of a citywide celebration and rumors that the war in Europe was over, Sarah searched and searched. Silvio was always with her. Sometimes Don Claudio joined them, and other times he wandered off on his own, looking in various places, working his beads. Milan was filled with partisans. They waved their rifles and embraced each other; they were treated as heroes, all of them. People bought them meals or gave them flowers, women kissed the men and men embraced the women. The morning before, the Americans had arrived, sitting atop their tanks and in their jeeps and armored vehicles. To Sarah, they looked dirty and exhausted, but some of them celebrated, too. A few of them even spoke Italian.

She wanted to go up to every partisan she saw and ask if they knew Luca Benedetto, but after she'd spoken with several of them, she remembered Luca telling her that the various bands of fighters operated separately from each other, and names—last names especially—were not often shared. So she gave up and walked and rested, tended to Lydia, scoured every face, watched the way every man walked, and listened for a familiar voice. Nothing.

After lunch, she took Lydia back to Silvio's apartment for a nap, promising to meet him at the Duomo at three o'clock and resume the search. Just as the three bells sounded, she found him there, standing with Don Claudio.

"The radio is saying *il Duce* has been caught," the priest told her. "Near Dongo."

"Could it be true?"

He shrugged, smiled. "In one way now, it doesn't matter."

"No, Father," Silvio said politely. "It matters very much. Mussolini, Hitler, the Japanese emperor. Wars are started by individuals, not armies. What happens to them matters very much."

"And what would you have happen to them?" the priest asked. "Trial? Execution? Imprisonment?"

Silvio waved an arm at a knot of partisans singing in the square, and for the first time Sarah thought he seemed envious of them. "*They* should decide, Father," Silvio said. "Those brave men and women are the ones who should answer that question."

Forty-Three

After an hour of hard walking, Enzo guessed he was still about halfway up the western side of the lake, somewhere above Menaggio. He decided to work his way higher into the hills, though he wasn't sure why. To be closer to Switzerland, maybe, in case he decided to try to cross the border. Or to be farther away from the traffic on the *statale*, where it was possible someone might recognize him. In the years of his service to Mussolini, his face had been in countless photos and news reports, always just to the side of the main figures, but there nevertheless. It was possible he'd be recognized.

He wasn't really sure of anything, though; his mind was a nightmarish circus of voices, images, and possibilities, none of them good. Thanks to Silvio's payments, he had a pocketful of money. He supposed he could find his way to Porlezza and try to bribe a border guard, though even Rachele had been denied entrance there, so maybe there was an order to stop all of *il Duce*'s people, something put in place to placate the Allies. It was possible he could sneak through: the Germans and Italians wouldn't be bothering with that border at a moment like this, though the Swiss guards would be alert.

The idea of living in Switzerland held as little appeal for him as life anywhere outside Italy. He'd be an alien among the Swiss, unwanted as disease, a man without a passport, profession, family, or friends. He'd end up begging on the streets or sweeping them for a few francs. In the back of his mind he still clung to the notion of making a life in Italy, possibly with Angelina. He thought of what the cardinal had said about forgiveness. There would have to be forgiveness, have to be. Or else the Italian nation wouldn't survive.

He saw the steeple of a church ahead, gray and white, more in the Germanic than the Italian style. At the sight of it, and a few tile-roofed houses nearby, Enzo felt a sudden stab of hunger and realized that, in the confusion and haste of the past few days, he'd eaten very little. But what was he supposed to do? Knock on the door of the church in his Fascist uniform and ask for bread? The uniform was the problem. The army coat might be fine—he could always say he'd stolen it—but the trousers and shirt with their decorations and emblems would be akin to a death sentence. He tore the insignia from his shirt, a red enameled *fascio*, and flung it into the trees, then walked farther down the hill and pulled on the church's front door. Locked tight. He went around back to another door. Also locked. Maybe the Nazis had chased the priest away. Or executed him for the crime of talking about God.

Enzo decided to try one of the houses. He'd steal if he had to, food and clothing. What difference did it make now for a man of no country and no loyalties? He owed and was owed nothing. The slate was clean. From this hour forward he'd have to build a new life from the ruins of the old one.

He saw a house with a garden plot behind it, a few dormant olive and apple trees nearby. A rotten apple would do just fine, he told himself, but the tree was bare, and there wasn't so much as a frozen cabbage in the garden. The house was a modest structure, stone, one story, with a peaked space that must be some kind of attic. He approached the door, knocked, and heard shuffling footsteps, someone fumbling with the interior handle: everyone, it seemed, had gotten into the habit of securing their doors.

It took Enzo a few seconds to realize that the man who opened the door was blind. Eyelids flickered over milky irises, and until Enzo spoke, the man moved his face this way and that, confused.

"I'm hungry," Enzo said. "Can you give me some food?"

"Certo, certo," the man answered, and motioned Enzo inside. "I'm Sabatino. I'm home now, two days. From Russia. I'm sorry, but I can't see. In the kitchen there's food—women come to help me in the afternoon. Take whatever you want, sit with me for a few minutes. Are you a partisan?"

"Yes," Enzo said. "I've just come out of the hills. Heading to Milan for the victory celebrations." Going through the kitchen shelves he found half a loaf of bread, an apple, and a small salami. He stuffed a fistful of bread into his mouth, cut the apple in two, took all the salami. The blind man had women coming to help; he wouldn't starve.

"Sit with me for a bit," the man said again. "The women tell me my son is also a partisan."

"I'm sure he's a great hero," Enzo said. "The Allies have reached Milan now. The war here is over. Perhaps your son will be home soon."

"I hope he will. The women say my wife was killed. For me, the world is only darkness now."

"Things will get better and better," Enzo said, trying to chew the apple without making too much noise. He cast his eyes around the living room. The corners near the ceiling were thick with cobwebs; a layer of dust coated the chairs and shelves. But he could see a small pile of neatly folded clothing on one table. "The women care for you well," he said, measuring the man with his eyes, wondering how much he could sense. "I see they've done your laundry for you. Do they cook, also?"

"They do. I'm hoping my son will come home, though."

"I'm sure he will, I'm sure. How bad was it in Russia?"

"A frozen hell," Sabatino said. "They pushed us back into Poland, and I was blinded there. Most of the men beside me were killed. I was able to get rides as far as Merano, and the nuns there helped me, put me on a train."

Enzo was half listening. He gnawed at the salami, went back to the kitchen, poured himself a glass of water, and gulped it down. He thought of taking the other half of the apple but decided to be kind and leave it, and he went back and stood not far from the blind man.

"The train took me to Bergamo," Sabatino was saying. "And then I had rides again here. From kind people."

"Yes, yes. You're a hero, certainly a hero."

"And you are also."

"Thank you, and thank you for the food. I took only a small amount. Do you have a bathroom?"

Sabatino pointed behind him. "No paper."

Enzo didn't need paper; he didn't even need a bathroom, but he walked in that direction, silently swiping a pair of pants and a shirt from the pile of clothing as he went. No socks. He'd have to keep his wet socks. The shirt and pants mattered. The only question was whether he should change here, or wait. He decided to change in the bathroom, stripping off the militia uniform and pulling on the shirt and pants. Tight everywhere, but good enough. He rolled up the uniform, pants and shirt together, and stuffed the wet bundle behind the toilet, making sure to take the money from his pocket first.

"Are you ill?" Sabatino asked when Enzo had finally returned to the living room.

"Yes, I'm sorry. The simplest things take my body longer now after years in the forests. I'm not well."

"May you get to a doctor, then," Sabatino said. He'd started giving the name of the man he claimed was the best doctor in Menaggio, started offering directions to the clinic, but by that time Enzo was out the door. He left it slightly open and hurried across the back yard, past a makeshift grave, just a mound of dirt with a cross at one end. *"Grazie,"* he said over his shoulder. "Thank you for being blind, comrade." He bit off another piece of the salami and felt himself carried along on a wave of energy, a new resolve, asking God to let his good luck continue.

He decided he'd go to Milan. The city was big enough that he could probably blend in without being recognized. He'd buy a pair of eyeglasses, a hat, maybe grow a beard. He cursed himself, realizing he should have asked to use Sabatino's phone and tried to call Angelina, another citizen of no nation. Lake Garda wasn't so far away. If she hadn't fled, there was a chance she could meet him in Milan and they could compose a new chapter there. A chapter in a new Italian story.

Forty-Four

When Masso arrived at the Dongo church, he seemed to Luca like an old, solid tree in a storm, gnarled roots holding it upright against the gale. A second group of partisans had come onto the scene, scampering down out of the woods behind their very tall redheaded leader, and there were discussions and arguments going on in the church, some of them, Luca knew, within hearing distance of Mussolini. To kill him, or let him live.

Luca was introduced to Domenico, the head of the other brigade, and they greeted Masso together beside the parked truck. To Luca's surprise, the old farmer had no interest in seeing *il Duce*. "I know what he looks like, Luca," he said. Instead, the three of them took a short walk to the shoreline, and Masso turned and faced them. "This is no ordinary prisoner. I've been told to hold him until we get orders from the National Committee of Liberation. They'll likely want to hand him over to the Allies."

Domenico spat into the mud to his right and swung his head left. He was a huge man, with bright-red hair that curled down onto the back of his neck. He was half a meter taller and thirty years younger than Masso. A subordinate, but he didn't act that way. "Hold him, *merde*," he said bitterly. "I'd kill him now, if it was up to me."

"It isn't up to you," Masso told him in a steely voice. "There are larger things at stake here than your anger."

"My anger has legitimate roots."

"As does mine and his"—Masso pointed to Luca—"everyone's. We can't keep him in the church. I know of a place just above here, an isolated house. An older couple lives there, good friends of the partisans. The DeMarias. I'll give you directions. Tell your people not to let the word out that Mussolini is there. Hold him and Petacci in the DeMaria house under guard—double guard, in fact—two fighters from each of your groups. I'll make some phone calls, and by morning we'll have our orders."

Domenico spat again, but said nothing and walked away.

"You did right," Masso said, "not to kill him."

"Although *assassin* is my new title, it seems."

Masso glanced sideways at him and then out over the lake. "It wasn't my idea, Luca, the Milan assignment. You can believe that or not believe it. I take orders, just as you do. Just as people take them from you." He glanced at Luca again. "I have news for you. Two pieces. You'll be pleased."

Luca watched him and waited. "Tell me."

"On one condition. If I tell you, you have to remain here for another day with me. I don't want to deal with Domenico on my own. He's reckless and always has been. I don't know how he survived this long. Give me your word."

"I give it."

Masso touched him on the shoulder in a friendly way, then said, "As of yesterday morning, your father's home. Wounded, but in his own house and being well cared for. I arranged that."

Luca stalled and took a breath. "Thank you. Wounded how badly?"

"He can't see."

Luca closed his own eyes for a moment and shook his head. "And the other news?"

"Your woman is here also."

"Sarah? You're sure? At the house with my father?"

"No, but she's here. I saw her at Orlando's. She was searching for you. I told her you were in Milan."

"When?"

"Two days ago."

"You couldn't have called me?"

"I gave her a description of the truck. Where was I supposed to call you?"

"At Anna's."

"Who knew you'd be there? I didn't know until this second that you even knew her name. Save your anger for tomorrow. You may be asked to do the job you once told me you wanted to do. Do you remember?"

"I remember everything."

"After tomorrow you can go find your lover in Milan and bring her to see your father. The very end is here. Tomorrow, maybe the day after tomorrow. Finish your work, Luca, and then you can be angry at me for the rest of your life—I don't care."

"Was she . . . did she have a child with her?"

"Yes, a child and also another man. A friend, she said. The child is a girl and seemed to be—I'm not sure of these things—about two years old."

"Eighteen months," Luca corrected him. "Who was the man?"

"A friend, that's all she told me. I saw them together at Orlando's. I heard her mention your name, otherwise I wouldn't have been sure who she was. A friend with expensive clothes and an expensive car. She said he was being very kind to her and would take her to Milan and help her find you."

Forty-Five

Silvio returned to the apartment that evening with another dress for Sarah and one for Lydia, too. "We must mark the date of my birth!" he announced happily. "The rumors are true: Mussolini has been captured. We're going out to celebrate."

Sarah did her best to summon a measure of enthusiasm, but she was beginning to despair. She, Silvio, and Don Claudio had combed the entire center of the city, seen hundreds of partisans, and there was no truck and no Luca. She wondered if he might be celebrating elsewhere, closer to their hometown maybe, and while she wanted him to celebrate, wanted him—if he were indeed still alive—to finally have some rest from what must have been almost two years of constant deprivation and fear, she wished in the deepest part of herself that they could celebrate together. She, Luca, and Lydia.

To complicate matters, these latest gifts from Silvio had a different feeling to them. The dress he'd bought her wasn't just functional; it was pretty. And the look on his face when he handed her the package—which had been beautifully wrapped—felt like it expressed something beyond simple generosity. Lydia was forming a real affection for him, as well, climbing into his lap when he was sitting with them, stretching her arms up to him, asking to be carried. That afternoon, when Sarah had been alone for a while with Don Claudio, the priest had asked, "Who is he to you, this fine Silvio?"

"A friend, Father, nothing more," she'd answered, and Don Claudio had apologized for asking, then said, "I've decided to leave the priesthood soon, something I should have done before you were born. I beg your forgiveness, again. I'd get on my knees and apologize to your mother, if she were still with us." Don Claudio had waited for a response, and when she couldn't think of one, he'd gone on. "And we have to agree on a different name for me, if you don't mind. I feel you're addressing me as a priest, and I am a priest, or have been, but . . ."

Sarah went up on her toes and kissed him on the side of his forehead, and then Silvio rejoined them and they left the conversation unfinished.

All three men—Luca, Silvio, Don Claudio—were on her mind as she carried Lydia along the sidewalk on the way to mark Silvio's birthday. It felt to her as though the war had somehow concentrated everything, distilled life into its most intense emotions and agonizing choices. Now that it was ending, she felt a deep, fast-flowing current of joy running through her, yes, of course. But below that lay a cold, muddy riverbed of doubt and confusion.

———

Silvio had said the restaurant was very close, so she hadn't taken the stroller. After a short walk, he led them through a doorway, then along a corridor, through a courtyard, through another doorway, and into what felt like a secret place, four beautifully set tables in one room, a kitchen half-hidden behind, a white-haired man who seemed to be both waiter and cook, and who introduced himself as Giampiero.

"I can offer you some oranges with fennel and oil," Giampiero said, standing by the table with his hands clasped at his chest. "Then spaghetti with clams. Then some beef and potatoes. And perhaps a small dessert. Is that suitable?"

Silvio assured him it was more than suitable, and Giampiero brought an open, unlabeled bottle of white wine. He served it with a flourish, then went off to his duties. The other three tables remained unoccupied.

"How does this happen?" Sarah asked. "How does he get beef and oranges when others can't get bread? It makes me feel guilty."

He smiled. "You haven't suffered enough, Sarah? Having had to climb twice over the mountains, once with child and once holding a child? Having lost your mother? Having been separated from your lover?"

The first course was served before she could answer. Sarah sat Lydia on her lap and fed her small pieces of orange, then some pasta, and very small bites of beef. When the girl grew restless, Silvio offered to hold her so Sarah could eat, and she accepted that, too. She could feel words bunching up at the back of her tongue. When Silvio asked what she planned for her future, she started to cry. Lydia watched her with wide eyes.

"No need to answer, no need," Silvio said.

But the words came tumbling out. "I grew up not knowing that my father was my father. I don't want that for Lydia."

"Ah, I see." He twirled his wineglass and, for the first time since she'd met him, seemed less than ebullient.

"You've been an angel to me, Silvio. I can't say how grateful I am."

"And is there nothing else? Beyond gratitude?"

"There is something else, yes. But you know I can't pursue that something else until I find Luca and see what his feelings are, if he's even alive."

Giampiero arrived with coffee and thin slices of cake, and Silvio grasped his forearm with one hand and said, "You're a genius. When you open a larger place, I'll send you every one of my rich friends."

"Thank you, it's all delicious," Sarah managed, but she was glad when he walked away.

"I hope he's alive, Sarah," Silvio said. "Honestly I do. I would never lie about something like that. But if he isn't alive. Or if, forgive me, if he's alive and has found someone else . . . then?"

The tears came again. Sarah patted her face with the cloth napkin and took Lydia back into her lap. "I need to wait, Silvio. I need to wait, but at the same time, I have nowhere else to go. I feel like a little girl who has no parents and is living with kind neighbors. I'm embarrassed, confused, guilty, angry."

Silvio reached across the table and covered her hand with his. "This is war," he said. "War tears off the skin and reveals every emotion. It offers us choices, but they are impossible choices."

"It doesn't seem to have bothered you."

He laughed but almost unhappily. "I haven't lost anyone. I haven't walked across mountains. I haven't fought in any battles." He gestured to his scar. "I've lost my good looks, that's all."

"You don't feel guilty about not having fought?"

"I've tried to help in other ways."

"I know, I'm sorry I said that. You must be very brave. I think I have to . . . I don't know what I have to do now. I can't keep walking the streets of Milan and living with you and accepting your gifts."

He squeezed her fingers once and let go. "The war has taught me patience," he said. "I don't know my future, either. Perhaps I'll go back to Roma, to my former contacts, my work. Why don't we enjoy these happy hours, this meal, this day, this song of happiness all around us, and let the future unfold as it will?"

"Good, yes, thank you," she said. "Thank you a thousand times. And happy birthday."

Forty-Six

After trekking for another few hours along an old path that ran parallel to the lake and well above it, Enzo felt even more certain that the only good option open to him was a return to Milan. He had no family or friends there, which was, at this point, a positive thing. Chances of living anonymously were much better in a large city than in one of the small lakeside towns. And, with his belly more or less full, he was beginning to believe the stolen clothes would provide him enough security to drop down into the nearest town and take his chances there, rather than continuing to hike through the sodden forest. He had money. Some buses were still running, and if not, it shouldn't be too difficult to catch a ride back as far as Como on a farmer's truck or one of the rare passenger cars still in use, then take a train from Como to Milan. There was a small risk, of course. He supposed that for the rest of his life there would be a degree of risk. Some Fascist-hater might recognize him as one of *il Duce*'s associates and turn him into the communists, who were surely going to take over the country now. But who really knew how a liberated Italy was going to treat the followers of *il Duce*? Most likely he wouldn't be able to defend himself by claiming to have been a betrayer of the defeated dictator—that was a secret he'd have to hold for the rest of his life. And he might never know how important his betrayal had been. Maybe *il Duce* had escaped, after all. Maybe the Germans, with their machine guns, grenades, and armored vehicles, could fight their way through any roadblock the partisans erected. Maybe, after the short delay at the tunnel in Dongo, they'd fired a few shots, killed a few partisans, and were now moving north toward Innsbruck and a warm welcome.

It didn't matter. He'd done what he'd done, and told himself he had no regrets. Having gone back and forth about it on this terrible day, he'd come to the conclusion yet again that he couldn't live in Austria, Switzerland, or Germany, no matter what kind of company he kept in those places, no matter what kind of reception the Fascist militia might receive, no matter what happened to *il Duce* and his Führer friend. Enzo Riccio was a proud Italian. Nothing could ever change that.

He drew near to another small town—he could see the top of the church steeple—and angled downhill toward the lake. Let people stop him and ask questions if they dared; he'd come up with a believable story.

The path led all the way to the *statale*, turning from dirt to gravel to pavement by the time it reached a small city the signs told him was Tremezzo Sud. To his delight, he saw an open café. He purchased a coffee and pastry from a pale young woman, carried them to an outdoor table, and enjoyed them there, with a view of the lake. No convoys of German vehicles plied the roadway below him. He'd made a point of not saying much to the young woman—no need to instigate questions that might lead toward dangerous subjects—but he caught scraps of conversation from the few patrons as they came in and out. Milan, it seemed, was in the hands of the Allies. There were wild celebrations going on, and rumors that both *il Duce* and Hitler were dead.

A bus, he thought, a bus would be safer than hitching a ride: less opportunity for questions. He waited almost an hour at the bus stop and at last saw one appear. Nearly empty, with the driver occupied by a friend sitting in the front passenger seat, it carried Enzo as far as the train station in Como. Another long wait there. One elderly woman walked past with a loaf of bread clutched to her breast and eyed him suspiciously. He smiled at her and she moved on, but it made him realize he needed a complete disguise.

The first errand, after the slow train had carried him to Milano Centrale—the station mostly in ruins now—was to find a store selling eyeglasses.

"What strength are you looking for?" the clerk inquired.

"I don't know. It's just become a bit difficult to see things at a distance. What do you recommend?"

He was fitted with the lowest magnification. Next stop was a store selling fedoras, the owner there so pleased to make a sale that Enzo guessed she hadn't sold more than two or three hats since the start of the German occupation.

Outside, there was a festive air. Crowds of people in the street, many of them looking haggard and tired, but happy. Church bells were sounding continuously, and from where he stood he could see the spires of the Duomo piercing the sky just above the place where he'd given information to the mysterious Silvio. He headed off in the opposite direction and came to an open square called Piazzale Loreto. A gas station there, a few open shops, people milling about in small groups talking happily with one another. A few blocks away he spied a small hotel and, inquiring at the desk, asked to rent a room for a week.

The clerk—another elderly woman; they seemed to have taken over the country while their men were at war—looked up at him, squinted, peered, and said, "Your face is familiar."

"Ah, it's a curse. A face so ordinary that I resemble half the not-so-attractive men in Italy."

"An honest face," the woman said.

"Thank you. I've been . . . I was fighting with the partisans closer to Roma, and when I heard Milan was about to be liberated, I decided to come here and celebrate with some cousins."

"The partisans haven't fought near Roma in a long time."

"Yes, I've been recovering from a minor wound."

"And your cousins are making you pay for a hotel room?"

"I left my bag there. They have little children. I like my privacy, and I think, you know, they're older and the war has been very difficult for them. I didn't want to be a burden. Is there a shop nearby where I can buy some clothing to bring them?"

The woman gave him the name of a shop not far away. Enzo climbed wearily to his third-floor room. It was small and musty, but clean enough, with a toilet in the hall. He took off the stolen clothes and wet socks, lay on the bed, and fell instantly asleep.

Forty-Seven

The partisans held Mussolini and Petacci in the church for only another quarter of an hour, then used Masso's truck to spirit them across the *statale*, up a smaller, winding road, and to a house deep in the hills above Mezzegra. Luca thought it was almost as isolated as the cabin where he'd hidden Sarah all those months ago. The elderly DeMarias made a meal of polenta for the two captives and the handful of fighters guarding them. When Petacci had eaten and gone upstairs to the bedroom, and the redheaded giant and his men had settled themselves outside, Luca felt an urge to speak with Mussolini, something he never would have dared to do before the war. All during the steep climb to this house, *il Duce* had said not a word. There were other captives—ministers of his Republic of Salò, as Luca understood it, some who'd been caught near the lake, trying to flee. They were being held in a different location, but even as they'd parted ways, Mussolini remained mute and pensive, silent as a priest in prayer.

Il Duce had eaten next to nothing, and sat now with his elbows on the table and his forehead in his hands. Luca sat down opposite him. The elderly couple stood to either side of an interior doorway, as if the house didn't belong to them any longer, as if they were merely servants.

"*Il Duce,*" Luca said, his voice vibrating with anger. Mussolini looked up. "Tell me. All the Italian families who lost sons in the fighting, all the beautiful Italian cities that have been bombed almost to the point of being unrecognizable and will never be the same again, the

German torture cells, the torment of the Jews, the abuse of women, the pain endured by your own family, tell me, do you feel any satisfaction now? Do you regret any of it? Anything at all?"

For a few seconds Luca thought Mussolini would refuse to answer, and he could feel the old fire burning in his belly. *Talk to me!* he wanted to scream. *Your life is in my hands now. Answer me!*

Mussolini drew a breath. He laid his hands on the table, one on top of the other, like a scholar about to deliver a piece of knowledge to his students, and met Luca's eyes. *"Soltanto gl' uomini grandi possono capire la chiamata della storia,"* he said.

Only great men can understand the call of history.

Il Duce broke eye contact like a disobedient boy. The words he'd spoken hung in the room, floating across the kitchen table and around the old couple in the doorway, who stood there, watching, listening. Luca studied the man opposite him. The face and voice were perfectly familiar, but *il Duce* seemed so puny compared to what he'd once been, so worn out and filled with defeat, that the fury Luca felt only simmered and simmered. He tried to think of something to say in return, but the comment was so absurd that it rendered him mute. *That a human being could think this way! That a man could do what Mussolini has done and feel no regret at all, no remorse, no compassion! This,* he thought, *this is what true evil looks like.*

Luca let out a short, bitter laugh, then stood, borrowed a blanket from the DeMarias, and went outside to wait for his orders. During the rest of that day and the long night, the tall redhead, Domenico, paced restlessly around the house, rifle looped over his shoulder. "I'd kill him," he kept saying. "If it was up to me, I'd kill him." At one point, he stopped and sat with Luca on the rock and suggested they do just that, orders be damned.

Luca told him for the fourth time that they had to wait. "We've followed orders this long," he said. "We've both lost people close to us, but we've followed orders. One more day, I think."

"He's the devil. When you have a chance to slay the devil, you take it."

Luca put his hand on Domenico's knee. "We'll live with what happens now for the rest of our lives. A few more hours of patience and then we'll do what the bosses tell us to do."

Domenico relented, but kept pacing around and around outside the small house, as if casting a spell. They each had a man stationed inside, but as the hours wore on, Luca worried less and less that someone might come to free *il Duce* or that he and Petacci might try to escape. Despite what Mussolini had said to him, despite his lack of "greatness," Luca felt he'd come to understand history fairly well. He sensed it as the slow turning of an enormous stone wheel, unstoppable as sunrise. *Fate*, people called it. *God's hand.* He thought of his father, blind now, Masso said, waiting alone in a house less than three kilometers from where he sat. Maybe Sarah and their child were there with him, or maybe she'd stayed in Milan with her wealthy new friend. He forced himself not to think of her, not to let his mind travel to the following day. The last fingers of duty had hold of him; that and a deep, deep weariness. A soul weariness. He lifted the automatic rifle from where it leaned against his leg and ran his fingers over it, turning it this way and that. A miraculous gift at one time, it seemed an alien creature to him now, something belonging to a different man. He tried to imagine pointing it at Mussolini and Petacci and pulling the trigger.

Weary beyond exhaustion, Luca fell asleep briefly there, sitting on the stone, hands supporting his head in the same posture as Mussolini at the kitchen table. Giovanni came walking around the house, and the sound of the footsteps woke him, and for one terrible moment, Luca worried that his trusted friend was going to say *il Duce* had escaped, or that Domenico had gone inside and shot him. "I got the radio to work again," Giovanni said. "Took me all night. Masso will be here momentarily."

"Domenico calm down yet?"

Giovanni shrugged. "I understand him. He told me his sister was raped by Germans, more than one of them. I understand."

They heard car engines, doors closing, and then voices on the path leading from the gravel road. Masso appeared at the head of a group of ten or so others, all partisans, Luca assumed, though he'd never seen any of them.

He stood, and Masso came up to him. "Anna has given me the word. I don't want to do it here, in front of these good people. Let's take him down the road. Him and Petacci. The others will be brought there, too."

Domenico will be happy, Luca thought, but his own feelings were a puzzle. He found Mussolini and Petacci waiting inside, *il Duce* sitting placidly, almost in a hypnotic state, in the small living room, and Petacci running the fingers of both trembling hands through her long, dark hair and walking back and forth. When she saw them enter and saw the looks on their faces, she started to sob in a pitiful way. Mussolini stood and wouldn't make eye contact with any of them. *As if we're beneath him still,* Luca thought, and the fire of anger burned hot again.

They marched the captives to the vehicles and drove them down to the gravel road, then took a side road that Luca knew ran along the face of the hillside, toward and just above the village of Mezzegra, a ten-minute walk from his own house. When they stepped out of the vehicles, Mussolini and Petacci were in the middle of the group, surrounded on all sides by fighters, with Masso and Luca in the lead and Domenico just behind them. They walked a hundred meters and came upon a beautiful villa—the Belmonte family had lived there, Luca knew, and before them, ironically enough, Austrian nobles, Hitler's true countrymen, who'd used it as a summer residence. There was a two-meter-tall wrought-iron fence in front. Beyond it spread a lawn spotted with fruit trees.

Without speaking, Masso took Mussolini by the arm, led him to the splendid wrought-iron gates, and stood him, and then Petacci and two other Fascists—one of them shaking uncontrollably—on the granite slab, facing forward. Petacci was weeping and clutching Mussolini's left arm. The two Fascists stood to either side of the couple.

"Shoot me in the chest," Mussolini said, in the same proud voice Luca had heard on the radio a hundred times.

Masso turned to Luca and nodded, and Luca spread his feet, one slightly behind the other, and raised the automatic weapon. His exhaustion caused the barrel of the rifle to wander a bit this way and that. He thought of his mother, remembered finding her lying in the dirt, poisoned and shot by the SS men she'd been forced to serve. He sighted the rifle on Mussolini's chest, but then he thought of *il Duce*'s comment. *History. Great men.* If he squeezed the trigger now, they'd be linked forever, he and *il Duce*, linked in history, in the lore of the lake and of the Italian nation. He hesitated two seconds, and in those seconds, he heard a furious burst of gunfire beside him, from where Domenico was standing. Luca saw the four torsos sprouting spurts of blood, the bodies slamming back against the gate and tipping over sideways off the slab of granite, Mussolini's boots twitching in a death dance, one of Petacci's muddy black shoes dangling from her right foot, then toppling to the ground and lying still.

Luca could feel Masso staring at him. He stared back and said nothing.

The bodies were loaded into the truck bed, the entrance to the villa left bloody and uncleaned. Masso sat behind the wheel, Luca in the passenger seat. Domenico, one of his men, and one of the women in Luca's brigade climbed up behind.

Masso started the truck but glanced over at Luca before engaging the gears. "I understand," he said.

"Do you?"

The farmer nodded, the corners of his lips twitching in a wry silence.

"My brain is a storm."

Masso nodded again. "You didn't have the pleasure of firing the shots, so I'll give you the pleasure of deciding what we do with the bodies. We have to go pick up the others, so you have time."

Luca didn't require any time. "Not long before Sarah left," he said, "a German soldier was ambushed and killed on the outskirts of Milan. The Nazis caught some partisans and blamed them for the killing. Do you know the story?"

"There are many stories like this. I believe you told me once, but go on."

"There were fifteen partisans, some of them boys. Teenagers. The Nazis brought them to Piazzale Loreto, lined them up, and machine-gunned them to death. Bad enough, yes? But then—the day was very hot—they left them there on the pavement to rot in the sun. For two days the bodies remained there. The families of the partisans, mostly mothers, but some children, too, and a few elderly men, came. The Nazis wouldn't allow them to take the bodies. They beat some of those people, kept them away by beating them with their rifles. The mothers were weeping, begging. All they wanted was to take their dead sons and bury them, but the Nazis made them wait. Two days, Masso. The bodies rotted and stank. Flies feasted on them. The soldiers made the families watch. I was there, near the end. A crowd had gathered. I lingered in the back, but I could see everything, all of it. I could see it and hear it and smell it. And I made a vow then that I would find *il Duce* and kill him, because, without him, those soldiers would never have been in Italy, those boys would never have had to fight, those mothers would never have been weeping like that. I made a vow that I would kill him. But when I had the chance, I couldn't do it."

"You're done with killing now. I understand that. I'm done with it also."

"Yes. I know where we should take him. We should take him and his friends to that same place. To Piazzale Loreto."

There were coals in Luca's belly now, hot coals, but no fire. He turned and looked at the old farmer, waiting for an answer, and after a long, quiet minute, Masso nodded and said, "There are no other orders," and pointed his old truck south.

Forty-Eight

Early in the morning, Sarah was awakened by a cacophony in the street outside her window. She threw on the new dress and hurried into the living room. Silvio had made coffee and was sitting at the kitchen table, enjoying it, when he heard the noise, too. He went over to one of the windows and pushed the curtain aside. He stood there a moment, his back to Sarah, and then said, "Get Lydia ready, put on your shoes, let's go."

In less than five minutes, they were out on the sidewalk, Sarah holding Lydia at first, and then placing her in the stroller Silvio had carried outside. They joined a crowd streaming northeast along Corso Buenos Aires. All around them they heard excited voices: "*Il Duce* is dead. The *partigiani* killed him. Yesterday, near Menaggio. He's dead, he's dead! They've brought him here!"

The crowd thickened; Silvio took one of her hands. Sarah pushed the stroller with the other hand and moved her eyes left and right, still searching for the familiar face, wondering if the voices around them were part of a communal hallucination, a thrilling, terrible rumor, brought on by the years of misery.

But as she and Silvio kept walking, it began to seem that what people were saying was true. *Il Duce* was dead. They arrived at Piazzale Loreto, and Sarah could see that a large crowd had filled the square and leaked out into the five streets that fed it. Walking a short distance in front of her, Silvio was clearing a path forward, but even with that, it soon became too difficult for Sarah to keep pushing the stroller through the crowd. Silvio turned around, and there was something different on his face now, a new emotion. Triumph, terror, satisfaction—she couldn't be sure. "I'll be back, wait here," he said, and he pushed his way toward the center of the square. Sarah could hear ghastly shouting going on there, a hurricane of fury it sounded like, the voices of men and women screaming in the most hateful ways. She hesitated a second—afraid and captivated at the same time—then lifted Lydia out of the stroller, held her tight against her breast, and tried to push forward, too, keeping her eyes on Silvio's fedora and following in his wake.

There was a swirling craziness all around her; she could feel it in the air, hear it in the wild shouts. Another few minutes and she'd managed to push a little closer to what seemed to be the center of everyone's attention. She squeezed up next to Silvio and heard him say, above the noise, "Keep Lydia's face turned away." Sarah did that, and then they shuffled forward another few steps and she could see that the crowd had left an irregular open circle on the piazza pavement. Another step forward and she went up on her toes and could see what lay in the center of that circle. More than a dozen bodies, men and one woman, all but one of them lying face down. Even at this distance, she could see that the body that lay face up belonged to Benito Mussolini. Feverish, maddened people were taking turns approaching it, spitting on it, kicking it. Two huge men had clubs, and they stepped forward and slammed them down against the *Duce*'s knees. Then someone who appeared to be very drunk was urinating on the corpse. She heard a shot, saw Mussolini's body jerk to the side. The people closest to the circle were screaming, "Monster! Devil! Friend of Hitler! You died a dog's death, and we'll bury you like a dog!" She felt Silvio's arm around the back of her shoulders. She stopped Lydia from turning her eyes forward, and then she was backing away from the scene, disgusted, terrified, fascinated.

She kept moving back until there was no chance Lydia could see over the people in front of them, and then she turned and found the stroller again, a bit farther off than where she'd left it. The noise and craziness were reflected in Lydia's eyes, so Sarah held her close and pushed the stroller with her free hand, singing a quiet lullaby in her daughter's ear, hoping Silvio would join them but not wanting to wait. She walked as far as the crowd's loose edges, then kept going, finally stopping on a slight rise and looking for Silvio. She thought she could see his fedora, then lost sight of it. She heard five gunshots, one after the next, in an even cadence. The mob was chanting in unison now, a sarcastic *"Du-ce, Du-ce, Du-ce!"* People were laughing hysterically, dancing, throwing things in the air. Sarah could see a few street children slipping between and around the adults' legs, reaching into pockets, scurrying away.

Just as Silvio emerged from the madness, just as he waved and called to her, she saw a police car pushing its way toward the center of the piazza and heard three loud reports, *bang, bang, bang!* Policemen firing into the sky. Silvio came up beside her, breathing heavily. As if to calm himself more than to calm Lydia, he reached down and kissed her on the top of her head. He was looking at Sarah now, his eyes glassy with disgust. "All the suffering," he said. "All the hatred."

She pointed over his shoulder. "Look!"

To try and stem the madness, the police had apparently tied the feet of seven of the corpses and dragged them over toward a gas station at one edge of the piazza. They'd thrown seven ropes over a horizontal metal bar there, above the station's roof, and begun hoisting the bodies into the air. The corpses were lifted, and a great cheer went up from the crowd, as if the thousands gathered there were all feeling the same emotion: a savage triumph, a mindless revenge. Neither she nor Silvio could turn their eyes away. The bodies were hoisted to a certain point, and then the ropes were tied off and the corpses swung back and forth like weary pendulums. Even from this distance—fifty meters or more—Sarah could see that Mussolini's face resembled a piece of raw meat, and that the woman's skirt—was it Petacci?—had been tied to her legs so it wouldn't hang down and reveal her underwear. *"Do-chay, Do-chay!"* the sarcastic chant went on. Ten meters away, Sarah could see a woman weeping so forcefully that at last she had to sit down on the pavement, face in her hands, tears running along her arms.

"*Do-chay, DO-CHAY!*"

"How long can it go on?" she asked Silvio.

"Until they take him away and bury him. Do you want to stay?"

She shook her head. They turned their backs to the crowd and had started to walk when Sarah thought she heard something between the chants, two syllables so faint she at first believed she was imagining them. She listened closely and heard them again: her own name being called.

Forty-Nine

Enzo had been having a breakfast of coffee—real coffee—and eggs in the dining room of the hotel when he heard the commotion in the street. He ignored it at first, thinking it was just more celebration. He wasn't in a mood to celebrate. The war was over, yes; he was as glad of that as anyone. But his mind was occupied with making a complete erasure of his past. As she served him that morning, the hotel owner, her hair in two gray braids, had given him a strange look and asked when he was planning to see his cousins, and what were their names. "Perhaps I know them," she'd said, in a sly tone. Enzo gave her the names of two of his friends, who lived near Avellino. They had the last names of southerners; it was unlikely the woman would be able to connect them to anyone she knew.

But the brief encounter and the tone of her question had made him uneasy. It wouldn't do to stay in the hotel, but where should he go?

As he was pondering, someone burst through the front door and yelled, "*Il Duce* is dead! His body has been brought to Piazzale Loreto!" The man turned and hurried back out into the street. The hotel owner followed him. And, so spontaneously that he left his hat and eyeglasses on the table, Enzo followed, and then quickly separated from her, merging into the middle of a stream of people, some walking at a fast pace, others running down the sides of the street. Two police cars were trying to push through, blaring their Klaxons, but the people paid no attention. Enzo walked as fast as he could, angling this way and that when he saw an open route. In ten minutes he found himself at the edge of a large square. Everyone seemed to be screaming or weeping, shouting vile curses into the air. A small boy, a street urchin, was going in the opposite direction, reaching his filthy hand into people's pockets, then ducking away with whatever he'd been able to steal. As the boy scurried past, Enzo slapped him hard on the back of his head and knocked him flat on his face.

The police cars pushed slowly along. Enzo followed in their wake, a woman beside him making the sign of the cross over and over again. Finally, he came to a place where the crowd was so thick he could go no farther. People were shouting, *"Il Duce! Il Duce!"* but in nothing like the way they used to shout it up to the balcony at Piazza Venezia, adoring the uniformed *Duce* there with his chest and chin thrust forward, his arm like a sword slicing the air, telling them they belonged to the finest nation on earth and he was going to make that nation great again, bring them all back to the glory of the Roman era, make every single one of them part of a heroic struggle for Fascism, for victory, for their rightful place in history.

Now the word—*Il Duce! Il Duce!*—was drenched in sarcasm and hatred. Enzo could feel that hatred all around him, vibrating in his bones, and he felt suddenly afraid. He maneuvered his way to one side, close against a gas station there, behind the police cars still, and then he saw the most horrible thing he'd ever seen. The bodies of *il Duce*, Claretta, her brother Marcello, Larracú, Scavolini, Grazanini, and Nazzacone, their heels tightly bound, were being raised up like the bloody banners of a lost satanic empire. This was the man he'd once adored; these were the people he'd labored with for years. Their limbs were stiff as tree trunks, the faces battered and broken. Fighting a wave of nausea, he followed the bodies upward with his eyes. Mussolini's face looked as though it had been stripped of its skin, one eye bulging, the mouth a bloody cavern. Enzo glanced away, and then back. Claretta's beautiful black hair hung straight down to either side of her face in filthy clumps. One of her feet was bare. The bodies of Grazanini and Nazzacone wobbled hideously, their pants soiled at the crotch.

Enzo stepped back but kept his eyes raised. He felt as though he were standing on the edge of a volcanic crater, but instead of lava pouring out, it was madness, actual madness, blended with the blood fever of violence. He'd never felt so afraid, never felt so evil, in his entire life. It was as if the crazed crowd were condemning him in the voice of a merciless God.

An image leapt into his mind: *il Duce's* son-in-law Galeazzo Ciano and the others being executed by the firing squad. That had been the most terrible moment of his life, a sickening display of inhumanity. This was a hundred times worse. Another strong wave of nausea gripped him. He turned around. A middle-aged man was standing there, leaning on a cane, and Enzo found himself face-to-face with him. "I know you!" the man cried out, over the voice of the crowd. "*Il Duce's* assistant. Everybody knows you!"

"No, no," Enzo yelled back, holding both hands up in front of him, palms forward. "You're mistaken, *Signore*."

The man stepped closer and started poking the end of his cane against Enzo's midsection. Enzo tried to turn away, but now someone had hold of his right arm. He panicked, wrestled it free, and turned again, but there were others there, pointing at him, men and women, pressing close. "It's him, it's him, it's him!" a teenage boy was yelling. Enzo spun halfway around and tried to make his legs move, but people were pushing against him on all sides, and he caught sight of two huge men moving toward him. Both men were holding clubs. The clubs were stained with blood. The last thing Enzo saw, the last thing he would ever see, was one of the men lifting the club up over his right shoulder and whipping it forward through the air.

Fifty

After picking up the other bodies, there had been a long delay on the road south—just outside Como a bus had twisted sideways into a ditch, cars backed up behind it—and then, near Saronno, one of the tires on Masso's old truck had gone flat, and it had taken them a while to make the repair. By the time Masso and Luca had arrived at Piazzale Loreto, somewhere in the early-morning hours, the area was littered with ribbons and flowers, but deserted. After dumping the bodies in the center of the square, he and Masso and Giovanni and several of their men had remained, while the others filtered away in the darkness.

Luca spent a moment standing over *il Duce*'s body, studying the bullet holes in his chest, glancing at his famous face—swollen now, raw and pitiful. He spat once on the corpse, said, "This is for you, great man. From my mother," and then he turned and walked over to a gas station at the corner of the square. He sat against one of the concrete bases of the light post there—it was cold against his back—and fell asleep instantly.

When he awakened, the first rays of sun were shining directly into his face, and he saw that a handful of people were standing around the bodies. A group of men, some in felt hats, others bareheaded, a police officer, one woman astride a rusty bicycle, gripping both handles. As he watched, the group doubled in size. One of the men kicked Mussolini's body and spat on Petacci's. In what seemed like minutes, the crowd had doubled again. The new arrivals were pushing forward to get a

Roland Merullo

glimpse. The crowd was filling the square, and a kind of madness had already infected them. Luca saw a man urinate on Mussolini's body. Others were kicking it, spitting on it, striking the face with clubs. A middle-aged woman, hair wrapped in a kerchief, shoved her way to the front, pulled a pistol from the pocket of her coat, and shot *il Duce* five times. "For each of my sons!" she shouted, and then she threw the pistol down among the bodies, took two steps backward, and collapsed.

Luca slowly worked his way back from the center of the mayhem. People—three-quarters of them men, with a few women sprinkled here and there—were screaming, cursing, pushing forward to have a look. There must have been a thousand people in the square by then, and the mob had a personality of its own, a personality forged by years of deprivation, terror, and grief. Nothing and no one could stop that from erupting.

His own feelings, a blend of bitter satisfaction, exhaustion, and disgust, simmered rather than boiled. He felt as though, with his killing of the Nazi torturer and then his narrow escape from the cell, the fire beneath his soul had been turned down. It flickered there still: he felt no pity for Mussolini and the others, nothing but hatred for all of them. But he wasn't bothered by not having been able to pull the trigger. The war's bloody torrent had been reduced to a thin red trickle, *il Duce* had been caught and executed, the last major cities of the north had revolted; Hitler was rumored to be dead. There would likely be no names added to the list of men and women who'd given their lives for a liberated Italy. Close as he still felt to his comrades in arms, it was as if he could already sense himself peeling away from them, an individual again, not a member of a fighting force. A kind of spiritual exhaustion weighed upon him, but beneath that weight, like one thin shoot of greenery pushing up through a thin spring snow, he sensed that he was standing between the end of one chapter of his life and the beginning of another. The craziness in front of him belonged to the past; he was finished with that kind of fury. It had propelled him all these months through all kinds of danger, but he sensed it wouldn't propel him into the kind of future he had dreamed of and so badly wanted.

He moved toward the back of the crowd, where people weren't pressed as tightly together and where the air seemed filled more with morbid curiosity than rage. He heard the sound of gunfire and realized that police vehicles had made their way into the crowd and that the policemen there were firing into the air, trying to calm those near the front. There was a pause in the screaming and shouting. Another few minutes and Luca saw the strange sight of seven bodies, legs bound at the ankles, being raised on ropes that had been thrown over the grid of metal beams above the gas station where he'd fallen asleep. Up and up the corpses went, to the crowd's crazed cheers, and they hung there, swinging back and forth. Luca noticed that Claretta was among them, and noticed, too, that her skirt had been tied tightly around her legs so it didn't fall down over her face. He wondered which of the policemen or partisans had thought to make that gesture—one drop of humanity in a sea of animalistic frenzy.

He stared at the bodies for another few minutes. Mussolini's face looked like ground veal. Petacci's hair hung down in clumps. The rope holding one of the associates—Marshal Grazanini, he thought it was— gave way, and the stiff body fell against the pavement with a snapping sound so loud even Luca could hear it. Another of the Fascists was strung up in the man's place. *Il Duce's* corpse had gone still now, the arms pointing downward on either side of his head as if he'd died sur- rendering. Luca remembered him saying, "Shoot me in the chest," and wondered if he'd wanted his famous face preserved for history. "Too late for that now, *Duce*," Luca said quietly. "Too late for that."

The bitterness was rising in him again, so Luca made himself turn away. He wanted to get back to Mezzegra and see his father, and won- dered if it would be possible to find Masso in the crowd and take the truck, or if he should look for another way out of the city. In front of him, the pavement of the square rose at an almost imperceptible angle. He lifted his eyes and, fifty or so meters in front of him, saw a couple pushing a baby stroller away from the scene. He looked at the uneven pavement and then back up, studying the way the woman's hair fell against her shoulders, the way she walked. He wasn't sure but called out anyway. "Sarah?"

The woman didn't seem to hear.

Luca hurried forward a few paces and yelled more loudly, "Sarah!"

The couple stopped. Luca yelled a third time and watched the woman turn around. "Sarah!" he screamed. She let go of the baby stroller and started toward him, but then Luca saw the man speak to her. She turned and made a few steps in his direction—the rich friend from Orlando's bar, no doubt, calling her back to him. But the rich friend had whirled the stroller around, and she bent over it and took a sleeping child into her arms. Luca was running toward her now. He watched Sarah lift and turn the child so he could see its face.

It was a gesture he would remember for the rest of his days.

Fifty-One

Very late that night—*the Day of Piazzale Loreto* is the way Silvio Merino would always think of it—he lay awake in his Milan apartment enjoying the feel of the warm skin of the naked woman beside him. He and Anna had made love not once, but twice, in playful fashion, and both of them were sinking slowly into a magnificent sleep. As he drifted toward that other world, Silvio let his mind wander back over the events of the past two years. He hadn't fought, it was true, and had no right to celebrate the way the partisans were celebrating. But it seemed to him he'd made a contribution, saved a few lives, perhaps hastened, by a small measure, the end of *il Duce* and the war that demon had brought to Italian soil. It also seemed clear to Silvio that he, himself, had evolved into a different man, somewhat less focused on his own pleasure, more engaged in the world that surrounded him. He thought of Sarah and wondered if she would ever understand that, in exchange for his small acts of generosity toward her and the wondrous Lydia—a bit of inconvenience, a few lire spent here and there—she'd given him a precious and unexpected gift.

In the darkness, he pressed his left ankle against Anna's warm leg and smiled up at the ceiling. "Do you think it might be possible," he asked quietly, "for people like us, people who've lived the way you and I have lived all these years, to turn onto a different road?" He hesitated before saying the next words. "A more domesticated road?"

Anna was quiet. He imagined her musing on the kind of future he was imagining now. *Tame* would be the word he'd use to describe it. Or perhaps *predictable*, if anything in this life could ever be predicted. Tame and predictable, but very fine, too. Very safe and fine. Silvio waited a few seconds for Anna to respond. When she didn't say anything, he turned his face toward her and saw that she was wrapped in the world of dreams, breathing peacefully in sleep.

Epilogue

They'd been living at the house in Mezzegra—Luca's family's house—for a week now, and, as if it had been waiting for the end of the bloodshed, the weather had warmed into its typical May mildness. Sarah's favorite month.

Word of Hitler's suicide had reached them; the war was officially over. But that news—like the news of arguments among communist, socialist, and Christian Democratic partisans, already fighting over the shape of postwar Italy—seemed to Luca very far away. Sarah had gone into what had been his bedroom as a boy, and she was changing and nursing the unbelievably beautiful gift named *Lydia*. His father was taking a nap. Luca brought one of the kitchen chairs outside and set it on the small rise in the front part of the property, a place that offered a view down across the rooftops of the nearby houses and out over the shimmering blue lake. The late-afternoon sun had swung around behind him and was dropping slowly beyond the range of mountains that separated Italy from Switzerland. He could see, above the clusters of houses on the lake's far eastern shore, green hills rising toward another range of mountains, in Lombardia, gray near the base, but turning a gorgeous rose color in the higher reaches. Minute by minute, he watched the light change there, watched the blue of the lake turn to purple, the lamps of a ferry tracing a path east from Bellagio.

Before full darkness fell, Sarah came out and joined him. "Your daughter is sleeping," she said. She sat sideways on his lap, wrapped her arms around his shoulders, and laid her head against his neck. He held her with his left arm and felt her chest rising and falling against him. "We have a garden here," she said quietly. "We can grow food. You can take your father fishing on the lake." Luca nodded, his cheek moving against her hair. "We can have Don Claudio marry us, if you don't mind, if he's still a priest. Silvio said he can get you some paying work. We could have another child."

Luca was finding it difficult to speak. He held Sarah a bit tighter and ran his right hand down across her hair, holding strands of it in his fingers and twirling them gently. Over her shoulder he watched the last touches of sun leave the lake's surface, then the tips of the far mountains darkening, as if the light there had been a scarlet vapor, not quite blood colored, and was now evaporating into a purple evening sky.

Begun: Conway, Massachusetts, November 10, 2022
Completed: Conway, Massachusetts, August 8, 2023

Acknowledgments

First thanks, as always, to Amanda for her patience, love, and support. I'm grateful, also, to our daughters, Alexandra and Juliana, who have endured, with their typical grace, some of the oddities of having a writer father. Their love sustains me.

My thanks to Erin Adair-Hodges for her excellent editorial advice, to David Downing for his superb line editing, to Haley Swan for a great job of copyediting, and to Jon Ford for a superb proofread. Over my long career I've worked with numerous editors, and these four are absolutely top-shelf. Thank you to Kyra Wojdyla and Karah Nichols for expert production management, and to the entire team at Lake Union Publishing for always going the extra mile.

About the Author

Photo © 2023 Amanda S. Merullo

With his older daughter, Zanny, Roland Merullo writes the popular Substack newsletter *Hi Zan, Hi Pa*. Merullo is the bestselling and award-winning author of numerous works of fiction, including the historical novels *Once Night Falls*, *From These Broken Streets*, and *A Harvest of Secrets*; *Breakfast with Buddha*, a nominee for the International IMPAC Dublin Literary Award; and *The Talk-Funny Girl*, an Alex Award winner. He is also the author of the memoir *Revere Beach Elegy*, which won the Massachusetts Book Award for Nonfiction. His essays have appeared in *Newsweek*, *Details*, the *New York Times*, *Reader's Digest*, *Good Housekeeping*, the *Philadelphia Inquirer*, and *Boston* magazine, among many other publications. A graduate of Phillips Exeter Academy and Brown University, Merullo lives with his wife, photographer Amanda Merullo, in the hills of western Massachusetts and travels frequently to Italy for research and pleasure. For more information, visit rolandmerullo.com.